Acclaim for
NANCY SPRINGER's bestselling
WINGS OF FLAME

"The finest fantasy writer of this or any decade. Her fantastic images are telling, sharp and impressive; her poetic imagination unparalleled."

—Marion Zimmer Bradley

"I read WINGS OF FLAME in one gulp . . . Nancy Springer's conceptions are always new and the ending of this tale is a very satisfying one."

—André Norton

"WINGS OF FLAME is fantasy at its finest . . . Springer's creativity brings a freshness and sparkle to delight the most discriminating of tastes."

—*Romantic Times*

The new novel by the author of
The White Hart

NANCY SPRINGER

A TOM DOHERTY ASSOCIATES BOOK

WINGS OF FLAME

Copyright © 1985 by Nancy Springer

First printing: April 1985
First mass market printing: February 1986

A TOR Book

Published by Tom Doherty Associates
49 West 24 Street
New York, N.Y. 10010

Cover art by Carl Lundgren

ISBN: 0-812-55484-1
CAN. ED.: 0-812-55485-X

Printed in the United States

0 9 8 7 6 5 4 3 2 1

The yellow dun treads on the topaz of the sun;
The hooves of the white have left his mark
  on the pearl of the mottled moon.
Black runs the charger in the clouds of the thunder,
The blood bay gallops in the hot sere wind.
Blue stallion of soft rain rears in the high lapis sky.
Mighty lies she, the great mare of earth,
  under the mountains brown.
Gray walks the steed of mist and the mysteries
  over the sundering river.
All are in Him,
  the firstborn of the mistral,
    numen most puissant and wise:
The spotted horse with the jewel between his eyes,
On wings of flame he flies,
On wings of flame.

Chapter One

"Shuntali!"

The title was not a name. It designated an outcast, an unperson, a member of the class that beggars could look down on, could shout at if they chose. The shouter in this instance was the master of the hut that served as hostelry, and the shuntali was a girl who did the unclean work. For this she was allowed scraps and a degree of tolerance, because no one knew she was a girl—she appeared to be a lad of about twelve years of age. She had been a boy for most of those years, so long that she herself had almost forgotten her own secret femininity. If it had been known that she was a female, she would have been driven from the shanty of an inn and put to prostitution.

"Shuntali!"

Far up in the red-budding blackthorn forest of the mountaintop, gathering kindling, she heard him shouting and came running.

The innkeeper was a member of the third class, the caste

of merchants, farmers and laborers. One of his several names placed him in that class according to his vocation, which had been his father's also. Another name described the order of his birth in his family, his sex and his rank in his clan, and another invoked his totems as determined by the date of his birth. He wore his lucky color, brown, and the hems of his clothing were edged with protective borders and tassels, and the shoulders crudely embroidered with the emblem of his totem animal, the onager. Being prosperous enough to have purchased it, he wore a pendant of jasper, his lucky stone, carved with the glyph of his planet, Jupiter.

The shuntali, on the other hand, had no names, no birthdate, no emblems, and her faded and colorless clothing served merely to cover her nakedness. Though most Vashtins were fair of face and red or russet of hair, she seemed nearly as colorless as her clothing, earth-dun, hair and eyes and skin, and her face was expressionless, silent. Barefoot, crop-headed, in coarse shirt and hemp trousers, she pattered up to her master and awaited his command.

But before he could speak, she gasped aloud in surprise. "By the old man," she breathed, "Devans!"

The innkeeper cuffed her, but she scarcely felt the blow. She stood rapt. Riders on horseback were filing into the inn yard. Horses! All the bright and solid colors of horses, barley red and golden brown and a splendid blue roan in the lead; the rider sat it in the royal fashion, legs straight, feet pointing past the steed's shoulders. The girl briefly noted him, his own shoulders nearly as broad and muscular as the stallion's, his jet-black hair all in curls under a tall red cap; then her gaze returned to the horses. Travelers from Deva were not so uncommon, for the hostelry lay near a pass of the Kansban Mountains that divided that kingdom from Vashti. That was why the innkeeper needed his shuntali. No proper Vashtin would ride or even touch a horse. The animals were sacred to the supreme god, the horse-god Suth. But the Devans used horses in their own arrogant fashion; they said the steeds were the gift of Suth to men, to make men victorious in war. Their most recent war with Vashti had ended a mere month before.

There might be trouble. But oh, such beautiful horses! "By the old man!" the shuntali whispered again, and the innkeeper cuffed her again, harder.

"Take that wood in," he ordered harshly.

She had forgotten the bundle of kindling, still in her arms. She hurried with it into the single room of the hostelry. Some few men loitered there, as always, and she could hear them grumbling as she stacked her sticks by the hearth.

"Devan devils!" someone quipped.

"Pompous horse-sitting infidels!" another voice joined in with more spleen than seemed usual. "Blasphemers! How dare they show their bodies here so boldly? Has their precious King Kyrillos even signed treaty?"

The shuntali stole a glance at the speaker. He was a weasel-faced man in gray clothing, no one she knew, certainly not one of the villagers from the few huts that huddled along the mountain track by the inn. In fact, there were several strange men in the hostelry, though they all wore the clothing of Vashtins, yellow or red or whatever color their day of birth decreed, with the customary magical stitchings and talismans. Devans wore no such talismans.

"Kyrillos and our good King Auron have come to spoken promise, I understand." The voice was that of an older man of the village. The stranger scoffed.

"Good as the vellum it's written on, is it not? Damned Devan horsebeaters, I wonder what they want here! Likely they're spies."

"Shuntali!" her master roared from the yard. She hurried out.

The care of the horses would fall to her, she knew. It was a task forbidden to all but priests in the service of Suth. She was liable to hell ice for doing it, but a shuntali deserved no more, the reasoning went. She approached the job with guilty pleasure. To rub the silky flanks, all of the seven horse colors and many of the seven times seven horse colors. . . . So many horses, and no merchant goods in sight. What, indeed, might be the business of these strangers?

There were no halters of soft rope such as a Vashtin might have used on a donkey, no loop of leather around the lower jaw, no harness of any sort at all. Each man in turn led his horse before her and touched her hand to the arch of its neck, giving her charge of it. Then they all strode inside—all except one. The rider of the big blue roan stood tending to his animal himself, taking the thick seat-blanket off its back and scraping at the dark patch of sweat it had left. His short black beard was as curly as his hair. His skin was not as dark as that of most Devans, and, staring at him, the girl thought he might be younger than the beard made him look. An older Devan turned impatiently, waiting for him.

"Kyrem, get within. It will be dark soon."

"Exactly. And you would have me entrust Omber to the care of a little lad with twelve others on his hands and no light to groom them by." He looked up, his tone edging toward arrogance. "Get in yourself if you're so hungry."

The other frowned and came back. "It is not good for you to be out here by yourself," he said in a low voice.

"Then stay." Kyrem stood rubbing at the mark the surcingle had left on his steed. The older man flushed and let go of courtesy.

"Kyrem, your father charged me to get you safely to Avedon, and I'll do it if I have to tie you up! Now get in!"

"Do you think I would fail to honor my father's bond?" The youth turned with threatening suddenness, and the little lad who watched found herself stepping back. The older man stepped back also.

"Go in," said Kyrem, not at all loudly, and the other went. Kyrem sent a black look after him, then abruptly escorted his horse to the meager stabling, left the steed there and followed.

The shuntali had gotten the blankets off of the others while listening. Though they were in no way constrained or confined, the horses made no effort to wander away from her; they stood still and let her tend to them. She did not understand how it was that the Devans trained their horses—infidel magic, some said. If so, she admired that magic. She went for sacking and dried them all off, whistling tunelessly under her breath and wondering. Avedon was the court city of King Auron in the lowlands of Vashti, the city by the Ahara Suth, the hoofprint Suthspring, and the Atar-Vesth, Suth's sacred grove. She knew that. But she wondered, who was this Kyrem who seemed to be both the leader and the led?

The stabling was directly beneath the hostelry itself, no more than a dug cave in the dirt and rock with entry toward the lower side of the sloping terrain. This arrangement was inimical to sweetness of fragrance in the single room above, and the flies buzzed up from the dungheap into the pantry, but it kept the animals close at hand and provided some warmth to both animals and humans in the frigid mountain weather. Even this evening, in springtime, the air was chill and the hearthfire was lit. The shuntali could not share the warmth of that fire. She also lived in the stable, along with the donkey that was used for haulage, two spotted milk cows and several chickens.

As the moon rose above the jagged rim of the Kansban, she sat there, watching from her bed of well-used straw, eating the bread and meat she had stolen from the pantry and listening to the contented movements of the blue roan. Stealing had been easy this evening, the cooks busy with so many guests. She felt contented herself—until lamplight began to creep into her retreat and she stiffened in surprise. It was very late; it had taken her a long time to groom and water and feed and hobble all those horses, and she had thought that everybody else would be in bed. Who could be coming?

It was Kyrem, in nothing but his soft leather sandals and red breeches cut off at the knee, striding into the stable from the yard. The stableboy felt her secret femininity stir at the sight of him, his bare broad shoulders and erect head—he must have crept from his bed, away from his guardian. She shrank into a corner, confused and shamed by the feelings that she, a boy, was not supposed to have. What did she care about him! And what did he want, forsooth?

He set the clay lamp on the dirt floor near his horse and greeted the stallion with the traditional Devan touch to the center of its forehead, rubbing the itchy place there where the hairs made a whorl.

Watching from her shadow, the shuntali felt surprise and a degree of jealousy. Vashtins said that Devans abused their horses to make them so tame, but this Devan hugged his around the neck and the big animal laid its muzzle on his shoulder, whickering. He caressed it, inspecting every inch of its body, running his hands over its black flanks with the frosting of white hairs that gave the blue tinge. The shuntali knew he would find nothing amiss. She had groomed the horse to a high polish in spite of its impatience, the mettle-some steed. Except—

"I could not check the hooves." She spoke up suddenly in a voice scarcely more than a whisper. "He would not lift his feet for me."

Kyrem jerked his head up, startled, and the girl edged forward so that he could see her. He relaxed with a grudging smile.

"You've done wonders with the brute," he said. "Come here, hold the lamp."

He approached the task of checking the hooves first in the traditional way, sliding his hand down the leg and pinching lightly between the shank bones with his fingers. He swore and smacked his animal when it attempted to kick rather than offering the foot. "All right, Omber," he muttered, and he stood at the horse's head, stroking its face and ears, gentling it. Then he closed his eyes.

The shuntali stood watching, openmouthed. Kyrem had not moved, but she saw a concentration in him that affected every muscle of his body, a focusing of power within himself in a way too quiet, too still, to be called force. When he stirred slightly and reached out to touch his horse's shoulder, the movement was tender, a caress. But though he had no more than stroked the swelling of muscle just below the neck, the corresponding foot came up at once and held steady.

Kyrem stepped forward and took the hoof, cleaning out dirt and straw and pebbles with the fire-hardened pointed stick the girl offered him. He moved to the horse's rump, touched the plump rondure of it, and the hind hoof came up. The shuntali watched in astonishment as he finished all four feet, then stepped to the horse's head and gentled it again, rubbing the soft fur at the base of the ears and murmuring.

She saw him ease something within himself, letting it go like a sigh, settling into the place where he stood. "Good fellow," he told the horse, and then to the stableboy he said, "Where are the others?"

"Out at grass. There is no room in here." She spoke so softly he could scarcely hear her. "They have had water and a scoop of barley each." Ah, the feel of the warm muzzles in her cupped hands. "This one has had hay as well." She stood watching Kyrem comb a black forelock with his fingers. Omber, the horse's name was. She wondered if all Devans named their mounts. Such a shame to turn the sons of the south wind into beasts of burden. And yet, that closeness, that caress, the silent magic that had passed between the two, beast and master—she felt a sudden, fierce tenderness toward this Devan and his horse.

Shouts sounded above, the hard, angry shouts that men use to incite themselves to warlike deeds. Then a scream, the hoarse, wrenching sound of a man's death scream, and a sort of gurgle. "Devan dogs!" someone roared, and a panicky voice was calling, "Kyrem? Kyrem!" The youth and the girl stood rigid, motionless.

"My men," Kyrem whispered, "they're beset!" He bolted toward the ladder that led up into the inn. It took the girl a moment to realize that he was running toward, not away from, the fray. And he bore no weapon that she could see. "Wait!" she called, perhaps as loudly as she had ever spoken, and she ran after him. He had not gotten far. A dark mass of men blocked the top of the ladder, and in that shadow she could see the glint of long knives.

"There he is!" one of them barked and came down in a single jump to confront Kyrem. The shuntali saw him in the light of the oil lamp she still carried; it was the weasel-faced, rabble-rousing stranger in gray. His knife flashed, already poised to dart at Kyrem's defenseless ribs. The shuntali did not have to think; she hurled her lamp at the attacker with force enough to shatter it against his face. Sparks flew along with shards of clay, hot oil splattered, and the man gave a startled scream as darkness fell. The girl had gone into an instinctive charge. She butted her head full force into the stranger's belly, and he toppled against the ladder, bringing it and his comrades down on top of him. But his knife, flying loose, struck the shuntali above the eye. She fell.

There followed a confusing time. When her head cleared, the girl saw Kyrem battling with three adversaries. He had found a long knife, and two of the others, by way of fate, had lost theirs, so the battle was not as uneven as it seemed. And Kyrem seemed to have that strange power in him again, swelling his muscles. . . . The others surrounded him but could not hold him, like so many jackals harrying a lion. He surged and swirled amid them as though he were an embodied energy, something elemental. . . . The shuntali watched, sitting up and blinking, wincing when they made him bleed. They might yet tear and worry him down—and there was a vague rustling noise she could not identify, a menacing hiss behind the panting and scrambling of combat. She could see the man she had felled stirring, that would make it four against one—she could see? By the light of flames. The lamp had set the straw afire.

She scrambled up. Oily smoke stung her eyes and set her to coughing. Among the men there was more blundering than battling now—no one could see. She scarcely could either, but her bare feet knew every inch of the ground she trod. She found Kyrem's arm and tried to tug him away, but he fought her. She was just another enemy in the smoky chaos to him.

"Come on," she urged, as if urging a donkey.

The soft voice, so soft that only he could hear it. He

recognized it and followed it into the cramped maze of pens and stalls. The stableboy knew the way quite surely even in the confusion of dark and smoke and flickering shadow. Wild shouts of men behind and screams of animals all around. . . . There was Omber, plunging in his place, too frightened to flee, panicked as a horse will be by fire. The stableboy slipped off her ragged shirt and tied it over the lurching, struggling beast's eyes, and Kyrem laid his hand on the neck. Omber calmed as soon as he felt that touch, for power still flowed in Kyrem.

"Lead us," he murmured to the girl.

They walked one on either side of Omber's head, coaxing him forward, coughing in the smoke, thinking they would die in the smoke—but in a moment they were outside at last, and the shuntali slipped the blindfold off the steed. Kyrem vaulted onto his mount. The stableboy got back into her shirt, silent and shivering. There was shouting in the darkness all around, pounding of hooves under the trees, and the inn—the inn was going up in flames.

"You can't go back there," said Kyrem. "They'll kill you. Come on." He hauled the youngster up onto the horse behind him. She went without question, even though she had never sat a horse before, for she had nothing to lose, and she was used to doing as she was told.

The other horses were gone from the place she had put them. Kyrem sent Omber plunging away into the darkness, whistling and shouting as he rode. The girl rested against his bare back, hanging on and paying little attention. Her cut head hurt. After a while she drowsed, and when she awoke, it was dawn.

Chapter Two

The sun came up at their backs. Straightening, the shuntali vaguely remembered a night of riding in zigzags and circles, Kyrem's shouting, other shouts answering his across the darkness. But with the dawn they were traveling mostly westward, down the mountain slopes toward Avedon. Half a dozen riders accompanied the youth and the girl now. She recognized the older man who had spoken with Kyrem the previous evening. He was blood-splattered, as were the others, and he looked grim.

"So much for the local hospitality, Captain," said Kyrem, breaking a long silence.

"The fault is all mine, my prince, I admit it," the other answered bitterly. "I spoke of danger, but I never truly expected—"

"Stop it," Kyrem ordered. "How could you possibly imagine that we would be so treacherously attacked? There will be no talk of fault. And do not call me prince."

They rode in silence out of budding blackthorn forest and into a high mountain meadow, the thin, rocky, brown soil studded with tiny red flowers, blood-of-Suth, amid moss. Lush new growth of bright green ferns showed where a small spring ran. "Let us stop here and breathe a bit, now that we can see about us," said the captain when they reached the open ground. "What is that rag you seem to have attached to your back?"

"That little rag-tag saved my life twice last night." Kyrem swung a leg lithely over his horse's neck and dropped to the ground. The girl sat up stiff and dazed on the horse's rump where he had left her. He helped her down.

"You are a prince of Deva," she whispered.

"Kyrem son of Kyrillos, gratefully at your service." He set her down on the ground. His men were drinking at the spring by turns; none of them had a flask or a cooking pan or even a hat to hold water in. They had escaped with only scant clothing, a few weapons and their lives. Kyrem still held the long knife he had taken. He sliced a square of cloth from his trousers with it, soaked the makeshift napkin in the spring water and came and plastered it on the shuntali's head. The cut above her eye was swollen. She reached up under the cloth and touched it, felt the stickiness of congealed blood on her fingers, felt weak and then angry at her weakness. Faintness was a girlish trait, and she was a boy, was she not?

"But what are you doing in Vashti?" she asked Kyrem sluggishly. "When folk are still roused in wrath about the war?"

"I am my father's hostage for peace. I am to take up residence with your King Auron." Kyrem's voice hardened. "Evidently someone does not want me to reach Avedon."

"But who?" she asked in her soft way, and Kyrem laughed without mirth.

"That is a very apt question."

The men had gathered around, listening. "If you fail to ʳrive," the captain said, "Auron will be able to accuse your ʳther of breaking faith. Perhaps he will use the pretext to ᵃarch."

"Then you say it is Auron himself who sets traps for us?"

"King Auron would not do that," the girl protested, and ᴵl the men laughed.

" 'Tis a tempting theory, Captain," Kyrem said judiciously. But in all fairness it ought to be said that Auron has not een one to march in the past. Also, my father seems to trust ᴵm, which is odd."

"King Kyrillos hardly trusts anyone," the captain wryly ᵍreed. "Even himself."

"But who else could it be but Auron?" a man spoke up.

"For the present, it scarcely matters," the captain grumbled. Here we are, half naked, our comrades slain, here in a ʳilderness without food or gold or gear, and three weapons ᵐong the seven of us. Yonder lad would be better off back ᵛith his family."

"I have no family," the shuntali said.

"None?" All eyes turned on the lad. "What might your ᵃame be?" Kyrem inquired.

"Name?" she repeated stupidly.

"Yes, your name." He smiled with genuine friendliness. ᵗYou know mine. What is yours?"

"I have none," she whispered.

"No name?" Kyrem sat down by her, dumbfounded. "But ᵒw can that be? What was it that they were calling you at ᵗe inn?"

She could not answer, could not bring herself to say the ᵃted word. "Shuntali, my lord," someone else told him.

"It is a sort of curse. Vashtins use it for those they consid
unfit to live, beneath regard. The boy is an outcast."

"But he is a mere slip of a lad!" Kyrem turned to the gi
"What can you have done at your age to deserve contempt?

She kept her eyes turned to the ground. Kyrem raised h
chin with two fingers of his right hand.

"Answer," he commanded.

She knew she must have done something. "I was bo
evil," she said, and Kyrem sighed with exasperated relief.

"You're a bastard, then? Well, so am I. So are we all.
The men roared with laughter and nodded their agreement.

"I'll give you a name," Kyrem said.

Her eyes widened enormously. Everyone saw, but no o
laughed anymore. Her world awaited redemption. Kyre
looked at her carefully, seeing a rather delicate boy, sensi
how brashly he had trodden on ground where no man had y
gone. Holy ground or unclean, it made no difference, the ri
was the same. . . .

He thought frantically. The name had to be right.

In Vashti people were named according to their place
the planets, the family, the clan, the magical chart of sev
times seven correspondences. But in Deva folk took th
names of things they found lovely or significant—flower
jewels, birds, the breezes that sifted through the bristli
black upland trees, the echoing mountains themselves—

"Seda," said Kyrem. "Your name is Seda. That is wh
the Old Ones would have called you, because you spe:
softly, like an echo, a whisper. Will that do?"

A tear brimmed out of one wide eye by way of answe
Kyrem tried to reach out and wipe it away, found that I
could not quite do it and turned his back instead.

"Crazy Vashtins!" he shouted at the distant peaks, and th
words came echoing back to him.

"Are you mad? That will bring all the rabble within hearing after us," the captain said sharply. "Let us ride."

Kyrem and Seda drank at the spring, for Kyrem would not be hurried. Then they mounted, with Seda on Omber behind Kyrem as before. Omber was the largest and strongest stallion of the lot. "Omber," someone remarked. "That means 'shadow.' The echo rides the shadow. You choose strange names, Kyrem."

The prince made no comment as they rode to the fern-fringed lower edge of the meadow and into the shadows of the black forest.

No rabble came after them, for the time. They rode through tree shade and out into yellow sunlight again, into another spring-green mountain meadow, this one contained by shelving red rock. The blue rose of the wilderness grew there. In spite of tense thoughts and an empty belly, Kyrem smiled at the beauty of the place. But as they traversed it, with ominous silence and suddenness a moving shadow swept over them. "Curse you! Curse you all!" a voice rasped from overhead.

The horses shied, coming dangerously close to the rocky edge, and the riders could not control them, for the riders themselves were staring skyward, as unnerved as their mounts. The horses spun and circled, striking against each other, and great black wings wheeled above them, the wings of a mighty raven larger than any ordinary raven, but the baleful face that glared down was that of—how could it be? A horse, a black bony horse's head with flaring nostrils and long yellow teeth. The yellow, scaly, reptilian legs of a bird were tucked under the thing's feathered tail, but instead of claws, the legs ended in two hard black hooves. They hung heavily from the bird's body, making it lurch and lumber in air, clumsy, ugly.

"Curse you!" the thing said again quite plainly, eyes rolling whitely in its black equine head.

"Demon," Kyrem breathed, gaining control of Omber at last, and he sent his long knife darting up at it like a javelin. The weapon flew both short and wide, out of its element, and came to earth somewhere on the rocks with a clatter. But the weird horse-bird swung away nevertheless and flapped off, lifting itself with difficulty toward Kimiel, the tallest mountain.

The men quieted their horses, soothing themselves as much as the steeds, and then sat staring at each other, pallid.

"What in the name of Suth was that?" someone faltered at last, breaking silence. At once a hubbub went up.

"Watch out how you mention the name of Suth! That might have been Suth himself, come to punish us."

"I have heard that Suth is a mighty flying horse, but I never thought of him in such form as that!"

"But it must have been a god, it was so big it blotted out the sun. Bigger than any natural bird—"

"Did I see hooves?"

"I saw blood in its nostril and fire in its eye."

"Had we not better pray and make sacrifice? If Suth is angry at us—but we have nothing to sacrifice—"

"Silence," Kyrem said, not too loudly, but the babble stopped at the sound of his voice. "You are talking nonsense," he said fiercely. "What reason could Suth have to curse us? That was some sort of demon, and a paltry one at that, not much bigger than a raven, forsooth! Not nearly grand enough to be a god. Think on what little learning you have, and be silent." Glowering, he slid down from Omber and marched off to find his knife.

Likely his men thought more of their own fears than of learning, but if they obeyed him, they remembered the legend.

In the beginning days the Mare Mother rose up, the brown

mare great of girth, she whose black, bristling mane forms
the forests of the Kansban, she whose ears are the holy
eminence, and this great mother of earth opened herself and
was impregnated by the hot, wild waft of the south wind, and
out of that union Suth was born.

And Suth's first and final form was that of a stallion, the
most splendid of horses, of what color men could not agree;
the Vashtins said that he was the varicolored horse of the
pattern that is or is not, but the Devans scorned the piebald
horse as a cousin to the cow, and they called Suth the *kumait*,
the shining and sacred bay. In his broad forehead between his
wise and dangerous eyes nestled a jewel, which jewel men
could not tell, but all men knew that he carried that treasure
between his eyes. And all men agreed that he was winged to
fly with his father wind, though the Vashtins sometimes said
that the wings were made of flame.

And the Mare Mother bore daughters as well, the lovely
twins Vashti and Deva—and men quarrel still as to which
one came first from the womb—and Suth came to his sisters
in his holy stallion form and wed them, and they bore him
seven sons to fly with him, winged on the wings of wind.
The white horse of moonlight and the yellow dun steed of the
sun, the red horse of red fire and of the fertile red soil of
Vashti (for in Deva the soil is as yellow as the sun), the blue
horse of love and leaping water, the sorrel brown of the
mountains, the gray horse of the mysteries, and the black
horse of death and thunder and the stardark sky.

And on the flanks of the mother the scurf and small
sheddings rose up and became people, men and women, and
they had children, and needed barley to feed them. Then
lovely Vashti came (said the Vashtins) and lay down as a
willing sacrifice, and the hero struck the blow of immolation,
he, Auberameron, first priest and first king of Vashti, and out

of the wound the red blood flowed, and bright green vegetation sprang up all around it. And ever since that day the good soil of Vashti has been as red as that blood, but the soil beyond the bourne, the boundary river, where no one goes, where magic grows and the melantha, that soil is as black as that black lily flower.

And in those days all the horses could fly, and they spoke to man as equals, or more than equals, for they were far wiser than men and possessed of prophetic powers. In the fall of all things from the glory of those beginning days, they had lost the wings and the power of speech, but Devans said that they still possessed the wisdom, and Vashtins, that they retained the power of prophecy.

But how could the horses be called wise and prophets, she wondered, the girl who was a boy who was newly named Seda wondered while sitting on a blue roan rump and waiting. How so wise, when they let the Devans use them so, suffered themselves to be sat upon, and so tamely? Being a horse was a godlike state. It ought not to be at all like being a shuntali.

Kyrem returned with his knife, and Omber lowered his head and neck to help him vault on. Silently the party rode the length of the meadow and down through the next belt of blackthorn. Shadow-tails moved in the trees—small furry climbing creatures; squirrels, the Devans called them. Thin and famished with springtime hunger, they scurried about to feed on buds, and at each scrape or clatter of the branches, every rider stiffened on his mount. Though none of them would say it, they were each taut and tense, ears alert and eyes roving, watching for the return of the horse-bird. Hunger and human enemies were almost forgotten, except by Seda, who was accustomed to thinking of the many foes at once, the rocks that came hurled from all directions.

They are not so accursed, she thought, though she did not

speak her thought, for she seldom spoke much. To Kyrem she said only, "Look. Devil's toe."

"What?" Startled, Kyrem glanced all around, for she was pointing at what looked like merely a weedy tangle to him.

"Good to eat," Seda explained. And enough for all, she thought, though again she did not speak.

"Show us," Kyrem said, signaling the halt.

She showed them, pulling the plant up boldly and rubbing the dirt off the fat root with her hands; it was the root that was to be eaten. They all ate after watching her bite into it fearlessly. The root was dull dun in color, crunchy on the outside and mealy within, and they found it oddly satisfying. Vashtins, even beggars, seldom came near this plant because of its fearsome name and its claw-shaped, red-tipped leaves, but Devans thought differently about such things, Seda already surmised. As for herself, she had eaten it many times. A shuntali had to learn to brave superstitious fear.

"Good," the captain said judiciously.

They ate their fill and stuffed their few pockets with more and rode on, their mood somewhat lighter. And as day wore away into afternoon and no ill chanced, they began to feel that they had outridden the curse, and they talked to each other and grew merry.

Chapter Three

Evening came on, the dusky melantha of night spreading her black petals in the dome of the sky, and they began to look for a place to stop. No dwellings were near, for they rode far off the track in hopes of avoiding their unknown enemies. Only the mountain wilderness surrounded them, fresh green of ilex and laurel and springtime white of blackthorn bloom—for the season advanced as they descended the slope; red bud had gone to white bloom here, and farther down they would find the green leaf of early summer. But these blackthorns were still bare, deep shade seemed caught in their branches, and twilight brought on again the feeling of danger. Men were shivering, whether from that or the evening chill. Few of them wore so much as a shirt to warm them.

"There," said the captain finally. "A dingle. We will be able to risk a fire."

A hollow had sometime been scooped in the flank of the mountain, as though by a god's hand. Laurel clustered thickly around the rim of it and tall iron-black trunks marched down within. The trees stood so closely ranked and the drop fell away so steeply that they had to cling to their horses. Once standing at the loamy bottom, they felt as if they were in another world. Relieved and eager, they set to work, some building a makeshift shelter of laurel boughs, some gathering last year's fallen thorns for fuel, some kindling fire with bow and bore since no one had flint and iron.

"We have no water," said Seda.

"We shall see," Kyrem replied, pointing at the horses. Off to one side Omber stood pawing at a patch of moss and ferns. Seda went over and discovered that the steed had uncovered a trickle of water and was digging himself a basin to catch it in. She ran back to the prince.

"A spring," she reported, astonished. Kyrem nodded.

"In Deva we value our horses for many reasons," Kyrem said obliquely. And Seda remembered that the great horse-god had made Ahara Suth, the sacred spring near Avedon, with a single blow of his mighty hoof.

Huddling together in their shelter after nightfall, eating their remaining roots and a coney caught in a snare, watching the fire that burned just outside their open entryway, the company felt nearly comfortable. Still, the men of Deva mourned their lost comrades. Talk turned to how they might avoid further tragedy, and to Auron of Avedon, king of Vashti, and how he might be plotting to kill them all.

"I keep telling you," Seda said, she who usually kept silence, "Auron is not like that."

They laughed at her, but not so loudly this time, and Kyrem glanced at the lad quizzically.

"How can you say that, Seda?"

"Auron is the king," she averred, her voice rising so that she was nearly speaking aloud.

"But do you know him, or know of him?"

"Have you ever even seen him?" added the captain.

"Of course not." She did not herself understand her own passionate certainty. She only felt, instinctively and unreasonably, that if Auron son of Rabiron were not a good and righteous king, the bright green buds would not be on the ilex nor the green grass growing from the sorrel earth nor the celandine growing so yellow or the wilderness rose so blue. "He is King, I tell you," she added with just a hint of whimper in her voice, looking at them all with pitiful eyes, daring them to laugh at her again, she, he, a poor shuntali. Seda was not above using her own misfortune to give her leverage on the scrupulous.

"Oh, let him alone," Kyrem said promptly. "Have you no family at all, Seda? Are you orphaned?"

"I think I am a twin," she said.

"What?" He did not understand.

"I sometimes remember a mother and a father and a . . . someone very like myself. When twins are born, one is cast out."

"What?" Kyrem spoke in astonishment this time. But some of his men were nodding. In Deva also, twins were regarded as unnatural. But rather than abandoning one, parents treated them as one child, and so did the clan and village as well, insisting that they take passage together, marry another set of twins and that on the same day, even die on the same day. Girt about with all these restrictions, twins were regarded as awesome and somehow unlucky.

"The one who comes second from the womb is cast out," Seda went on. "That is the bastard. And the mother is lamed for adultery. . . ." She let her words drift away, recalling the dark, pretty mother who hobbled around a mistily remembered cottage.

"Great galloping Suth!" Kyrem exclaimed, shocked.

"So you do not do these things in Deva?" Seda was also capable of a certain dry humor.

"Most assuredly not!" Kyrem started to stand up in his discomfiture, remembered in time the low roof of the hut and sank down again. "Although," he admitted, "I do remember hearing an old curse, 'May you be the mother of twins,' or some such. I thought it was because of the hard labor." He winced at his own words.

It is hard on all concerned, Seda thought, not speaking the thought.

"My lord," a man said urgently, "send the lad away. He is bringing us ill luck."

"Silence," Kyrem snapped. "Seda, how did you live if they cast you out?"

She shrugged. "They had to keep me until I was three, that is the rule, so that it would not be murder."

"Great Suth," Kyrem said again. "Murder might have been kinder."

"They . . . they never killed the babies outright. In the old days I would have been taken to a mountaintop and left to die."

Kyrem sat gazing at her, engrossed, ignoring the mutterings of his men. "So you have a brother somewhere, a twin, whom you have never seen," he said in wonder.

Seda shrugged again to hide her confusion. It was a sister. Try as she might, she could not remember the name, but she remembered the infant face, mirror of her own. The years since were all confusion. How had she lived, and how had she become a boy?

"Lord," said another of the soldiers, "we are half naked and shivering in a wilderness; is that not ill enough? Send the lad away, before he brings worse on us."

Kyrem turned on the man. "You fool, you sound like a Vashtin!" he said hotly. "They with their stars and their talismans and their charts and rules and their lucky this and unlucky that! Remember you are a Devan, you carry your own magic with you in your very body! You have no need of luck." He glared at the man and turned back to Seda, still fuming. "We value people more in Deva," he said darkly.

Seda had to smile, a small, shadowed smile. The Devans had not always been particularly valuing of people in their warlike dealings with the Vashtins. But there were no shuntali in Deva, or so it seemed. "Here, people are cheap," she said in her soft voice. "Only horses are precious."

"How so, lad? Will they try to rob us of ours?"

It was the captain. But she never answered him, for a dark, winged form swirled by and landed with a thump just at the verge of night, beyond the fire. They knew at once that their demon had returned, even before they saw the sheen of firelight on two unlikely hooves and the red reflection of firelight in equine eyes.

"Devan dogs!" the thing sneered.

As one man all the Devans sprang up and charged it, demolishing their hut. The horse-bird lurched up and away, just out of reach of their angry, grasping hands. "Dung of Suth!" another voice said blasphemously from behind them.

They jerked around, puppets pulled by someone's string. Another winged and horse-headed black demon sat there almost companionably by their fire. Behind it, in the ruined hut, the lad Seda groped for a rock, preparing to stun it. But before she could strike, yet other voices took up the chant.

"Dung of Suth! Balls of Suth! Bowels of Suth! Die! Die! Devan dogs!"

The men clustered like frightened horses, circling, staring in every direction. The black birdlike things faced them on every side, weird in the firelight and ominous, darkling, beyond it. How many? Perhaps a dozen; no one could see clearly. Quite enough to make their hearts sink in unreasoning despair, for they had thought there was only the one.

Beyond the dingle the laurel bushes rustled, though there was no breeze. Shadow-tails, Seda thought. But the men seemed not to think so, nor did the steeds. At the far end of the hollow near the spring she could hear the horses milling and whinnying. The animals were alarmed, but they hated to leave their masters.

"To mount," the captain ordered, and his men were glad to obey him, for every sinew of every one of them cried out for flight, though the demons had threatened them with no bodily harm. The horse-birds, each sitting on its two hooves, moved aside before their rushing exodus, and the dingle echoed with a sort of whinnying laughter.

Kyrem, as panicky as the rest of them, stopped only long enough to take the erstwhile stableboy by her arm and hurry her after the others. She tugged against him.

"What is the matter?" she protested softly, and though he did not stop, he slowed his pace to argue with her.

"Have you no sense?" he whispered furiously, fear turning to anger; he felt mockery in her words and mockery in the presence of the demon birds. "The night is full of danger. Anyone can feel it."

"Where?" she asked.

He stopped for a moment to hearken. The night was still and, this far from the fire, quite black. Omber stepped softly up to them, the sound of his hooves muffled by the forest loam. Kyrem felt a pang of despondency as sharp as that of an abandoned child.

"See now what you have done?" he said bitterly. "They've gone off and left us."

Shouts rang out harsh and fearsome across the night, and the scream of a stallion hurt or enraged. Kyrem stiffened, turning toward the uproar at the edge of the dingle.

"There," Seda murmured.

"They've been attacked again!" Seething, he flung himself onto Omber and galloped off, leaving her standing where she was.

They never knew whether the fight was with the weasel-faced man and his followers from the hostelry or with some commonplace robbers, for it was too dark to tell. Though they had little enough to be robbed of, except perhaps the horses, which no Vashtin would touch. . . . Kyrem hurled himself and Omber into the slashing confusion under the trees, bellowing for his men to rally to him, and the suddenness of his charge gave them some small advantage for the time. They cut themselves away and broke free, fleeing down the mountainside, but the dark and the unknown terrain soon slowed them. They stopped after a bit in a dense stand of cover and stayed the rest of the night there, tensely standing guard, no one sleeping. Dawn showed them each other somewhat cut and bloody, tired and pale. The captain was there, and Kyrem, and three men. Two others were missing, and Seda.

"We must go back," said Kyrem.

"Take the wise path, Kyrem, and go on," said the captain grimly. "Those who are gone are gone for good and aye by now."

"We do not know that. They could have hidden themselves, as we did."

"I heard at least one give his death cry at my side. And remember, your first duty is not to them or to your rag-tag youngster, but to your father's bond."

That thought gave Kyrem pause for a while. But then he stubbornly shook his head.

"You young fool—" The captain lost patience and temper, but Kyrem stopped his words with a black glance.

"I may be a fool and young too, but I know myself. I cannot merely ride away and leave them. I will go back, with you or alone."

In the end they all retraced their tracks, riding warily. They found the dingle and the battle-scarred soil amid blackthorn, and they found their two comrades there, quite dead. There was no sign of Seda, though they circled the dingle.

"Now may we go on?" the captain snapped.

They rode away westward, heavy-hearted, the soldiers on account of their comrades, and Kyrem, though he frowned hotly to admit it even to himself, on account of the lad he had so unceremoniously deserted. But before they had gone much beyond the next belt of trees, they heard a clatter of quick, light hooves coming up from behind. They turned, half fearfully, wondering if certain black birdlike things preferred walking to flying. But there came two donkeys, each heavily loaded with packs and blankets and gear, and leading one and bouncing about on top of the other was Seda, driving the creature forward by twisting its ear.

She presented the booty wordlessly. There was food in the packs, and a few garments, and flasks and cooking pans, and many of the things they lacked. The captain spoke to her harshly.

"Where did you get all of this?"

"Those who attacked you last night—they left their train unguarded." She faced him blankly, wrinkling up her nose a trifle at his tone. "I make a better thief than a brawler," she added finally. "Are you not glad to have food? Do you still say I bring you bad luck?"

No one said a word, but Kyrem put down his hand to her and hauled her up once again onto Omber's back. The others took the packs and blankets and sent the donkeys away with a whack.

"What is the matter?" Seda asked after they had ridden for quite a while in silence.

No one answered her. No one would say what it was that preyed on their minds: that the two who had died were the two who had spoken against her.

Chapter Four

Down from the mountaintop, the holy mountaintop, the highest in the Kansban range, called by the Devans Anka, by the Vashtins Kimiel, down came the cursing, flapping, black demon things. For days they followed above the riders, hurling their imprecations. "Devan dogs!" would come the neighing shout, causing the soldiers to mutter angrily. "Curse you! Curse you all!" A dozen or thirteen at a time would be lurching about in the air, shaking their black-maned heads crazily or thumping into the trees. Each one had its own litany of ill will. "Dung of Suth!" one would cry, and others would join in, "Blood of Suth! Balls of Suth! Bowels of Suth!" until the whinnying chorus deafened those below and made them shout. Outrage filled them, not just on their own account, but on their god's. They could see these black things only as monstrous, blasphemous parodies of the horse-god's greatness.

"Let us take to the trail again," the captain said heavily.

"We can have no thought of secrecy anyway, with these cousins of vultures wheeling above us."

So they rode on the track, which grew ever wider as they neared the foothills. One-roomed inns and small villages dotted that way, each about a day's journey from the last, but the travelers did not stop at them—they had no coinage, not even coppers, and also they remembered what had happened the last time they had stopped at such a hostelry. They avoided each small settlement, making their camps in the surrounding wilderness. They soon were out of food again. No wild berries were ripe so early in the season, but they found the devil's-toe root from time to time, and mushrooms were growing in the loam that was constantly damp from mountain fogs and dews. Seda gathered odd fungi that were large, bluntly pointed of shape and bright red, for all the world like Kyrem's lost cap, long since turned to ash in that fateful inn. She cooked them by the dozen in a panful of steaming water, and they were pleasing to the taste as well as filling. Sometimes—not often enough—they would manage to down a squirrel with a stone, or snare a rabbit. And in the night Seda would pay brief and clandestine visits to the local cooking sheds, returning with bread, cheese, and sometimes even meat.

No one came after them or troubled them on account of these thieveries. But the horse-birds still flapped above them and cursed them with never-lessening fervor.

"Can the things know what they are saying?" Kyrem wondered aloud. "I mean, each of them has its own little tattle-taunt, quite short—could it be that the creatures have small wit of their own?"

Even that thought was unpleasant. "If that is so," the captain asked, "then who or what trained them and sent them to harry us?"

No one knew. A nameless enmity hovered over them and followed them like their own shadowing cloud.

The nights were, if anything, worse than the days. The creatures always stopped with them at their camp, thudding heavily to earth at some small distance or attempting in a clumsy fashion to roost in the trees. There they shouted mindlessly all night and rattled the branches with their weight, turning sleep sour. The soldiers tried to shoot them with makeshift arrows, to stone them, trap them, snare them, drive them away by any means, but it was a business like the swatting of midges, doomed to frustration. After a while they would turn surly and pull blankets over their heads, letting the birdlike things be. Seda suffered as much from them as the others. "Shun-shun-shuntali!" one of the black things would cry, "Shun-shun-shuntali!" until she had turned into a taut knot of misery and could scarcely eat or sleep. Since the others were nearly as wretched, no one noticed her particular discomfort. But after a few days of this siege of curses, Kyrem set his jaw and willed himself to combat it.

"Come here," he said to Seda one evening at their beleaguered campsite.

She came listlessly. He had her sit down beside him and he took up one of her small hands, began wordlessly to trace with his own stocky finger the narrow bones that showed whitely through her skin. After a moment she looked up at him in astonishment. Comfort and strength were flowing through her, marrow-deep and bone-strong, and as she saw him truly, she realized that the power was in him again, as it had been that night at the inn; he looked bigger than himself and solid as the mountains, and the squawking demon creatures seemed of no importance beside him.

"What is it?" she whispered.

"Devan magic," he replied softly. "We carry it with us,

in our bodies, our innermost selves. We have no need of chants and charms and lucky colors." He touched her head lightly with cupped hands, turned her by the shoulders and gently traced the line of her spine, caressed her thin shoulder blades, sending a tingling joy and wonder through her. He would not have done so had he known she was a girl and not merely a boy younger than himself. For her girl's heart was touched, and body magic is the most binding of magics. Kyrem was yet a virgin, but when the time came that he would lie with a woman, that one would be his mate for life, such was the power within him.

With a final gentle touch he left her and went to his men. "Now you four," he said to the soldiers, "help each other."

They did not have gift for the magic such as Kyrem's. But, watching them, Seda began to understand something of the bond between the Devans and their horses. That constant touch throughout the day, gentle squeezing of knees and guidance of hand on the crest of the neck—no wonder, with the magic, that man and beast became nearly as one, the man's will guiding the steed, the steed warm and generous in its submission. Did something of the steed's strength come through to the man, she wondered? Did the magic work two ways? She knew what Kyrem had given to her—but what, if anything, had she given to Kyrem?

"Peckernose!" a cursing creature shrieked with passionate abandon from the darkness just beyond their camp fire. "Prince peckernose!"

Kyrem swung like a bear where he stood, and for a moment rage darkened his face; Seda thought he would go after the horse-bird with one of his useless charges. But the next moment his face cleared and he threw back his head and laughed, a wild, free, ringing laugh, the beggar's laugh that mocks any adversity.

"Peckernose yourself!" he shouted back at the bird with no beak, and all around the camp fire men smiled.

"What makes you think it means you, lord?" a soldier joked quietly.

Kyrem grinned and answered not the jester but Seda's inquiring glance. "My name," he told her. "It means 'phallus' in the language of the Old Ones. No dishonor intended, only that I am called after the emblem of love and fertility. My father's name means 'lion.' So I am the phallus out of the lion, do you see?"

Seda felt her heart go hot and spoke before the feeling could reach her face. "Who are the Old Ones?" she asked. The question had been with her for days, waiting.

Kyrem's grin faded. "I scarcely know. Those who lived in Deva before us. All that is left of them is their sacred language and their saying that souls go up as birds. They worshiped birds, their great god was the simurgh. Folk say that their horses were as yellow as our yellow clay, tarpans, and that they themselves were colored as if arisen from earth itself, dun of skin and hair. They might well have returned to earth, for all I know."

"It is said also that someday their great king who lies asleep under the mountains will arise and smite us all," a man added.

"And folk say as well that it is unlucky to speak of them overmuch," the captain warned.

"Let us have no more talk of luck," Kyrem said, though quietly. "That is not fitting for Devans." And they all fell silent, for they knew two who had once said that Seda had brought them bad luck, two who no longer lived, and now they wondered whether to feel foolish or afraid. But for the time, their magic ran strong in them. They smiled and slept that night with no thought for noise or luck or curses.

The next day the first one of their remaining number met his fate.

It was one of the demon things that did it to him, the one that whinnied out, "Devan dogs!" The soldiers were beginning to be able to tell them apart, almost as though they were pets, and they had lost most fear of them, for the things merely mocked and followed. But on this day the company was riding along some steep terrain, picking a winding way amid shelves of rock, and the horse-bird swept low overhead, catching a man on the side of his head with its heavy, dangling hooves, knocking him off his mount and over the rocky edge. The fellow went crashing and tumbling down the mountainside, coming to rest finally far below, smashed and dead. The others never knew which killed him, the blow or the fall, but his head was half crushed, and either way, the blame fell to the account of the cursing horse-headed bird.

After they had made their way to the body and stood for a while around it, stunned, Kyrem's three remaining followers turned on him in open rebellion.

"It has been nothing but ill fortune ever since this shuntali joined with us!" a man cried, shaking.

"I do not believe such stuff," the captain said, "but you know, Kyrem, the lad was there at that inn, and no mishap had plagued us before then. Perhaps Vashtin magic does hold some sway—in Vashti."

"We'll all be dead," the other soldier groaned.

"I know the lad means us no harm, Kyrem," the captain continued, "but perhaps—"

"You're talking craven nonsense, all of you!" said Kyrem hotly. If he felt an inward chill at what had happened, that was his secret, for an unreasoning bond now held him to the unfortunate he had befriended. "Seda has done us all good and no harm. He is to stay by my side for as long as he wishes."

"I will go," said Seda. She turned and without another word started walking back the way they had come, uphill and away from them.

With mingled guilt and relief, the men watched her depart. Kyrem felt some more genuine distress. "Seda, wait!" he called after her. "Where will you go? What will you do?"

She turned for a moment, shrugged and waved and kept going. Her situation was not new to her—why, then, the tug at her heart?

"Well," said Kyrem tightly to his companions, "let us tend to this dead one and be on our way."

They hastily covered the body with scree. The dead man's horse had panicked and bolted, long since out of sight, gone off to join the wild horses on Kimiel. And as ill luck would have it, packs had been on it that contained most of their meager gear and supplies. Kyrem decided against pursuing the mount, and the others did not object; they were eager only to be gone, to make their way out of these mountains that now seemed to loom so ominously.

They rode silently until sunset. Then in the afterglow they turned and looked at each other. They had no food and little comfort in blankets or each other's company.

"There are some of those ruddy mushrooms beneath the trees," the captain said at last. "Let us see how they taste raw, since we have no pan to cook them in."

They were good. But Kyrem ate only a little, for appetite left him whenever he thought of Seda. The others ate heartily, lazing by the fire and ignoring the voices that called from the shadows all around them.

"Peckernose! Peckernose!"

"Where is your father? Bastard! Bastard!"

"Die! Die! Devan dogs!"

The captain bent over where he sat with a groan. As Kyrem stared, the others did likewise. Then, as he rose to go to them, the pain struck him in his turn. His belly, poison working its way through his vitals— His men were screaming. He did not scream, but the gut agony bent him and felled him like a strong blow; he landed nearly in the fire, lying on his side in the dirt and writhing. His head swam, and sparks not of the fire flashed before his eyes. Was he losing his mind? He seemed to see Seda, one hand on the neck of the missing horse, standing just at the rim of the firelight and staring. Horror on the lad's thin face. Horror—Kyrem remembered horror and nothing more.

The horses fought. Stallions all—for mares were not ridden but used for brood and milk, and gelding was scarcely whispered of, an enormity as blasphemous as the mating of mare to onager—once the control of their masters ceased to restrain them, the stallions fought.

The white went first—soft, posturing, suitable only for ceremony and show; rearing, it was soon toppled over backwards and broke its neck in the fall. The black was more dangerous—the pure, clear black, not a brown hair on it, not even the fine hairs of forehead and muzzle—very dangerous, but it took a smashing blow in the jaw from Omber's hind hooves and fled to die a lingering death from starvation. The falcon-speckled gray, lean and swift, favored as resembling the raptor, fared little better, running off with the blood flowing bright from a deep meeting of teeth at the jugular. And the red bay, the *kumait* with the lucky star of Suth on the forehead, took a striking blow on that star, strong enough to send it crashing to the ground. Omber alone, the blue roan, remained, and a wisp of a girl of a stableboy scarcely noticed the battle, intent on the fate of the one remaining human sufferer before her.

When at last he awoke, yellow sunlight was streaming through the trees. Morning, he thought. How the leaves have spread. Where has the night gone? He tried to rise and discovered to his hazy surprise that he could not; he felt too weak. He could see to either side. No sign of the captain or the others, but one of their blankets was stretched, tentlike, over his head. He noticed a steady pain in his stomach, not so much the familiar pang of hunger as a more sluggish ache, the feeling of illness. Then Seda appeared above him, carrying a pan of something.

"Seda," he said, wondering that his voice came out as a quavering whisper.

The lad sat down wordlessly beside him, folding her long legs, and without preamble, she began to spoon the stuff into him. It was a very thin gruel. Kyrem swallowed a few spoonfuls, astonished and insulted, before he mustered strength to bring an arm up from under his covering of blankets. He intended to take the spoon, but his hand, wavering, blundered into the pan of gruel, sending it splattering over Seda and the ground.

"Stop that!" said Seda as sharply as he had ever heard the lad speak. "Lie still."

Kyrem glared—the ungrateful youngster! But in a moment all his attention was taken up by a phenomenal sensation in his innards. The gruel seemed to be eating its way through them. Pain attended every inch of its progress, and Kyrem doubled up and lay on his side, moaning. Seda came over and inserted her hand into the tight curl of his belly, rubbing it hard. At first Kyrem wanted to shout in protest, but then he realized that the warmth and pressure of the lad's hand eased him somewhat, and by cautious degrees he relaxed.

"What is going on?" he panted. "Was that poison you fed me, Seda?"

Somewhat to his surprise, the lad replied. "The redcaps," she said tightly.

"Those mushrooms? But you had eaten them with us many a time."

"They are good food cooked, deadly raw."

The few spoonfuls of gruel reached the end of their agonizing journey. Seda turned back the blankets and cleaned Kyrem without comment. He forgot to be mortified, for a sense was growing in him that he had wet one foot in the river of death.

"The others—"

"Dead," she said. "Dead within a few breaths. I could not help them."

He had eaten less than they. How long ago had that been?

"Sleep," said Seda, and he did.

It had been nearly a week, he found later. Seda had nursed him constantly during that time. She had dragged the bodies of the dead men away and had covered the bodies of the horses with boughs, and she had found pasturage for Omber. She had stolen bread at the nearest village. She had gathered herbs such as she thought might help Kyrem. She had endured the mockery of the cursing demons through long nights alone with a sick and insensible prince. She had foraged for wild food for herself, snared coneys and shadow-tails, and she had boiled stolen barley meal into gruel.

"You have to eat," she told Kyrem when he awoke.

He ate and suffered, and in a few days the suffering grew less and he was stronger, able to sit and hold the spoon for himself. At first he nearly hated the shuntali who tended him, somehow irrationally linking her with his misfortune, his pain. But along with his strength there grew in him a sense of gratitude. This lad, this stableboy, what Seda had done for him was extraordinary. The quick rescue from fire and foes at the inn had taken courage, but this slow helping of him back to health took more; it took constancy. Not many would have seen it through. They would have left him on a doorstep perhaps, or left him worse off than that. Those were harsh times. But Seda had showed true in every way.

The fourth evening after he awoke, Kyrem sat silently beside Seda at the fire, watching the flames and listening to the familiar noise of cursing in the night.

"Folk say that the souls of the dead go up as fire, that they make their way to the sun," Seda said.

He glanced at her keenly and kept silence. In his experience, Seda was not one to talk for the sake of conviviality.

"I never thought," she said.

"Never thought what?" Kyrem asked after the curse-filled night had waited for a while.

"I never thought to tell you about the redcaps."

"You are never likely to make a blabbermouth," Kyrem wryly averred.

"I never meant to be a curse to you," Seda said, and Kyrem exploded into speech.

"You are nothing of the sort! How can you be a curse, you who have done nothing but good for us? You who showed us paths and brought us food and risked yourself, saved our lives, saved mine at least twice, maybe more."

"Your ill luck began when you met me," Seda said.

"Our ill luck began that night, it is true, the night of our crossing over into Vashti, and you are the only thing here that has combatted it. No, if there is a curse, I think it comes from out yonder somewhere." He glanced away toward the darkness and the mountains and the noise of the demons.

Then he reached over and lightly touched her hand. They both felt the ancient magic in that touch, the bone-deep comfort and the bond.

"I am not sure I believe in curses," Kyrem added, "but if I do, then you must be my talisman, the jewel that sends harm away from me."

Chapter Five

After the camp fire had burned down to embers, Seda went out a-thieving, as was her custom, and Kyrem lay in his blankets and dozed. When her thin hand shook him awake, he blinked in surprise. It was not yet morning. Darkness lay all around.

"I have seen a familiar face at the hostelry," Seda said.

"What?" He did not understand.

"One of those who fought with you. A pinched face, small eyes like those of an animal. Weasel-face, I call him to myself."

Fully awake now, Kyrem threw off his blankets. "They have followed us here? But weeks have gone by. I thought we were rid of them long since!"

"Vashtins do not ride." Seda had grown more talkative of late. "If they have followed us, likely they have only now caught up to us. And it is to be hoped that they do not yet know we are here."

"Those cursing demon things mark us! If they know the

meaning of them. And I wager they do. Why else. . . ."
Kyrem left the thought unfinished and rose to his feet, standing unsteadily. Urgently he felt the presence of an enemy, a
relentless agent of misfortune that tracked him and pursued
him, paring and paring away at his strength. "If only I can
get on Omber—"

He could not. Try as he might by the faint light of embers,
he could not, nor did he have the strength of body to control
the steed, strength to focus his Devan power. Swaying but
still determined, he coaxed Omber alongside a fallen log.
The stallion was confused by what was happening, starting to
feel restive.

"Give it up, Devan dog!" a horse-bird shouted. Enemies
in the night. Kyrem suppressed his terror and ignored it.

"Seda," he said, "get on."

"But what of you?"

"Do as I say. Get on him."

She scrambled onto the horse from the log, dragging after
her a pack full of hastily gathered gear and supplies. Kyrem
had just strength enough to boost her into her place.

"Now hang onto his neck and pull me up behind you."

"Behind me?" she repeated stupidly.

"Yes. I am going to have to hold on to you, and you are
going to have to learn to ride like a Devan, lad."

Omber was a prince's steed. No one except Kyrem had
ever sat him to control him. By his training, no one could.
Now Seda was to try.

"Hold on by the mane," Kyrem directed, his head already
resting against Seda's thin shoulders.

The long, silky black mane. She laid the pack before her
and grasped it.

"Squeeze with your legs just a little to send him forward."

Omber did not move. He felt the presence of his master on

his back, but strangely; something was wrong, and though he would not rear and hurl his master off, still, why should he obey this other? He pawed the ground angrily and flung up his head, shaking it, sending mane flying.

"Squeeze again, and concentrate your thoughts on going forward. It is his will against yours."

Stubborn determination stirred in Seda, and her jaw grew hard, the line of her lips straight and narrow. She nudged with her legs again, then yelled and kicked.

Omber gave a stallion's scream of rage and sprang forward from a stand into a hard gallop. Seda hung on by the mane, and Kyrem hung on to Seda. And as the girl struggled to keep her seat and her balance, her legs fastened ever tighter around the horse, urging it on and on. There was no question of control; Omber took his own course. Back to the track and down the mountain straight through the village they sped, Omber snorting, the others riding intently, silent and pale, and the cursing demon things flapping above. A few late-goers saw the blue-black horse bearing down on them, unknown riders, weird retinue, and they sprang out of the way, clutching at the talismans they wore around their necks and holding them up to ward off evil.

"We've marked ourselves now for certain," Kyrem gasped.

Seda nodded, for she had seen a pinched face peer from the shadow of a doorway. But Omber plunged on down the valley track, shying and swerving at every reaching tree, running crazily. Not until dawn did exhaustion slow him to a walk, the lather of his mad exertions shining whitely all over him, steam curling up from his flanks in the morning chill. Kyrem was leaning hard against Seda, nearly unconscious, and the girl set herself to learn on her own how to handle the beast that strode under her.

She came to understanding with Omber gradually, directing him with the tug at the mane, with the pressure of one hand against his neck, with the pressure of the opposite heel against his belly, bending him to the way of her choosing, with the shifting and settling of her body weight, and above all, with the focusing of her will. A sense grew in her slowly that was unlike anything she had ever felt before, a sense of power. It sang in her, and she listened, unbelieving. Her, power? She had always been powerless in every way and shut off from all Vashtin magic. She who had always had to struggle even for scraps to eat, she could not believe she was controlling the stallion between her knees.

"It is in your blood," Kyrem said, recovering somewhat. "Born in you—you are doing beautifully. Are you sure you are not a Devan, Seda?"

She shrugged. She was neither as dark as a Devan nor as fair as a Vashtin. She looked like dirt, they had always told her. No matter.

"It is the air," she said, meaning the freedom, the mountains, the ways of the open road. Getting away from her bondage and the scorn of Vashtins. Knowing the company of Devans. It smote her that all but one of the Devans were dead. And the strength of their bright horses—she remembered the names of the horses, Chert, Agreeable, Topaz, Alabaster, Superb, Sard of Suth, My Difficult—that was the black. . . . She mourned the horses too.

"We are in the foothills," Kyrem marveled.

They had, indeed, made good speed. The land had turned grassy, red earth contained by shelving terraces of blue rock; wild goats gamboled on the outcroppings, and only the rounded crests of the grassland were forested with thorn. They could see to all sides, and for the time they had certainly outdistanced their enemy, if the weasel-faced man were their enemy.

"Look," said Kyrem. "Even our demons are fewer."

It was true. With the dawn and the foothills, several of the black horse-headed birds had circled away and left them, flapping back toward Kimiel.

Kyrem laid his head down again. "I hope I am in better fettle before we reach Avedon," he muttered.

Seda was feeling weak and sore as well, battered by that first wild ride. But they kept on at the quiet gaits throughout the day, eating a few scraps of bread from Seda's pocket, drinking from her flask, fearing that if they stopped to rest, they would not be able to go on again. The sun grew hot, for in these parts it was already summer, and the heat sapped their little remaining strength. When at last evening came, they stumbled from their mount with no thought for fire or food. Seda stood swaying for a moment and rubbed Omber's forehead where the sweat had dried on it, giving him Devan thanks or greeting, and he stood gravely. Then she unblanketed him, pulled her own sleeping blanket from the pack and tossed Kyrem his, and they both nearly fell into them, sinking to the ground.

"Besides me, you are the only one who can ride him," Kyrem murmured. There was a warmth in his voice, an ungrudging generosity that made Seda blink and moved her to words.

"Thank you, Ky," she said softly. Sometime during his illness she had started calling him Ky.

"He is starting to like you," Kyrem added.

"Shuntali! Shuntali!" shouted a demon from the dark.

The next day as she rode, Kyrem still weak and leaning against her, Seda learning more and more of an accord with the horse, she felt an odd, sticky sensation under her and realized to her horror that she was bleeding. The onset of women's flux—she could not realize for a moment what it was, for she had almost forgotten that she would be a woman.

Then her eyes opened wide in consternation. This must some-how be hidden from Kyrem. They could not be together if he found her out.

She rode the rest of the day in a paralysis of worry. Luckily Kyrem, faint and weary, noticed nothing. Luckily also the blanket on which they rode was red, like Kyrem's lost cap. They stopped that evening by a stream, and Kyrem lapsed at once into a sleep that was almost a swoon. Seda washed out the blanket, wet with more than the horse's sweat, and washed her own clothing and herself, and that night she stole more than food. She came back with someone's old patched tunic swaddled and wadded underneath her trousers. Then after they had eaten, she slept contentedly and dreamt of riding Omber.

In the nighttime of far away an other opened her dark eyes, startled awake. This dream, this sense of a great beast, a stallion, moving between her legs, what could it mean? And the sun, the warm breeze—and the grasslands, the blue rock, and not so far behind, the mountains! Great lofty crests of sorrel with their mane of black trees—things she had never seen, yet she saw them so clearly—and she herself, had she not been . . . a boy? A stripling half drunk by a wayward power?

But how could she have dreamt such a strange thing? She was a maiden, humbly born and just thirteen, just entered on her first flux. Soon there would be the ceremony of passage, the lengthening of her skirts to below her ankles, and already her mother and her mother's noble mistress had been adjuring her to sit more gracefully, walk more sedately as she grew into women's estate, speak more demurely and more seldom and with circumspection, conduct herself always in such a way that her chastity would never be questioned. And it was true that she had never slept far from her mother's bed.

Then who had been the man, the youth, pale of face, comely, curly of jet-black hair—and how could it be that she had dreamt of sleeping by his side? Only a dream, she told herself. Yet even on waking she remembered his face as clearly as though she had seen it in flesh and in fact, as though she had gazed on it with longing. And her heart throbbed with the memory.

Atop the mountain, the most holy mountain that men called Kimiel or Anka, the enemy heard report from his black horse-headed servants and frowned. All the Devans destroyed except the one who mattered the most! And this little Vashtin, this shuntali, what was he to thwart the most holy rage? The Old One bent his mind that way and frowned again. Something was wrong; he found no outcast lad, but a virgin girl in her first red moon dew and full of powerful magic.

He frowned yet again and sent orders winging to his other, human servants.

As Seda and Kyrem rode past one last rampart of the mountains the next day, orange rock came roaring down at them, and Omber's best speed barely took them out of danger. Looking back, Seda saw human figures, black and tiny with distance, standing where the landslide had begun. A few of the cursing, black demon things circled above them, and a few more from their own unofficial entourage left them, flapping back to join the others.

"If those are our enemies from the inn back there," said Kyrem, "they will be hard put to catch up with us afoot."

They pressed the pace a little. But they could not ride long or late with Kyrem still so weak. And the next day, as they threaded their way down the rocky valleys of the foothills, an arrow flew at them from some distant thornwoods, barely missing them, parting the air between them with a rush. As Omber leapt forward in response to their panic, another flew just behind his haunches, and as they fled, another fell to the track at their feet.

"Bowels of Suth!" Kyrem muttered, having learned blasphemy from black mentors.

They rode as long and hard as they were able, camped in secrecy with no fire, rose early to ride again. Each day, as Kyrem grew stronger, they made more miles, and for a while there were no more incidents.

By the time Seda was over her flux and had secretly discarded the old tunic, Kyrem had mostly regained his former fettle. Once again he took his place as rightful rider of his steed, and once again Seda rode behind him. Though she was not as timid with him as she once had been, she felt too timid to speak her mind about this arrangement. It was his horse after all.

They had come far down the foothills; they would soon be in Avedon. All but two or three of the cursing demons had deserted them. But those few reminded them constantly of danger and the enemies and misfortune that had followed them thus far.

"Die! Die! Devan dogs!"

In Avedon there would be safety for Kyrem, Seda felt sure. All the energy of her will was bent toward bringing him safely there. Kyrem also pressed on toward Avedon, but with a different feeling, not thinking of safety and hardly thinking he would ever actually arrive. The journey had become its own reality to him.

"There it is!" Seda exclaimed, and Kyrem stared, unbelieving.

Atop the breast of the last soft foothill, they looked down on Auron's city. It seemed all white and brilliant, sparkling gemmily in the strong Vashtin sunlight. City walls, spiral towers, stately buildings were white-plastered and ornamented with mosaics, some of them, Seda had heard, made of real semiprecious stones; they blazed in the sunshine, and beyond the city stood a blaze of red, the flamelike trees of the sacred grove. They marched up the sides of the flat-topped promontory called Atar-Vesth, the place of fire, and they surrounded the spring of Suth whence sprang the welling river, Ril Acaltha. Mirrorlike, blinding bright in the light, it looped and spiraled clear around the city, winding its way under narrow bridges, rimmed with yellow sand. . . . And flowers: the yellow flowers that gave the river its name, and other flowers, tall spires of red, pillows and froths of white and blue and pink—every terrace was bordered with flowers. The red land was all done up in such terraces to either side of the river, with troughs and buckets always working to bring the water up. Avedon fed on the Ril Acaltha.

"Look," Seda said. "The red-tiled roof—that is the temple." Where the priests of Suth read the great charts and kept the horses at the sacred stable. "And the gold dome— that is King Auron's dwelling." At the very center of the city, amid all the glitter, and outshining it all.

"I must be out of my mind," Kyrem said abruptly. He backed Omber until the court city vanished like a vision behind the crest of the hill. Then he wheeled his horse and headed at a canter back up into the foothills, toward the wilderness and its sheltering woods.

"What is the matter?" Seda asked, startled.

"I can't go in there! I look like a beggar!"

He was variously put together with pieces of looted gear and clothing borrowed from dead men. He had a black-enameled helm that rose to a stubby point, and he had a belt, his long knife and a curving sword. He was thin, but he had his strength back; he looked dangerous and lean. Seda sniffed at him.

"No one would ever take you for a beggar," she told him, "and especially not on Omber."

"Omber needs grooming," Kyrem muttered. He had dismounted and was poking about the woods with a fixed intensity of expression but with no purpose that the girl could divine. She slipped off the horse in her turn.

"Whatever are you looking for?"

"Isn't there a sort of bush that makes black dye?"

"Yes, it grows by streams. But what . . ." She broke off and stopped where she stood, her hands on her narrow hips and her bony elbows pointing out to either side, weaponlike. "Ky Crazy," she stated, "we are not going to stay in this wood for another minute! Something has been hunting you for weeks, and now, half a mile from safety, you take it into your head to decide you want matching clothes!"

"You've grown louder since I've known you," Kyrem remarked.

"You are out of your mind if you spend another night away from Avedon."

"For all I know, the one who is trying to kill me sits on the throne in Avedon."

"I keep telling you," she shouted, "King Auron is not like that!"

"How would you know?" he retorted, and he turned on her in harsh, unwilling anger. "Damn it, Seda, I have come weeks on a starving journey to a place I hate and fear, harried like a rabbit by Suth knows who or what, some malevolent, faceless enemy—damn it! I can't just walk in there like someone coming to pay a morning visit!" He stood breathing raggedly. "Twelve brave men lie dead between here and Deva," he added, more quietly but more fiercely. "Don't you understand?"

"All right. I'll help you dye your mourning!" She threw up her small, twiggy hands and marched off downhill, toward where she judged a rivulet might run. "Don't expect to sleep," she added sharply over her shoulder. Until then she had taken the main burden of nighttime watching, reasoning that Kyrem was mending and needed his rest. Until then.

They found the plant, made their small camp, stripped the needed bark and placed it in a kettle of water to boil, all in silence. There was nothing to eat and no pot to cook it in. Seda shrugged and sat by the fire. Kyrem scowled.

Three mocking voices sounded in the dusk. "Where's your mother?" one neighed. "Where's your lover?" chanted the second. "Bastard! Bastard!" the third one cried.

"That's right, demons dear," said Kyrem morosely. "Curse me all you like. Here I sit, hungry, twelve comrades dead on my account, called mad by the one remaining"—he cocked a sour eye at Seda—"attended by flapping monsters, sent off into unknown peril by the command of a father who probably uses me more than loves me—" He stopped.

"You think your father has betrayed you into danger?" Seda asked, astonished.

Kyrem jumped up and paced, as if to outstrip his anger. "It is hard to say," he hedged. "He chose me out of the dozen of us, and I am not the eldest—he would never send his eldest son, the heir, on such an errand. Nor am I the youngest, or the cleverest, or—or anything. He sent for me and told me without a word of explanation that I was to go as hostage to Deva, without encouragement or sorrow or emotion of any kind. That is his way, and I should be accustomed to it by now, but I can't help feeling like . . . like an outcast.''

Though they had shared much in the course of their journey, he had not yet shared so much of himself with her, and she felt all the honor of it. Instantly peace was made, anger forgotten and only empathy left. She knew that outcast feeling well. ''Surely your mother was sorrowful to see you go,'' she said anxiously.

''I have no mother.'' He laughed at her expression, the warm laugh of a friend and equal. ''It is true! We princes are all bastards. The king sows his seed where he will, that is the custom, and he brings home his choice of the crop. We boys were all raised together in a big barracks.''

''So that is what you meant,'' Seda said. ''What you and the others told me that first day.''

''That we were all bastards? That was part of it.'' He sat beside her again. ''It's a sort of joke also, the Devan way of saying that we are none of us any too sweet. Devans are a tolerant folk.''

He was forever extolling Devans. That was his inner defense, Seda guessed in a quick rush of insight. There was a vulnerability about him she had not seen before. . . . He stood up and unlaced his shirt, preparing to place it in the dye pot, and the girl turned away from the sight of his strong, naked shoulders, feeling a thrill she refused to acknowledge or admit to.

''Seda,'' said Kyrem rather suddenly, ''have you ever thought of looking for that twin you think you have?''

Odd that he should mention that scarcely remembered other. Odd; since her flux she had felt for the first time that absence, that lack, like an ache or an empty place, like hunger.

"Your brother whom you have never known."

Sister. She had told him something of herself during their weeks together, but not the secret that troubled her the most. Her young breasts were swelling, a development she noted with dismay; she bound them sternly beneath her rough shirt so that he would not feel them against his back as they rode. She was still a boy to him.

"Do you think you might be a Devan? You somewhat resemble the nomadic folk I have sometimes seen in Ra'am."

Ra'am was his father's capital city, with its walls of yellow clay. Thinking of herself, of her sister, of hidden parts and secret feelings, full of confusion, she did not answer. But he was used to her silences. Noticing nothing amiss, he began to groom his horse.

"High polish for you, old nuisance," he said to the steed softly, "for in the morning we'll be riding you into Avedon."

"I'll walk," said Seda, and Kyrem looked at her in surprise. "I am a shuntali to everyone except you," she explained. "They could kill me for sitting on a horse."

"But how can they know," Kyrem asked, "if you do not tell them?"

"They'll know." The question seemed nonsensical to her. She fully believed that her taint, her unworthiness, was manifest in every aspect of her being as plainly as if it had been branded in black glyphs on her forehead.

"May your breasts droop!" a voice whinnied from the darkness, and Kyrem roared with laughter, not knowing that such nonsense made her wince.

Chapter Six

Shirt and tunic and short cloak and trousers were dyed a rusty black and hung up on prickly bushes to dry. Girl and youth kept watch that night or dozed uneasily, but no danger threatened them, and they arose with relief at dawn. The city gates would not open until sunrise or later.

"I hope they have something to eat in there," Kyrem muttered as they waited. "Ride with me," he urged when it was time.

She shook her head again. "I will walk." And he knew better than to coax her; the lad could be very stubborn in her quiet way.

"Well. . . ." He vaulted onto Omber and stroked the steed's neck, gaining courage. Then somehow, subtly, he transformed himself into the Prince. Seda knew his power as a person, his innate magic, his gift, but for the first time she sensed the power of his rank and his office. Straight and sober, all in black, sword at his side, black hair curling from under his black helm, he sent the splendid blue-black horse

forward at the slow and collected ceremonial walk. The
hostage rode forth to meet his fate. In a moment he would
crest the last rise and ride down into Avedon—

"Game ho!" a voice shouted, the cry of a hunter who
sights his quarry.

And arrows flew at them from several directions. One
clanged against Kyrem's helm, and one pinned his cloak to
his shoulder from behind, striking the bone beneath the skin;
for a moment he was almost blind with pain. Some swished
beneath Omber's belly and through the grass at Seda's feet.

"Come on, Seda!" Kyrem called, turning and offering her
his hand to pull her onto the horse with him. But her thought
was different. "Ride, Ky!" she shouted at the same instant,
and she gave Omber a fierce swat on the rump with her palm
to send him plunging forward. Then she scurried back toward
the shelter of the thicket they had just left. Omber's rush
carried Kyrem over the rise toward the safety of Avedon. Or
so Seda hoped.

Kyrem let Omber run as far as the first bridge, then drew
him to a halt, cursing. The few peasants who were about
scattered at the sight of him, for a man on a horse was an
omen, awful, a harbinger of war. And the black horse was
the darkest omen, the worst. The blue roan, black of skin,
not much better. . . . Kyrem laid his head on Omber's neck
and tried to think.

Wounded. What might they be doing to Seda? Raise the
garrison of the city, hundred men or more, go find the
boy—obstinate pride stirred. For all he knew, those within
the walls were his enemies as well. And they were Vashtins,
they would care little for him, and for the shuntali even less.
Painfully he sat up and reached around to where the arrow
jutted, removed it with a jerk, letting the blood flow down

and soak his black clothing. He would have to find Seda
himself.

And to do that he would have to circle around behind the
lines of his unseen enemies. Hills hid him for the time. . . .
He turned Omber and set off northward at the canter, following the yellow verge of the river. From the topmost tower of
Avedon a watchman studied him curiously until he vanished
around a curve of the terraced land.

"Find Seda, Omber," Kyrem murmured to his steed, his
head bent low to the horse's ear. If somehow by the focusing
of his thoughts and his will he could make the animal
understand. . . . Omber's half-wild senses were more likely
to find the lad than his eyes would ever be.

Omber snorted and carried him yet farther northward.
Kyrem could only assume that enemies were in those woods
the horse avoided, and he cursed them since he could not
confront them. Curse their eyes and their strong, recurving
bows that could shoot such parlous distances. . . . Curse
them. No curses in the air above him . . . what was this
unaccustomed silence? Where were the flapping demons, his
black entourage? They had left him. His heart rose at the
thought, though for a moment he felt, irrationally, almost
resentful. No retinue for the prince—but at least their presence no longer marked him.

The day wore on into hunger and confusion. He wound his
way up the foothills toward the Kansban in a different valley,
one studded with spicules of bright pink flowers among the
blue rocks, and he had to fight his way through thorn forest
at the end of it and make a crossing when he judged he was
out of danger. There was no knowing where the mysterious
archers were, but one could assume that they went afoot and
Omber had moved far faster. Still, the sun was high when he
at last found his way back to the track and prepared to

approach Avedon all over again. Somewhere along the way, he hoped, he would find Seda.

She was in the selfsame copse by the stream where they had camped during the night. He took a long time getting there, starting and shying at every movement and cloud shadow as if he were half horse. Twice Omber took him on a circuit off the path. His wound had stiffened and his stomach had ceased protesting its fate and the day had passed from pain to faintness when he saw the shuntali at last and could scarcely believe his eyes. For her own part, she was as startled as he.

"Kyrem!" she hissed, rather sharply. "You ought to be in Avedon."

"Leave you here?" he murmured, sliding off of Omber and collapsing beside her.

"I can take care of myself!" she retorted.

"Forward urchin," Kyrem grumped. "Ungrateful malapert. Have you seen any of our friends?"

"*What* friends?"

"The flappy-flappies?"

"Gone."

"How about the arrow-zingers, then?"

"Listen," she whispered.

The tramping of many feet, with no attempt at secrecy. They crept to the edge of their cover. Looking out between the leaves, they could see the movement of many helms and lances and the scarlet and yellow colors of Avedon. Auron's men were scouring the demesne.

"Come on," Kyrem breathed, inching back.

"Go to them!" Seda protested out loud. "They are clearing away your enemies, they are looking for you."

"I can take care of myself too," Kyrem said stubbornly. "Come on!" He tugged her back to where Omber stood.

"Ky—"

"I am going to Avedon, I'm going! Do you think I would break my father's bond? But I'll not be brought in like a captive by a bunch of hirelings. I'll go on my own." He lifted her onto the horse and they set off southward, eluding the foot soldiers.

"Ky, you are out of your mind." Seda was no more than mildly annoyed, for she felt blissfully the passing of danger. All day she had spent on the move and in hiding, going to tree or to ground like an animal, eluding the weasel-faced man and his brigands. She had come back to the copse at last only because they had already hunted through it twice and might not search there again. . . . Safe, now. She settled comfortably into her place behind the prince. It would be good, this one last ride before he entered the city. The sun beat down hotly, sending clouds piling high overhead in the brilliant turquoise sky. She dozed.

Crack of thunder, and torrential rain poured down. Seda awakened with a jolt to darkness and confusion. The storm had brought on an early nightfall, and Kyrem had slowed Omber to a walk, peering about him. In the gloom and blinding lightning nothing could be seen clearly except the occasional momentary sheen of the river off to their right.

"Vashti is a senseless country," Kyrem muttered. "Dry as old bones one moment and all in a flood the next. Well, it is time to double back toward Avedon, I suppose."

The river made a maze of itself, meandering around the city. They rode toward where Kyrem thought he remembered a bridge, and failed to find it. Then they thought they had strayed onto a spur of land within a river loop, and they changed direction and lost the river altogether. Lightning showed them a flash of white somewhere off to the left; might it be the white clay walls of the city? They rode toward it and found nothing. During the next hour they rode in several directions as the darkness deepened and the rain poured down, until at last they admitted to themselves, though not to each other, that they were wet to the skin and quite lost.

"What now?" Kyrem complained. "Trees. Surely we cannot have come all the way back to the foothills."

They rode under the shelter of—what? They could see little, but they could sense the branches far above them that rustled in the rain and broke the force of its fall, sending down large, plopping drops instead of stinging spicules. No undergrowth impeded them, and a sort of hush, a distancing of the thunder and roar of the night, told them that the trees were mighty, the woodland large. They came up against a steep slope and turned away from it.

"We *cannot* have come back to the foothills!" Kyrem insisted, although no one had contradicted him. "No, wait, here is a clearing."

They could sense the space by the pouring of the rain. Then lightning blazed, turning it all at once brighter than a dozen suns, and they both screamed.

A horse, a monstrous horse perhaps fifteen feet tall, towered over them, curveting, collected to spring; their startled, fearful eyes stared up at its flexed head, the gaping mouth with teeth bared, the distended nostrils, the fearsome, white-ringed, staring eyes—and between those eyes, set just at the center of the forehead, a great gemstone that flashed blue in the lightning—but there was no lightning, yet the stone continued to blaze! Omber reared with a scream of his own, a stallion's scream of fear, for he was as unnerved as his masters. With a squelching thud, Kyrem and Seda landed on the ground, and Omber plunged away.

Prince and girl sat where they were, staring. On that huge

head above them the jewel flared purple, then red, giving off its own fiery light in the dark woodland clearing. And on the shoulders of the steed . . . were those wings of flame? It had not moved from its gathered stance. With a shaky laugh, Kyrem stood up.

"It's made of stone," he said. "A sort of statue—but, Suth, doesn't that flickering light make it look alive?"

"Don't touch it!" Seda warned, still seated and gasping.

"I wouldn't go near that jewel yonder for anything." The gemstone had turned a greenish hue, then yellow. By its light Seda could see Omber peering cautiously from between the trees at the edge of the circular clearing.

"But the horse itself I dare touch," said Kyrem, and stepping onto the pedestal, he reached up to stroke a shoulder. The wing, or flange, that sprouted from it was rudimentary, flame-shaped, and not large enough to carry the bulk of the beast had it indeed been alive. The stone of the body was splotched and discolored with rain and lichen. Seda could see a large patch of pink lichen on the chest, flowerlike in shape and darkened to the color of blood in the rain. Brownish patches mottled the flanks and haunches. The head seemed white. The mane streamed moon-gray in the jewel's light, which had gone from yellow to white.

"Get away!" Seda exclaimed, standing up. "Do you not believe in the vengeance of Suth? You swear by him."

Kyrem stepped down but ignored her question. "Look," he remarked, "the ears are broken off. When might that have happened, I wonder."

"The statue looks very old," Seda muttered.

"Well, at least we know now where we are." Kyrem sighed, forcing his body to relax. "The sacred grove. Yonder hill is the altar, and the spring must be somewhere about. And we are just outside the city walls."

"And the gates are closed by now."

"Then we might as well spend the night here as elsewhere," said Kyrem with a fine, reckless air. "We have shelter here of a sort"—he eyed the dripping trees—"and our very own light to see by, which is well since it is too wet for us to make a fire."

Seda scowled. "I am sure the light is not for our benefit," she snapped.

"And, by Suth, food!" Kyrem had found a niche in the pedestal, and from it he pulled a flat round of bread. He sank his teeth into it even as Seda ran forward with a cry of indignation and fear.

"Ky, you'll be killed by the priests if the wrath of Suth does not strike you down first!"

"You pious Vashtins." He offered her a second round of bread, still chewing hungrily. "I would not care if a hundred screaming priests surrounded me at this very instant, I am so starved. Eat, Seda! What else but this has Suth ever given you?"

"I am used to hunger. I am going to find Omber." She marched off, her back angry and stiff, and the light of the jewel gently faded out behind her.

Warm in her sheltered bed under the eaves, the faraway other awoke with a start to stare wide-eyed at the thatch close over her head. What had it been, this vivid dream of—Suth himself? The treasure of wisdom and of the one true wish gleamed between that god-stallion's eyes, she had seen it. Did the dream mean she was to be a vestal for him? She shuddered at the thought, for Suth made a demanding master. But had there not been that youth in the dream also, he of the handsome face and the jet-black curls? And once again, that sense of her own trousered self, a lad?

Often of late she had been troubled and frightened by feelings she could not explain. In the midst of her maidenly tasks, laundering the fine fabrics her mother embroidered for lords' daughters, spinning the bright threads, stirring the dyes, she would feel the oddest sensations—surge of strong beast between her knees, wind keen in her face, rough touch of fur or trees or rock, taste of sweat, pull of strong muscles as if she could climb and run forever, she who sat daintily stitching. She wondered if she could confide in her mother, if her mother could help her, but she doubted it, and her just-budding sense of womanhood and independence kept her silent.

In the dark she lay and wondered. Suth the stallion, the god-steed—was he not but a steed after all? Winged with fire maybe, but a steed? And what might it be like to sit such a steed, or to serve him?

She paled, then blushed hotly, shaken and shamed by her thoughts. Blasphemy—but no god struck her dead.

Kyrem saved the second round of sacrificial bread for his lad, even though his own stomach wanted it badly. And sometime in the privacy of night, after she had brought Omber back, after the storm had rumbled away and she and Kyrem had supposedly settled into an uncomfortable sleep, Seda ate the bread. No god struck her dead, and morning dawned fine and bright. Before priests could come to serve their god, or before anyone else was likely to be up and about to see them, they slipped out of the grove, Kyrem on Omber and Seda afoot, as she insisted. When the gates of Avedon opened at sunrise, Kyrem entered his fateful city at last.

Chapter Seven

The gates were flanked by spiral-twisted columns inlaid with mosaic, and within, mosaics in glass and gems and tile adorned the walls of homes and shops: mosaics in the stylized melantha and acaltha pattern, or depicting the Mare Mother and Suth and his seven wild sons in their seven colors and with manes streaming to signify their grandfather the south wind, the mistral. The streets were cobbled or paved in saffron brick, and multicolored tiles bordered the small, square courtyards and the gardens with their ornate vases and statuary, their blossoming fruit trees. Though she had heard tales of the loveliness of Avedon, Seda had not truly comprehended them. The beauty of a city given over to craftsmen—the very bricks she trod were impressed with a spiral design. For the first time since she could remember, Seda felt her own shabbiness as she strode at Omber's side. Kyrem sat his steed stiffly erect, the blood of his arrow wound blackened on his black clothing, his jaw set and the lines of his face hard. Seda wished he would not look so forbidding.

Auron's palatial gold-domed dwelling fronted on the city center with its wide square of tile and brick and garden. At the steps they had to leave Omber on his own, for no Vashtin servant would touch him. They ascended the broad, shallow stone risers past porcelain tubs full of scarlet-blooming quince. At the top a doorman met them.

"Kyrem, prince of Deva?"

"Who else?" Kyrem's manner, usually the youth's proper mixture of civility and arrogance, tipped the balance this time toward arrogance.

"And your servant?"

"My friend Seda."

"Go in," said the man. "Straight ahead and—"

But there was no need for directions. Auron was hurrying to meet them, his crown and its crimson turban in his hand, picked up in haste from their ebony stand.

"At last!" the king exclaimed. "I have been worried. You were seen yesterday with an arrow in your shoulder, and I sent out my entire household—" Auron seemed ready to throw his arms around Kyrem, but he came to a stop as Kyrem stared at him in open scorn. For the king of Vashti was not a king as Kyrem knew kingship; not much like his warrior father Kyrillos, forsooth! Auron stood short, balding and plump, looking like any ordinary merchant except that he wore sumptuous robes in all the seven colors, embroidered with every sort of glyph and flower or animal emblem, and on his short fingers sparkled at least one of every sort of lucky jewel; there were forty-nine in all, and more draped his neck and studded his clothing. In his excess of ornamentation he seemed foolish, unmanly. On his feet were buskins of gilded leather, their high wooden heels covered in scarlet leather. Flamelike flanges of the same leather rose up to flank his ankles—were they meant to be fire or wings? Even with the tall footgear, Auron stood half a head shorter than Kyrem, and the buskins made him mince along rather than stride. To Kyrem they seemed the crowning affectation, utterly ludicrous.

"But what is the matter?" Auron asked softly. "What has happened? I sense . . . bereavement."

Kyrem gave only the briefest nod of greeting. He looked haughty and angry to Seda's eyes, not bereft. "Your realm is not kind to travelers, King," he said harshly. "All those who came here with me are slain, and I bear wounds. Six men killed by brigands at an inn, the rest by treachery and poison; only Seda's nursing saved me, and my horse, which carried me out of constant peril."

Seda stood staring at the fine floor of inlaid wood beneath her bare feet, but as Kyrem spoke, she risked a glance at Auron. He looked gray with shock, anguished rather than angry, as stricken as a mother facing a hurt child, and slowly he settled his crown onto his head.

"But this is terrible! That you should have been so beset on your way to me, in my kingdom."

Seda felt a sudden impulse to fall to her knees. Auron's soft robes suited him, for he was more than king—he was parent, the kind father and loving mother she had scarcely known. Her legs trembled and weakened, but as she watched, he set aside emotion for the time and his face grew still and thoughtful.

"Prince Kyrem, you are most warmly welcome here," he said quietly. "Please come in, sit down." He gestured, nearly touching Kyrem but thinking better of it. "Have some wine, tell me everything. I need to know places, dates, the circumstances."

Kyrem remained standing where he was. "I have sometimes thought," he said evenly, "that those might have been men of your hiring who sought to kill me." Seda trembled at his boldness. But Auron did not seem affronted.

"Yet you are here?" He glanced appraisingly at the youth, the dart of his eyes keen and seeking beneath the foppish headdress and crown. "Then you are very brave. And I cannot condemn you for your thought. But it is not true."

"I can believe nothing you say," Kyrem stated flatly. "I look only for falsehood. You are my enemy."

"Ky, what are you saying?" Seda whispered, then found herself speaking aloud. "What are you saying?" She spun to face him, a small fury. "Show some decency! He has greeted you as an honored guest. No, more. As—"

She would have said as a son. But Kyrem had turned on her in astonishment and anger. "Seda, what has gotten into you?" he shouted. King Auron looked as astonished as he.

"You apologize at once!" Seda shouted back.

"That will not be necessary!" Auron exclaimed, and Kyrem drew back in disgust.

"I will go see to my horse," he said, "if that is permitted. Or did you intend to have me put in chains?"

"I had not thought of it," Auron said mildly.

"Kyrem, you proud fool—" Seda began, shocked anew. But Kyrem glared at her and strode out, the heavy carved door banging behind him. King and shuntali were left alone in the hallway, and Auron was studying Seda with friendly interest in his eyes.

"You are a Vashtin," he said. "I can tell that much. But how is it that he calls you Seda? That is not a Vashtin name."

She said nothing and started to tremble yet again, her eyes transfixed by his and terrified. She could not allow herself a name before him, before her king, she the shuntali; she felt sure she would die if she did. Falsehood, and her own manifest unworthiness—

"Oh, I see," Auron murmured thoughtfully. "Never mind that then. Tell me, how did you come to travel with Kyrem? You two make an odd pair."

She could not answer. Fear bound her speechless, and she looked as if she would faint.

"Lad, believe me, there is no need to be so afraid." Auron drew closer as he spoke, stooping slightly, putting his face on a level with hers. "A king also makes an odd sort of outcast creature. We are not so unlike."

She did not hear him, for floor and walls had begun to spin at his nearness. His presence demanded an answer from her, a confession, or so she thought— She closed her eyes.

"Shuntali," she whispered, that terrible, that hated word she had never before spoken. Then she fell to the floor. She had meant, when she began, to seek succor of the floor, but by the time she reached it, she had fainted.

She awoke a few minutes later to find herself lying with her head in the arms of the doorkeeper and the king himself kneeling beside her, dosing her with wine. She turned her head to hide her eyes from him. But Auron placed a hand by her cheek and gently held her gaze with his.

"Seda," he said. He himself had titled her with that name now. "That was very courageous, but unnecessary. 'Shuntali' is not a legal term within the code of this kingship."

She stared, not understanding. Auron sighed and tried again. "Seda, you also are my most honored guest, the companion of my guest the prince."

She did not feel that she could stay on those terms. She wet her lips three times before she could reply. "Let me be his servant," she whispered at last.

"But I have servants enough for him and for you! You both have suffered. Rest a while."

Her eyes, the look in them of a small, trapped animal, gave the answer. Auron saw and acceded to the need in her.

"All right," he said. "Serve if you must, but remember that you will not be able to work your way into wholeness, Seda. You must seek for better truth."

He placed his other hand against her head, comfortably, almost casually, and she sat up, suddenly stronger.

"The body I can heal," Auron told her. "I am a king of Vashti; I have that power. Suth help you with the rest. Now come and eat."

The stable was large, with clay-floored horse-bays for nearly fifty steeds opening onto a central courtyard. Finely sculpted spiral columns supported the red-tiled roof that overhung the stalls deeply, making them cool and shady. The brick walkway behind the columns was as tidy as the hallway in a lady's home, each horse-bay piled deep with yellow straw, and the stone trough in each one brimming with clean water. Scores of paupers in Deva scarcely lived as well as the steeds here.

Into this scene of equine bliss came Kyrem, scowling, his hand on Omber's neck.

Stable and yard swarmed with priests and would-be priests, many boys in brown robes and youths in gray, a few men in blue or red. These were not their own colors, but the hierarchical colors of their calling; they had forgone their own personhood to become priests. None of them greeted their visitor or so much as glanced at him; they busied themselves. The boys scurried about like so many brown beetles. But Kyrem had only just started to look around him when a tall man in a yellow robe stepped from the shadows of a stall and strode to meet him.

"Kyrem, prince of Deva, greeting," he said, inclining his shaven head slightly, his tone gravely courteous.

"And who might you be?" Kyrem demanded, his tone not nearly as courteous.

"Nasr Yamut, atarabdh, at your service." Atarabdh meant fire-master. This priest had reached the highest rank he could hold without entirely retiring from the world into a life of meditation as did the atarashet, those beyond the fire.

"I need stabling for my horse," said Kyrem curtly. As a member of the warrior elite, he held rank above that of the priest, whose calling exempted him from the obligations of war. Or at least in Deva the rank of a warrior aristocrat was above that of a priest, even a powerful priest.

"This way," said Nasr Yamut, seeming not at all affronted.

A priest in a green robe and a green skullcap, two in red robes and two in blue were exercising horses in the central courtyard, leading them about by brightly colored braided ropes of cotton. The steeds pranced and skittered on their strings like so many kites, or like huge fish, Kyrem thought. They seemed almost unmanageable, but the priests never reprimanded them. As he and Omber skirted the group, Kyrem looked carefully for the first time at the sacred horses.

"Their ears are clipped!" he exclaimed aloud in shock. The creatures had only stubs of ears left, nearly level with their polls.

"Of course," Nasr Yamut said. "The more closely to resemble Suth."

Kyrem remembered the statue and looked again at the sacred steeds. All of them were oddly mottled and dashed with white—cousins of cows, he thought scornfully. Three had white legs and hooves, soft hooves that would never have withstood the rocks of the upland steppes of Deva, as Kyrem did not fail to note. On their faces they were marked with wide blazes of white that took in their eyes. Kyrem nearly shuddered; of the bald-faced horse it was said in Deva that he carried a shroud. But that was superstition. These horses looked fat, and so sleek and polished that the veins showed through the thin hair of their legs and muzzles.

"Will this do?" Nasr Yamut asked.

Kyrem blinked. It was a big cavern of enclosed horse-bay into which Omber could be put loose rather than being tied by the head as in the other stalls. There were only a few such enclosures in the stable, Kyrem saw at once, and he felt sure they were intended for the royalty among horses.

"It will do admirably," he said, trying to keep any hint of surprise or gratitude out of his voice. Certainly Omber deserved no less.

"We do not want such a fine stallion to become restive," Nasr Yamut said.

Kyrem darted a glance at him, wondering what might be his hidden purpose. For a priest of such high station to be found at the stable seemed odd. Was it he who had decided on this special stall, or Auron? No matter. Enemies, both. Though this priest at least seemed more like a man than Auron.

He lingered at the stall door while Kyrem tended to Omber, clapping his hands and calling in quick succession for brush, rubbing cloth and scraper. Brown-robed boys came running.

"I do not want any of them touching Omber," Kyrem said rather sharply. "I will care for him myself." He almost added, "If Auron permits," but stopped himself in time. He would not become a hostage in his own thinking.

"Of course," said Nasr Yamut smoothly. "They would not touch him in any event," he added after a moment's awkward silence. "The browns, the boys, are allowed only to sweep and fetch and clean, and the grays, the novices, may polish the ceremonial gear and carry water and food. But no one is allowed to touch a horse until he is confirmed to the priesthood for life and is a blue, an epigone—and then only under the supervision of a flamen."

"Red," said Kyrem involuntarily. He was being lured into conversation in spite of himself.

"Correct." Now it was the priest who stood silent.

"So what rank is next?" Kyrem asked, trying not to sound peevish.

"There are three greens, epopts, and then myself."

I am indeed dealing with an exalted stableboy, Kyrem thought wryly.

"The epopts and I, we tend only the oracles and the kingmakers."

Kyrem could not help raising his dark brows in inquiry.

"Here is one in the next stall," Nasr Yamut offered. "If you are finished. . . ."

The prince stroked his stallion's high crest and silky mane, glancing at the full manger and suppressing a starving urge to take some of the corn for himself. But he was a prince of Deva; he could go for a while longer without food. He followed Nasr Yamut out of the stall and watched as the priest, with quiet but evident pride, led a tall horse out of the next bay and into the sunshine. The creature kicked and reared dangerously, and the priest brought it down without comment.

"The colors, the markings," he said, "they are the finest we have yet attained."

Mud colors, Kyrem thought contemptuously. The horse's coat was mottled and blotched with gray, dun, brownish hairs and speckles of white. But it was not only the body markings that made this the oddest creature Kyrem had ever seen. The entire head, halfway down the neck, was white, giving an impression of hoary age, and the eyes were white as well. Kyrem wondered if the creature could see. When it turned its head his way, it seemed blind and at the same time secretly spying, as if it could see inside him, and he felt a chill of sudden revulsion or horror. Irrationally he thought of the demon horse-birds he had left behind in the foothills. The shape of this horse's head reminded him of them somehow, except for the clipped ears. Splatters and dashes of reddish hair grew on the steed, with a broad patch of red spreading down its chest. The priest laid his hand on it reverently.

"The bloody wound," he said.

The horse attempted to bite him. Nasr Yamut pulled back.

"Hit him," Kyrem exclaimed, "if you do not want him to do that."

"These are sacred steeds!" Shock and indignation showed plainly on Nasr Yamut's face, and just as plainly he struggled to suppress his anger. "We never strike them or restrain them in any way," he added more quietly.

Stalls and ropes, not restraints? Horses were kicking and pawing and biting in their stalls all the way around the stable. Kyrem took breath and let it go again, refraining from further comment.

"Does the beast have a name?" he asked at last, cautiously. Best to be courteous, since he had offended.

"No, of course not."

No names for the sacred steeds. Somehow he felt he should have known as much.

"And it is an oracle?" he asked, still trying, if distantly, to be polite.

"Of course. Our finest." As the horse reared again.

"But how does it speak to you?"

"In the paddock, the holy enclosure. It is outside the city walls, near the sacred grove."

Nasr Yamut seemed fully mollified by the prince's interest in this matter, but Kyrem stared blankly.

"We study and interpret the neighings and movements of the steeds when they are released. The direction taken, how many bounds, the bearing . . . it is a subtle art," Nasr Yamut explained with evident patience.

And the poor beasts are never freed except at such a time, Kyrem thought with an intuitive leap to truth. *The sons of wind tied in stalls, led in circles and rune figures, no gallops across open ground, not even under a rider. And they call Devans cruel. . . . They will not want Omber to use that paddock, and I want to stay far from this wrong-headed magic. I will take him to the hills outside of the city to romp and play—beyond the terraced land. If I am permitted.*

"I thought you read charts," he said to Nasr Yamut.

"We do that too. The prophecies of the oracular steeds apply only to the king and his kingdom." The priest spoke with a teacher's eager zeal. "The charts are for anyone who cares to learn his personal destiny. Come, would you like to see them and the temple and the Ahara Suth, the sacred spring?"

Even though his stomach was shouting, Kyrem went with him, not so much out of interest as a reluctance to return to the ruler's dwelling and face Auron and Seda. He did not know how to confront Seda.

The way led through a postern gate to the interior of the temple, a tall building standing against the outside of the city wall, cool and dim and thick of clay-brick wall, a fortress terminating in red-tiled towers spun out into javelin points against the sapphire sky. Kyrem did not see the towers until later, for his eyes were on the guardian above the entry, the stuffed and mounted head of a real horse, indeterminate of color and evidently very old; he could not meet its shriveled and sunken eyes. More such horses' heads were inside, to the number of thirteen of them, rangèd above the charts, some of them with clipped ears and most of them with white faces, or at least plentiful white markings about the forehead and muzzle. Some of the less ancient ones had polished stones set in for eyes. Those were only a little easier to face than the others.

"The kingmakers," Nasr Yamut explained, seeing Kyrem staring at them. If Kyrem had asked, the priest could have recited the names of the thirteen kings of Vashti and pointed to the head of the sacrificial horse that had ushered in each one. But Kyrem did not ask, for he did not wish at that time entirely to understand.

A pair of silent, gray-robed youths stood flanking the charts, expressionless, holding the fragrant lamps and guarding the flagons of chrism and the repositories of the mysteries. This was part of their training. The charts themselves were gigantic, finely detailed mosaics that filled the whole of the tall white wall of worship, the nave of the place, the sanctuary. Nasr Yamut genuflected and then approached them, chanting.

> *"Moon-white owns second sight,*
> *Yellow dun is essence of sun,*
> *Ardent, of Mars, is the sard-red bay,*
> *Blue is the steed of the evening star,*
> *Brown is sturdy, its emblem earth,*
> *Quicksilver fleet is the mystic gray,*
> *The black as significant as the white."*

The chart of seven. Kyrem knew it only by hearsay. The colors all Vashtins wore except priests, and to each horse color a star or planet and a glyphic symbol, an element, a jewel, a flower and a beast, so that the chart made a perfect square.

"Aside from the horse itself, the stars and the jewels are the most important," Nasr Yamut said. "For stars are the jewels of sky and jewels the stars of earth. . . . Come, I will give you a reading and require no offering. What were the day and time of your birth?"

"I do not care to say," Kyrem said, though not discourteously. Conversation had taken some of the edge from him.

"Why not?" The priest gave him a keen but smiling glance. "I know you Devans honor the name of Suth."

"We keep far from charts and symbols and all such subtlety," Kyrem replied promptly. "Princes of Deva are taught only to ride, to shoot the arrow from the bow, to use the curved sword and to speak truth. It is enough."

"It seems little enough learning for one who may someday rule," Nasr Yamut said, still smiling. "Here, we believe in wisdom. Before I became an epigone, I had hundreds of lines of lore taught to me, all committed to memory and chanted daily, and before I became a flamen, thousands, and the disciplines of the mind as well. But if you speak of subtlety, see here."

He bowed low before the chart of seven, and they moved on to the larger chart, that of the seven times seven.

"Forty-nine colors of horses."

He named some of them. Seven kinds of white—the pure candid white, and the porcelain, ash white, argent white, ermine, alabaster, and the aureate, or fire white. Seven sorts of yellow—the fallow dun, clay dun, saffron, barley meal, amber, sand, and the scorched, or fire-fanged. Each of the forty-nine tiny mosaic horses was shown in a different posture, curveting, running, rearing or standing at the alert. Looking at them all, Kyrem felt his head spin from hunger—or from a reluctant wonder.

"Sard, ruby, copper, cynoper, burnt bay and fire bay and murrey." Nasr Yamut recited the seven reds.

"I have never heard of a purple horse," Kyrem murmured.

"It is puce, a brownish dun purple, the color of a flea," Nasr Yamut said offhandedly. "The fire-touched colors are the most significant, the flame or scorch colors."

"Is that so?" Kyrem sounded only faintly sarcastic.

"But beyond even this chart there are yet other colors—the leopard-spotted horse and the horse of spreading flowers and the trout-speckled horse, the rose roan, the dappled horses and all those who bear white markings or the lucky star of Suth, or mane and tail of different colors; and then there are the whorlings of the hairs of the coat to be considered, wheat ears and shooting stars and cornflowers. As for the sacred horses, and the oracles and kingmakers in particular, they are quite beyond any chart, transcendent."

"I should think so," said Kyrem with a certain fervor. The sacred steeds were undoubtedly the oddest horses he had ever seen.

"Come," said Nasr Yamut. "Would you like to see the hoofprint spring and the stone Suth?"

"Thank you, but no. Some other day." Kyrem had decided to heed the importunities of his stomach. Also, he had seen that stone horse not long before, and the memory still flickered eerily in his mind, casting a shadow of vague unease. He had no desire to see it so soon again.

"Come here to the temple, then, any time between the bells. We priests live overhead. Ask for me."

Kyrem only nodded. He was not too eager to seek friendship in this city of his captivity. He turned and took his eave, wondering what welcome would await him this time at Auron's dwelling.

It was dinner, nothing more or less. The doorman directed him to his chamber, where water for washing awaited him along with a linen towel. Then he was summoned to a small room just off the golden-domed audience hall, where Auron sat studying his hands, his crown on a small table beside him and dishes with covers of silver on a larger table before him.

"Oh, there you are," he said, his tone warm but quiet. He sat up straighter and offered a chair. "Sit down, eat. Here is wine. I know you are starved."

Kyrem sat down and accepted the food with the best indifference he could muster. To his annoyance, his stomach would not let him muster much, and the viands were superb. Lamb in mint sauce, pastries, pomegranates, a salad made from the blooms of violets—he ate heartily and silently. Auron took only the salad.

"Your servant Seda has been lodged in suitable quarters," said Auron after some time, and Kyrem threw his head up with a snap.

"Seda is my friend!"

"I thought as much," Auron said. "But he is to be your servant now, it seems. He did not feel that he could remain here otherwise. Shuntali, he called himself."

"Ah." Kyrem's tone was dark with irony and his scorn for Vashtin ways. "And would you have known it of him had he not told you?"

"I would have known well enough." Auron met his hostage's hard gaze steadily. "But I would not have cared. Nor do I now."

Chapter Eight

"That arrow wound," Seda said. "You should have it looked at."

She had brought Kyrem pitchers of hot water and was watching him bathe. New clothes of red and royal blue were laid out for him on a vast tiled washstand below a tessellated wall; linens and pillows and blankets of the finest soft mohair clothed his bed, which swung from ornate chains fastened overhead; the room was luxurious in every detail. Kyrem had forgotten any vexation against Seda in the press of the day's events. He remembered now only that Auron had made his lad a servant, and anger warmed him at the thought. And he would have to take his meals with that monarch or else starve, it seemed. He was considering the merits of starvation when Seda spoke of the wound.

"It is only a scratch," he said.

"It is not. It is a piercing wound, and it was never properly cleaned, and it is starting to swell. You should have the king take care of it."

"Auron?" He swiveled around to stare at her.

"Yes. The king is a healer."

"I'd sooner swell." Kyrem turned back to his washing, finished it and reached for a towel of milky white cotton. He pushed aside a new tunic in the process.

"Bullheaded," Seda said. "You will be wearing your old rags next, and refusing his food. Or do you not scorn the king's food?"

He gave her a hard look, not failing to note that she wore new clothing which was soft and whole, though plain.

"I will eat Auron's food and wear this gaudery and even accept gifts and courtesy if I must." Kyrem turned away with a gesture of decision. "But I will have no part of any devilish Vashtin magic. And it does not surprise me to hear you say that your dear king is a sorcerer."

"A healer!" she protested.

"It is all the same. One capable of the sending of certain horse-headed birds."

He had told Auron the tale of their journey after dinner, grudgingly and only because justice demanded that the Vashtin king should be allowed a chance at vindication of himself and his kingdom. Auron had given orders immediately. Patrols were to go forth, men on foot with donkeys carrying their supplies, to find the mysterious archers. Kyrem cynically expected that they would find nothing.

"I am going to bed," he said to Seda, and she went off to her own bunk in the barracklike servants' quarters—the male quarters of course.

The next morning, quite early, Kyrem went to fetch Omber from the stables, speaking to no one, not even to Seda. He rode the horse out of the city gates as soon as they were open, and at trot and canter he sped far up the terraced farmland to the hills where sheep grazed and over the rise of the first one, out of sight of Avedon. There he dismounted and let Omber graze and roll and play, himself sitting on a blue boulder patterned with lichens of pink and whitish green, contentedly watching the horse and expecting at any moment to be surrounded by Auron's retainers come to march him back to captivity.

The sun reached its zenith and moved past it, and Kyrem's stomach took up arms against him. No Vashtin came near. Finally, reluctantly, he rode back to Avedon and stabled his horse. In his gold-domed palace, Auron sat waiting at the table as before.

Kyrem ate hungrily and silently, also as before, feeling cross and somehow outwitted. Auron ate little.

"It seems I am permitted to go out and exercise my horse," Kyrem said, keeping his voice as toneless as possible.

"Of course," Auron replied rather sleepily. "Take a packet of food from the kitchen next time. There is no need to go without."

"And if I ride away?" Kyrem challenged.

"That is as it comes." Auron glanced up from under delicate, highly arched brows like those of a well-bred woman. "It is true, you are unhappy here, perhaps you have comrades or a sweetheart in Deva whom you miss, perhaps you dream of yellow cliffs and great spaces. But you know the value of your father's bond or you would not be here."

Kyrem felt startled and angry, for Auron's words were accurate except concerning the sweetheart. Dismayingly accurate. Still, he would play his game out.

"And if I pack myself two weeks' worth of supplies and ride out of here bound for Deva," he said, "what will you do then?"

"Why, nothing." Auron met the youth's shocked gaze blandly. "Assuming that you would return to Deva by a different route so as to avoid those pertinacious enemies of yours. But you would have your father to deal with when you arrived there.''

Kyrem applied himself to his meal and said nothing more. Inwardly he seethed, knowing that he had been bested. He spent the afternoon exploring the city, staring with hard eyes at elegant houses, shops, stalls and tile-bordered streets. He took supper in his room, having Seda bring him fruit and bread from the kitchen, and he went early to bed.

The next morning there was some coinage lying on his washstand, some coppers, a few silvers and a single small gold coin, no extravagant amount but enough to provide some amusement at the gaming stalls, some sweets perhaps, a bauble, a small gift for Seda. Kyrem looked at the coins and let them lie. His shoulder was swollen and sore, hurting him so much now that he found it difficult to move the affected arm. He felt sullen.

"Come with me today," he said to Seda.

"That is not fitting," she told him. "You have rank to uphold, and I am a servant."

"I need a friend worse than I need a servant," Kyrem said.

"You have a royal friend, if you would only notice." She glanced at the coins. Kyrem scowled at her and stalked out.

The servant was honest. The coins stayed on the washstand for the next three days, and Kyrem continued as sore and sullen as ever. He was bored most of the time, for there was little for him to do while he was avoiding Auron. One can spend only just so much time with one's horse, exercising and grooming—though the priests and their boys seemed to be fussing over the sacred steeds constantly, leading and grooming and combing mane and tail and braiding lucky beads into the forelock—but even had Kyrem been inclined to spend all day brushing Omber, his painful shoulder would not allow it.

"May I do it?" Nasr Yamut asked, seeing Kyrem wince as he attempted to pick up the stallion's feet for cleaning. The priest sounded eager. It pleased Kyrem that Nasr Yamut so badly wanted what was in his, Kyrem's, power to bestow. In a more sane frame of mind he would not have thought of sharing Omber with a smiling stranger, but he was in a fit mood to swagger. Also, he hoped Omber might kick the priest.

"Go ahead," he said grandly. He placed Nasr Yamut's hand against the curve of the steed's neck, giving the man authority to touch him. Nasr Yamut cleaned the hooves deftly, and Omber did not threaten to kick. Watching, Kyrem felt an inexplicable prickling of dismay.

"Such a beauty," Nasr Yamut declared, stroking Omber. "So noble, so mannerly. Truly a paragon among horses."

Perhaps, Kyrem decided to still his dismay, this priest might be a friend of sorts after all.

When he was bored thereafter he would go in search of Nasr Yamut, if he had not met him at the stable, and find the priest in the temple teaching the novices or reading the charts for some wealthy suppliant or tending to the spiced barley mash that was always brewing on a gilded brazier for both the priests and their sacred steeds. And Nasr Yamut would greet Kyrem as a friend and an equal, leaving his work to walk and talk with him.

On Kyrem's fourth day in Avedon they walked out to the place of fire, the Atar-Vesth, and Kyrem studied the blunt promotory of blue rock and its strange red-leafed trees that were shaped, leaf and tree, like flames or perhaps like a horse's ear. And they visited the stone Suth, and Kyrem looked warily at the gem in its forehead, but it neither shone nor took on color other than a smoky crystal hue, shadow of the stone Suth beneath it.

"It is said in the lore that every horse carries the treasure of the world between its eyes," Nasr Yamut said, "but none of our foals has yet been born bearing such a gem, only the lucky white star."

"Is that the meaning of that gem then?" Kyrem asked. "That Suth owns the treasure of the world?"

Nasr Yamut hesitated. "It is not known exactly what is the meaning of that gem," he replied at last. "For many years men have feared it."

Kyrem had felt that fear, but he chose not to reveal it. "Why?" he asked blandly.

"People have died of touching it. We priests recite their names on our days of sorrow and fasting. No one nowadays will touch it, and no one comes here except we priests who serve the effigy of the god. Folk used to come more commonly at one time, it seems." Nasr Yamut pointed at the pedestal, and looking more closely, Kyrem could see a glyphic inscription in the stone, worn nearly smooth with the touch of time.

"Do you know what it says?" he asked the priest.

"Yes, and . . ." a delicate hesitation, for effect, Kyrem felt sure. ". . . I dare say I may tell you. It reads,

> *"Come hither, pilgrim, bearing*
> *your heart's desire.*
> *See whether your boldness*
> *will win your desire*
> *or death."*

"Grim," Kyrem remarked.

"Yon is a dangerous jewel, and an oracular one in some

way, we feel. It changes color when great events are in the offing. We watch it with awe.''

For once Kyrem did not scoff, inwardly or outwardly, at the words of the Vashtin.

Not far from the stone Suth ran the hoofprint fountain, Ahara Suth, the great crescent curve of blue rock where the river welled up. "Suth must be as big as the world," Kyrem said.

"What is the Devan belief concerning the shape of the world?" Nasr Yamut asked him.

"Belief?" Kyrem shrugged. "We know little enough. Our own land is the center, and beyond it lie places where souls go or where gods dwell or where the Old Ones went when we drove them out. Perilous places. And a great river surrounds it all, and then the edge of nothingness. But no one really knows except from dreams.''

"There is a great river at the edges of Vashti," said the priest. "Lore tells us that beyond that bourne the soil is black instead of red, and black lilies grow there, beyond the deep water. The river is called Ril Melantha, and it is always hidden in mist. That is a magical stream. No one crosses that river except the white-robed ones, the atarashet, those who are beyond the fire, to enter upon their life of meditation, and they never return.''

"I do not understand this matter of the atarashet," said Kyrem. It sounded like none of the customs of his land.

"When fire-masters go beyond, they cross the Ril Melantha to the Untrodden Land, the place of powers, of the numina and the puissant dead. From that moment they are atarashet; they become as if dead to this world. They speak with the spirits of potent kings of old, of seers out of the past. They meditate amid the black lilies. They grow wise.''

"Are they not wise, then, before they go?" asked Kyrem. This seemed to him to be an odd way to make a mystic.

"We hope all fire-masters are wise."

There seemed no safe answer to this.

"Are mystics honored in your land, Prince Kyrem?"

"Of course," he replied automatically. "The mystic is the third eye of being, that eye through which the world beholds itself and knows itself divine. Of course we honor our mystics."

Behind his back the jewel in the forehead of the stone Suth winked and glittered as he spoke. Nasr Yamut saw and stiffened and opened his mouth as though to speak, but thought better of it. If the jewel was the third eye of Suth, then what was this prince?

"And do you honor priests?" he asked Kyrem instead.

"Of course. But not—" Kyrem smiled sourly. "Not as much as you are honored here."

"How do you mean?" Nasr Yamut spoke smoothly, and Kyrem, who had begun to trust him, did not notice the tension around his eyelids.

"Priests serve the god. Rulers and warriors tend to the real business of the world." Kyrem shrugged, smiling, then grimaced as the shrug reminded him of the wound in his shoulder. "In Deva we raise men of might to rule," he added obliquely, saying nothing more scornful of Auron.

The king of Vashti was no warrior, no ruler to Kyrem's way of thinking. He did no mighty deeds, uttered no proclamations, received no ambassadors, made no appearances of state. He did not ride forth, nor even walk. Indeed, to Kyrem's knowledge, he had not yet set foot outside of his own palace. But within it he busied himself with councils and accountings, with the thousand petty affairs of his kingdom and city and servants; no detail was too small for him, Seda had said.

And sometimes for hours on end Auron would simply sit, as passive as so much pastry dough, and stare. Nasr Yamut, on the other hand, always seemed to be concerned with something important, even when he was not. He took command, gave orders to underlings, brushed aside the trivial, strode away to pace and brood, dynamic. Kyrem stood somewhat in admiration of the intensity of the man, the force of his intelligence, the scope of his conversation. Nasr Yamut made a superb teacher, he felt sure, he who had always had small use for teachers. Yet the priest honored him by asking him his opinions.

"Do your priests not prophesy, then?"

"In Deva," Kyrem answered promptly and with feeling, "prophecy is the province of old women who delve for the bones of murdered children. We of the blood take things as they come."

Nasr Yamut stood silent for a while. "Well," he said at last, "I must return to my duties. Do not come here alone, my prince. This is forbidden ground except on the great occasion of a sacrifice." He accompanied Kyrem back to the temple, then left him.

The prince went back to the gold-domed palace at the hub of Avedon to find Auron waiting at table for him as usual. And as usual they ate their dinner in silence—until Auron broke silence.

"These buskins of mine are ridiculous, as you've thought many times," he said, his voice quite gentle, though not at all apologetic. "But I do not wear them as an affectation, to make myself appear taller. They are royal footgear. The heel of the Vashtin monarch is never to touch the floor or the ground, not even in the privacy of his own chamber. And these silly things keep the royal heel from even coming near it."

Kyrem tried not to gape. To be sure, he had made no effort to keep his face from showing his thoughts, but it startled him that Auron should have guessed them so accurately.

"In the days of my grandfather's reign," Auron went on rather dreamily, "they lamed the king as well. Though I can hardly understand why."

"In Deva we do not hobble our kings," Kyrem said automatically. He felt dazed, and uneasy.

"That shoulder of yours," Auron said, his eyes suddenly keen. "It should not still be so sore. It troubles you, I know. Will you let me tend to it?"

Kyrem stood up, backing away from the table, shaking his head. Then he turned and fled, leaving his dinner unfinished.

The next day he awoke feverish. He rose anyway, ignoring Seda's entreaties to the contrary, and rode Omber out to the river and let the horse bathe in it, and he spent most of the day in the water himself, numbing the ache from his wound, trying to wash the fever from the rest of him. He arrived very late to dinner and found that Auron did not await him, to his surprise and somewhat, oddly, to his discomfiture. He ate little, finding himself queasy, and went early to bed. In the morning he was too ill to arise.

"Ky, let me bring the king. Please," Seda begged.

"No. For a certainty not," he muttered thickly. "Are there no other healers here in Avedon?"

"Midwives. I trust you don't want them. King Auron—"

Kyrem flung himself upright to face her. "No!" he roared with a force that turned his feverish face purple and started blood running from his nose. Seda jumped to staunch the flow with whatever cloth came to hand.

"All right, all right," she soothed, easing his head back onto the pillow and cooling his face with a wet piece of toweling. "Bullheaded. . . ." She sat by him until the bleeding stopped and he lapsed into a troubled sleep. For the sake of his pride she could do no more for him that day, and after dark she went first on a private errand and then to her own bed. She did not sleep. By herself she could not tend Kyrem in the nighttime, for if it ever should become known that she was a woman, he might be dishonored in the minds of all Vashtins—she was a shuntali, after all. But he would not die overnight. She had already seen to that.

That night the faraway other dreamt that she was a servant, a manservant, living in the crowded servants' quarters of a great king's dwelling. The other servants teased her, the shy young newcomer, often but not unkindly. She was a shuntali— what did that mean?—but they made nothing of that, for Auron would never have allowed it. Auron was the wisest, kindest king Vashti had ever known, and his ways of dealing with matters of the judgment hall had already become legendary. The servants knew all things about him, and they found no fault with him. Was Auron the comely youth with the black curly hair? No, that one lay abed, as sore in spirit as in body. Would Auron heal him? My king, heal him, please. He should not be like this, he is not like this inside; he has a nature as generous as yours, only younger, more ardent, less wise, and some things it is hard for him to understand. Already you know these things of him? My king, you will help him? Then must I slip away through these crowded barracks in the silent mid of night, slip away for the prince's sake, hushed, creeping. And look, King Auron awaits me near the prince's chamber door; he would have come without my pleading. Kyrem sleeps, I have checked, and Auron allows me to hold his candle—

The other awoke and lay staring at the darkness, puzzled

and afraid, as usual. Auron's name at least she knew—but only as that of an enemy.

Kyrem awoke in the morning feeling as well as he ever had in all his youthful life, as though sunrise sang within him, and he sat up in wonder. His fever was gone, and so was the ache in his shoulder. Raising his arm, he tested the joint, flexing it in every direction, and he could feel no pain in it; as far as he could tell, the wound was dry and healed. He stood up and for once did not call for Seda, but dressed himself thoughtfully. Seda was late in coming, and when she entered his room, she said nothing, only glanced at him with a shy smile, almost a wary smile, wary of too much show of gladness. He stared at the lad, not answering her smile.

"Has some one been in here to see me during the night?" he asked her, his voice low, toneless.

"How am I to know?" Seda shrugged extravagantly. "You know I do not sleep here. To be sure, I checked on you from time to time. I rejoiced when I found that the fever had broken."

Kyrem stared at her for a moment longer, still unsmiling, before he turned away with a shrug of his own, a shrug rendered mercifully free of pain. He went slowly to the washstand and picked up the coins that still lay there, fingered them briefly and then slipped them into his leathern scrip.

Chapter Nine

"Seda, you stink, boy," he said to her a few days later. "Don't you ever bathe?"

She hung her head, blushing. "I can't," she whispered. "There is no—nowhere in those barracks—"

No privacy. Servants were expected to go down and bathe in the river, where a section was set aside for men and one for women. Kyrem laughed, for he had noted his lad's modesty on their journey hither, a modesty that assorted well enough with Seda's soft voice and quiet ways. Indeed, he could hardly picture the lad bathing in the river, under so much open sky. His laughter quieted, and he thought.

"Barracks," he said softly, feeling a sudden surge of homesickness. "By the sound of it, just what I am used to. This room is far too quiet for me. Seda, let us bring a bath up for me, and you take it."

She stared at him, and he laughed again.

"Oh, I'll keep out of your way, never fear. I'll take your place down below."

"Ky!" She sounded incredulous.

"I am quite serious. Come, show me where we get the water."

He was both enthusiastic and adamant, and within a few hours it was done. Seda had bathed herself, hair and all, wrapped herself warmly and settled into Kyrem's soft, swinging bed. For once her poor young breasts need not be bound—such a soft bed, a bed like an embrace. And Kyrem was stretched on Seda's harder bunk down below amid many bunks, feeling clever and content.

"You Devans are a peculiar folk," a servant said to him. "Do you often change places with your varlets?"

"Yes," Kyrem replied promptly. "It is traditional." He flexed his feet and stretched luxuriously, feeling very much at home, and the others accepted this in him and talked before him freely. He lay and listened to the chatter. The doorman was a cuckold, but he did some wenching of his own. Nasr Yamut made a veritable devil of a master. But all good and no evil was said of King Auron.

"Tomorrow is the eve of the summer solstice," Auron told Kyrem some several days later. "Time for the king to take a bride by the traditional reckoning, but you know I have none, so every year at this time an oracle is done for me, as at other times. And there are the usual festivities, bowers and bonfires, and the parade of sacred horses, which I must review. Will you stand by me?"

Kyrem nodded with the faint beginnings of a smile.

"You would not take it amiss," Auron continued, "if I found you some more elaborate clothing?"

"No," Kyrem said, "I would not take it amiss."

"I do not go to the fires and the dancing," said Auron. "I seldom go anywhere lest I should endanger my dearly beloved heels.'' He sounded more whimsical than bitter. ''But you can go of course. I am sure your friends among the servantry would be glad of your company.''

Kyrem glanced at him sharply, but he found no censure or mockery in Auron's tone or face.

So it was that the following afternoon he stood beside Auron on the portico of Auron's gold-domed palace, looking down over the railings into the crowded street below. He wore a brocaded tunic and a tabard of velvet and a cloak of the Devan royal hue, dusky purple, which was flung back and fastened with a brooch of gold; he wore chamois breeches and boots of soft tooled leather, also gilded; he wore bands of gold that spiraled up his powerful arms, and a ceremonial sword too fine for any battlefield, and a tallish red cap with a tuft of feathers at one side. Auron's seven-colored robes were of brocade, and he wore his usual crown and buskins. Kyrem towered over him, fidgeting and feeling awkward, suspecting that his finery had been made especially for him, for none of it bore any of the embroidered emblems or talismans customary in all Vashtin clothing.

''We don't want the steeds to outshine us,'' said Auron.

The crowd parted and began to arrange itself along the sides of the street, and in a moment Kyrem saw what Auron meant as the horses came through.

The priests who led them wore only their usual robes of the single color, plain and unadorned. But the horses were in glorious caparison: headstalls of peacock blue or scarlet leather sparkling with gold or semiprecious gems and with plumes of the simurgh, folk said, floating and bobbing above their clipped ears; mane and forelock all braided with beads and bright ribbons, ribbon rosettes on their cheeks. And then the great leather poitrels around their shoulders, studded with gold and with gold talismans hanging down to ward off evil.

And then fastened to it a sort of garment too ornate and useless to be called a blanket, heavily embroidered and hung with tassels, and more tassels hung from the headgear and lead rope, and tassels danced at the fetlocks, and tails streamed with braids and ribbons, and even the hooves shone with black lacquer, clattering against the brick and tile of the roadway. All the flutter and glitter combined with the motion of the mottled steeds to make Kyrem blink dizzily. As usual, the horses were curveting and prancing dangerously, barely under the control of those who led them. They circled and blundered sidelong into the throng that lined the street. Screams arose as the crowd surged and struggled to avoid them.

"Someone is going to get hurt," Kyrem told Auron softly.

"Someone always does. It is supposed to be rather an honor, being kicked by a sacred steed," Auron said softly in reply. "And often they have to be brought to the palace to be healed."

Kyrem looked at him. He did not seem to be joking, but a wry edge was in his voice.

The epigones came first and the flamens, blue and red, leading the lesser horses, those with the least spotting and mottling of white and divers colors. Caparisons grew ever more splendid as the procession of forty-nine went on, the garments of the horses layered and intricately cut, the head-stalls ever more heavily laden with tassels and talismans. Finally came the three epopts in green, their splotched and spotted steeds draped in leopard skins, and last of all, Nasr Yamut, resplendent in yellow, shining like the sun, in fact, with his white-headed favorite fitted out in a massive jeweled poitrel from which sprang, one on each shoulder, large flame-shaped wings of red satin limned with thread of gold. The fire-master stood for a moment in front of the palace, bowing gravely to Auron and Kyrem as his steed shook its head and reared, fluttering the false wings, sending red shimmers flying—a gasp murmured through the throng. Then he walked past, and the crowd closed in behind him.

"Now onward they go to the place of oracle, the paddock," said Auron. "But the people may not follow them there." He sounded tired.

"Will they let all the horses run?" Kyrem asked hopefully.

"No, only two or three. As the god guides them. But certainly Nasr Yamut's beauty." Auron sounded wry again. He went in to sit and stare as was his wont, and Kyrem went to change out of his grand clothes. Then, on impulse, he fetched Omber from the empty stable and rode him far out into the countryside, letting him gallop as long as he liked.

Every two or three days Kyrem and Seda had been changing places that she could bathe, and he had come to know the servants well and know their ways and skills and the back passages they used. So it was that on the day of the summer solstice, the day after the processional of sacred steeds, he walked softly along a narrow serving-way toward a back entry that gave on the street nearest the stable. He was still within the palace and thinking of Omber when very near to him he heard Nasr Yamut's voice.

"I tell you, my king, beware." That intense voice. Kyrem could not mistake it. But where could the priest be speaking to Auron then, and why?

"The auguries were unmistakable," Nasr Yamut went on. "Your reign is nearing its end, and a usurper will take your throne."

A small serving portal stood close at hand. Kyrem eased it open a trifle and peered through the crack. It gave on the dome room, the audience chamber, and Kyrem's mouth came open, for he had never before seen Auron sit in state.

The rounded interior of the room was finished in gilded filigree and bright tile and velvet hangings, but Kyrem knew that. He had not known about the footbearers. Auron sat on the high golden throne, his head above that of the priest who stood before him, and his buskins sat on their own stand of carved ebony at his side, perched as if ready to take flight with their leathern wings. But Auron's feet did not touch the parquet and tile of the dais, for two of the most comely damsels Kyrem had ever seen held them in their laps. The girls were dressed in flowing, filmy robes of white, and they were redheads with alabaster skins, as alike as twins, although they could not have been twins in Vashti. Auron seemed not to notice them in the least, for all that they held his feet. His eyes were fixed on Nasr Yamut, and in some way he seemed larger than Kyrem had thought him before.

Suddenly ashamed of his spying—though every child and servant in every royal household survives by spying, and Kyrem had done it often enough when he was small—he started to ease the door closed. But then the mention of his own name froze him in place, and he listened.

"Usurper?" Auron was saying mildly. "Are you sure this is not just another way of indicating that I have no heir?"

"The signs were strong and dark for enmity, Sire," Nasr Yamut replied. "And you know Prince Kyrem bears you no love."

Kyrem scowled and bristled at that, surprised at his own anger. He felt the more surprised at Auron's reply.

"Prince Kyrem is an honorable youth."

"He has sneered at you openly, my king!"

"He was sent here with no explanation and no regard for his own wishes and no promise of reward. What do you expect from him except hostility? He makes no secret of his feelings; he is all honesty. And I have never scorned honesty, Nasr Yamut.'' Auron cocked a keen eye at the priest.

"He may make a very honest usurper then!" Nasr Yamut exclaimed. "Send him away, Sire."

"There is no such thing as an honest usurper," said Auron quite without heat. "Moreover, Prince Kyrem has a generous heart."

"Him? That haughty Devan?"

"The very same." Auron sounded faintly amused. "If he is sometimes arrogant, it is because he feels . . . needful, I think. There was little enough nurture in his rearing."

Kyrem listened in increasing astonishment, and Nasr Yamut's ardor grew in proportion.

"You are far too kind, Sire. You have always been so, to your own disservice. Prince Kyrem means you no good. Already, even without the aid of the oracle, I can see the beginnings of his scheming. He has grown familiar with the lower classes, those who are most likely to serve him without compunction. He rides a horse openly, and all the poor and uneducated folk look up to him with awe. Even the well-born youths admire him. He is young, handsome, he makes free of your city—"

"And worse than all that, he is a Devan, and Devans do not hold priests in such high regard as we do here." Auron's voice had become suddenly stern; Kyrem stiffened at the sound of it. And the king's gaze—Auron's eyes seemed to flicker with an unearthly light, colorless and all colors, light as of the statue's deadly jewel, the third eye of Suth. That eerie stare held the priest as motionless as if he were pinned in place by an invisible weapon. "The truth, Nasr Yamut, if you please," said Auron grimly.

The fire-master licked dry lips. "He blasphemes everything we honor," he whispered.

"To your way of thinking. What else?"

Nasr Yamut winced and wriggled, trying to escape, but he could not break free from the force of Auron's stare.

"Prince Kyrem possesses an immense gift for power," he blurted at last. "His whole body is crisp with it, but he does not yet know himself and the usages of it. Please, my king, send him away before he learns."

Kyrem stood incredulous. He could not believe he possessed any power comparable to that which he was witnessing. Nasr Yamut sweated where he stood. And he had thought the king a fop, and the priest a man!

"Certainly you will be the last one to teach him." Auron sounded amused again. "All right, Nasr Yamut. The exact content of the oracle, if you please."

The priest was allowed to lower his eyes at last. He looked at the exquisitely tiled floor as he spoke. "A short running for the shortness of your remaining reign, my king," he said, his voice shaking. "And a strong neigh for a strong new ruler. And much kicking."

"That last might signify you priests," Auron said. "All right, Nasr Yamut. You may go."

The man looked up. "Good my sire, everything in me abhors this prince! I beg you—"

"Is that why you have befriended him so prettily, helping him to while away the days, because you abhor him?" Auron interrupted. "Go."

Auron had not moved from his place, had not moved so much as a finger, and there was not a retainer in sight. But Nasr Yamut turned and went at once, in haste. Power was in that command beyond his reckoning.

And Kyrem stood thinking how that power could have been used against him at any time, and how it had been withheld. He stood for a moment gathering courage, and then he pushed open the door. He strode across the dome room, a long crossing, and stood before the dais and throne, at Auron's feet, looking up at the king.

"I heard," he said.

Auron gazed back at him, saying nothing, showing nothing.

"I have not listened before, nor did I intend to this time," Kyrem said. "I happened by. I hope you believe me, King of Vashti."

Auron smiled slightly at that. "I can tell when people are lying," he said, "and you have never lied to me, Prince. Not even in kindness."

Kyrem winced. "Least of all in kindness." He forced himself to continue to meet Auron's eyes, those wise, sleepy eyes, and he gestured toward the main door. "There went one whom I had thought was perhaps my friend." He turned back to the throne. "And here sits one whom I had thought was certainly my enemy."

Auron smiled and shrugged, reached for his buskins, put them on and sent the footbearers away with a wave of his hand. "Nasr Yamut is not an evil man," he said. "I do not think he would knife you in the dark. He plays at politics, that is all. And he understands power just enough to fear it in others, not in himself."

"And he fears me? That is laughable," Kyrem said.

Auron looked at him quizzically but did not reply. He descended the steps of his dais, teetering on the buskins, and came to stand beside his hostage and guest.

"I have had word," he said, "from the patrol I sent out."

Kyrem sensed the news that was coming—from the tone of Auron's voice, or by some other sense? He kept silence and waited.

"Three men returned. All the others were killed, they say.

And they made it no more than halfway up the mountainside toward Kimiel.''

"Killed? By what? Or whom?''

"Arrows and misfortunes.'' Auron paused long enough to remove the crown from his head and tuck it under his arm. "Kyrem, if you are ready,'' he said, "I really think it is time that we talked.''

Chapter Ten

The odd thing, Auron thought, was that Nasr Yamut's oracle might be in some sense inspired.

He and Kyrem had settled into chairs in the king's small personal chamber, and the prince faced him without speaking, waiting to hear what Auron had to say. So, how to begin. . . .

"What are these powers of yours, Kyrem," he asked, "of which Nasr Yamut thinks so poorly?"

The prince arched his dark brows, taken by surprise. "Only the usual ones," he answered.

How the youth underrated himself. Auron wanted only that he should see his own prowess. "What are they?" he persisted.

"Well," said Kyrem, "in Deva . . ." He was not boasting this time, only telling Auron the truth as he saw it. "In Deva, one who wishes to be called a warrior must be able to command an untamed stallion colt to bend the knee and bow before him. He must be able to stand immobile, with his feet in a ditch, armed only with a blackthorn stick, and fend off the shafts of nine spearmen who let fly at him in concert from a distance of nine paces. If he does wrong, he must speak truth of it and take the blow that follows, and he must lead the chase of his fellows across the steppes and escape them, and he must starve himself on the steppes until he meets his genius and understands his name.''

His genius, his personal spirit, living emblem. Kyrem's would have been that old phallic deity, genius of fertility. "And these many things you have done," Auron stated.

"Yes." All pride was kept out of that word.

"Most remarkable," Auron murmured. "Well . . . what do you know of me, Kyrem? Of my powers?"

The prince moistened his lips, sensing that the tests of Auron's boyhood had been quite different from those he had just named. "You are a healer," he said.

"Only at close range. I have to touch. There have been kings of Vashti who could heal with a thought."

"And you read thoughts."

"Again, only at close range."

"Your servants say you are just and good, and I have not observed otherwise."

"I try. I feel a great responsibility." Auron leaned forward slightly, preparing himself for a disclosure. "I am mother and father, spirit and nurse and nurturer of this land, Kyrem. I am not merely man or merely king. I am all things, all colors, all emblems, all hopes, and being so, I am no thing, neither mare nor stallion but more like the mule that is neither mare nor ass." Auron spoke without bitterness, lightly even, but as he spoke, he willed Kyrem to understand, and Kyrem understood. The king was not speaking in symbols merely, but meant exactly what he said.

"You are—part woman?"

"An androgyne. Yes."

Kyrem stared, his feelings teetering between reverence and

horror. What Auron had just said was abomination, a blasphemy, unnatural, as was the offspring of horse and ass, but like all things unclean and untouchable, it was also awesome. Kyrem could scarcely draw breath to speak.

"So that is why you have no queen," he managed to say. "And no offspring."

"I am quite sterile. I lack vitality of body. I think also that in the course of my reign, Vashti has become sterile as well."

"But surely you have not done that," Kyrem murmured impulsively, irrationally, before realizing what he had said, that he had understood instantly what Auron meant: the customs, the classes, the dry and constricted lives of the people, the arid, fierce blue sky. "Has not Vashti always been so?" he added awkwardly.

"Somewhat. It has formed me, to a degree, and it has its own being, which I cannot change—"

An androgyne, Kyrem was thinking dazedly. An epicene, a morphodite, a he-she or an it. The many freakish names spun through his mind along with nastier words and images, no matter how he tried to dismiss them.

"—but lately I feel the presence of a threat, a doom I wish to forestall. The cows drop fewer calves, the hills have only a few stunted trees, even the people seem old before their time and take little joy in children. And of course there is the drought. It has all come on so gradually that folk scarcely notice, but I notice. The land lies as red and dry as ocher."

"Do not blame yourself," Kyrem said abruptly and with unnecessary heat.

"I am not," Auron answered mildly. "I am of Vashti as it is of me; how can anyone place blame? But I can see what is happening. Before long it will be only the river that sustains us."

Kyren had no answer. His mind was in an uproar, whirling like the yellow dust devils that scorched over Deva.

"Does it trouble you," Auron asked gently, "that I am . . . what I have said I am?" And Kyrem looked at him and smiled suddenly, all uproar calmed.

"I shall grow used to it, I am sure."

"Well, it is, I suppose better than being a fop. No reproach intended," Auron added, not allowing Kyrem time for embarrassment. "Hearing thoughts makes one prize truth." He leaned back judiciously where he sat, and in a moment his eyes grew focusless and heavy-lidded, looking past Kyrem.

The prince sat for a considerable time, reluctant to disturb him. Finally he rose to tiptoe out, but his chair scraped. At the noise Auron came back to life with a start and looked at him.

"I am sorry," he exclaimed. "Do sit down."

Kyrem took his seat again.

"It has become habitual," Auron said apologetically. "Powers of mind are all I have, so when this dumpling of a body comes to rest, I tend to use them."

"You are a seer," the prince breathed, awestruck, and Auron almost laughed but thought better of it. Kyrem was not ready to be laughed at, or at least not by him.

"Not really. My visions know nothing of past or future."

"But of the present . . . you . . . see everything?"

"No, no!" Auron spoke hastily in reassurance. "Surprisingly little, really. It is as if I were a bird flying through the skies of Vashti, a swallow, or an animal on the hilltops, a hare—something swift, not soft and lumpy. But I cannot see into parlors as people seem to think I can, and I cannot be more than one place at a time, and sometimes I cannot even control where I am. I see bits of this and that, all across Vashti. It comes and goes." Auron gave a rueful grimace. "Often it seems that I find out everything and anything except what I truly need to know." He paused for a moment. "I cannot see the mountains at all, ever," he added softly. "And though I looked long and hard, I did not see you coming until you were quite close to Avedon."

Kyrem nodded wordlessly, remembering the king's concern for him that day, remembering his own curt responses with discomfort.

"I have never had the consummate control of thoughts such as my forebears possessed, not even when I was young," Auron said. "And as I grow older, I can focus them less and less."

So the king of Vashti conceived of himself as less than illustrious. Kyrem smiled, feeling a surge of warm affection for the man—no, for the androgyne, the oddity. No matter. They were not so much unlike.

"So, no wonder you never leave the palace," he said, his tone light, nearly teasing. "You never have to."

"I am scarcely allowed to," Auron retorted. "Even for war. I can see and comprehend the clash of armies, but I have never set foot on a battlefield."

"By what power did you defeat my father?"

He would not have been able to ask that question so easily a month earlier. Auron glanced at him in some small merriment.

"You underestimate your father," he said. "I did not defeat him."

"No? Then why am I here? I am his hostage to peace, am I not?"

"Let me start at the beginning." Auron took pause to think. "The curse started it all," he said at last.

Kyrem only stared.

"Have you not been aware of the curse? A deadly curse on the lands of Suth, on Vashti and Deva both. It has been so for several years. Have you not felt it? I feel it plainly, no very happy sensation. It is a curse of war. I do not know the name of the enemy who pronounced it, but I know the ways of curses; they go where they will be best received. This one goes whispering into the hearts of those who dream of glory. . . ." Auron hesitated. "Your father is a good man, Kyrem, but it took some small hold on him."

The prince stirred restively, not wanting to believe any of this but not knowing how to disbelieve. Auron would not lie, he felt sure.

"It prickled at me also," Auron added. "I searched and searched my kingdom and tried to venture to the Kansban, seeking a hidden enemy who opposed me with a will as strong as my own. For years I did that, and by the time your father came with his army, I was exhausted and not thinking clearly. I tried to fight him."

Kyrem looked up in bewilderment.

"I should have been fighting the true enemy," Auron explained. "Instead, I raised a force of callow youths, exhorted them to mighty deeds and sent them into battle. Your father's horsemen slaughtered them. The blood, it was my own . . . the pain brought me to my senses. The enemy had bested me after all."

Still, Kyrem realized, Auron did not speak of Kyrillos as his enemy. He listened in growing amazement.

"I threw all my remaining strength into the conflict and grappled with the nameless one. And in my desperation I was able to withhold that enemy a while from your father's mind, and he looked around him and wondered what he was doing. He came here to talk with me, to make peace. So you see, Kyrem, there has been no defeat, no victory."

"The report," said Kyrem cautiously, "is that your people resisted valiantly."

"Why, I suppose we did. There was a standoff of sorts. But the real enemy remains to be defeated. Your father knows that, and he sent you here as surety for both of us."

He got up and poured wine from a cruet, handing a cupful to Kyrem and taking one himself.

"My men saw one of those black horse-birds of which you spoke," he said, sitting down again. "The sight of it frightened them half to death, but it did not speak to them."

"Let them count their blessings then," Kyrem said wryly.

"Yes. You say the things—birds, demons, what you will— troubled you less as you neared the lowlands?"

"Aye. A few at a time they left us and flapped back toward Kimiel."

Auron stiffened at the name of the holy mountain and peered at Kyrem. "You really think they came from there?" he asked softly.

"I do not know. Our path lay close by that mountain. It sometimes seemed that they did, but we were never sure. Why?"

"Well, if the focus of this curse is there, then I am the more confounded, that is all. Kyrem, do you in Deva tell the tale of the mountaintop Suth?"

When Kyrem shook his head, Auron leaned back, and turning his wine cup in his hand, settled himself to relate it.

It was in the primal days. There had sprung up on the flanks of the Mare Mother a race of beings called men. They saw the beauty of Suth and his seven winged sons; they painted images of the steeds on the walls of their homes; they laid the seven colors on their bodies and their possessions, but they could not fly on the wind. And whenever they saw Suth, the varicolored stallion of the pattern that is or is not, they cried, Why? until it seemed to Suth that of all creatures, men were the most clever and the most to be pitied. And they could not understand him when he spoke, for his fearsome voice made them fall to earth and hide their heads with their hands. So he said, I will take that form of men and go teach them.

Therefore he became a man and went and lived on Mount Kimiel, sending wisdom among men by the mouths of the birds that can be taught to speak, the sooty starlings and blackbirds and ravens. He did this until he was old, but men grew no wiser and no more content. He lived and labored until he was so old that his hair had gone bone white and his eyes blind and white, but still he sent forth his birds from the mountaintop. Then the princes of Deva and Vashti went to him and demanded, Who are you that lived when our great-grandfathers were but youths?

And he answered, I am Suth.

Some fell down in supplication, and some shouted in anger. Prove it, they cried, and he replied, You have seen proof.

Give us wings, some pleaded, or let us fly on the wings of the wind. But Suth said, All my wishing or commanding will not give you even the wings of a gnat, for the pattern is set.

Then they became angry and some shouted Fraud, and others grumbled Come away, he is of no use. For there is nothing man likes less than the pattern that is or is not. Blasphemy, one strong voice shouted. He blasphemes the name of Suth. And all their angers joined into one.

You have said you are Suth, they roared; therefore let you be used as a horse. You will make a fine mount for us. And they forced the old seer onto all fours and sat on him and lashed at him with sticks. Be a horse then, and trot! they shouted. For the times were hard and they waxed bitter at the god even as they upheld his name.

But the seer truly was very old and frail and could not withstand such ill usage. And before long, he slumped over dead. Then they all stood and were ashamed, muttering Bury him and No, let him lie. Before they could decide, a fog and a chill wind moved across the mountain. And the dead body stirred and rose, but it was no man that stood there. An immense horse faced them, splattered with red as of blood, white of head and staring eyes, and the jewel between those eyes flared like flame, and of blood-red flame were the wings that rose from its mottled shoulders. And though Suth did not move, they all scattered and ran. Some ran until their hearts burst and they died; some ran over precipices, and some reached home insane and died soon after.

Only one man ultimately lived to tell the tale, and he became king of Vashti, the first Rabiron, a legendary king and the best that country had ever known. And he pledged that Suth should never again be ridden there in form of horse or man. Therefore horses were not ridden in Vashti but were cherished tenderly and suckled with human milk, and after they were weaned, they were let to run wild and at freedom for a year on the slopes of Mount Kimiel.

"Are you saying," Kyrem demanded, "that Suth is my enemy?"

"Whatever enemy there is, is mine as much as yours. No, I do not say that it is Suth. What have we done to deserve the anger of Suth? But there are similarities, parallels. . . . Perhaps a sort of dark Suth, or a parody of Suth. Those demons you describe seem to be mockeries of his greatness."

Kyrem sat shaking his head.

"I must send another patrol, I suppose, by a different route," Auron muttered. "I cannot see what else to do. The focus of my mind is much weakened from this long conflict, and it avails me nothing.''

"I do not believe in this enemy," said Kyrem levelly. "I am scarcely able to believe anything that you have told me." He sounded tired.

"Why, what will you believe then?" Auron asked.

"I . . . I don't know." His confused thoughts included a half-formed affection toward his peculiar host, and his admission of unbelief hurt him. It was the pain that put an edge of arrogance in his voice.

He went to his bed early that night and slept restlessly, dreaming of the odd androgyne king and a great white-headed horse with staring eyes and of black birds with the grotesque heads of horses.

And in his deep cave atop the mountain, the Old One dreamed yet more twisted dreams: visions of things he had never seen, but still the knowledge of them flowed to him through his ancestry. Of yellow horses on yellow wind-sculpted plains, dun tarpans, their buff-edged manes stiff and erect and the black eel stripe running down mane and neck, withers and back and rump to the broomlike tail. Heavy-headed, mealy-muzzled, the tarpans galloped through the seasons of his dreams, white in winter, the black stripes still on their backs until they writhed up and twisted and became black serpents, sprouted wings and flew up and clustered, sucking, on the sun. Let the ravens croak as they would. Lion of Deva and silly sacred horse of Vashti would both know that black wrath of the dun folk, the Old Ones. Mare Mother was a tarpan, black bristling mane of thorn trees, black, but men forgot. Black wings in black trees. Souls went up as birds. The Old One dreamed then of the simurgh, huge bareheaded bird like a vulture, feeder of the sun, feeder also with its beak of the chieftain who lay beneath the mountain. Was he that one? He thought not. Only starlings brought him food. But it might be that he was that revenant of power, that uprising avenger, for as far as he knew, he was the very last of the Old Ones, and all the generations of his people's longings formed a sharp peak of vengeance within him.

Chapter Eleven

The next morning when Kyrem went to the stable, Nasr Yamut strode toward him with a broad smile of greeting.

"Prince Kyrem! We missed you yesterday. Were you ill, that you did not come out?"

Kyrem did not answer the smile. "I was talking with King Auron, that I did not come out," he said grimly. "And you are no friend of mine, priest."

Nasr Yamut arched his brows in well-bred surprise. "You think there is something amiss between us?" he asked after a moment. "But what has King Auron told you? Perhaps—" He lowered his voice. "Perhaps I can tell you better truth."

"You would accuse your own liege king of lying?" Kyrem's shout rang throughout the stable courtyard, and Nasr Yamut winced, for many priests turned to stare. Nor did Kyrem trouble to lower his voice as he went on.

"Nasr Yamut, you are beneath contempt. Nor can you tell me that my ears lie, for I stood less than a stone's throw from you as you spoke yesterday beneath the dome. So you abhor me! That is why you meet me wreathed in smiles." His tone turned yet darker. "Get away from me, priest."

Nasr Yamut had heard Kyrem's words in shock, seeing himself fairly exposed to all who listened—but truth and honor were not of paramount concern to him. Power was. He abandoned his friendly stance and assumed the crouch of one who fights on the defensive, gathering to himself the powers of his priesthood. "Speak me more fair, Prince," he said in a voice low and dangerous, "or I will blight all of the poor life that is left to you."

Kyrem snorted and gestured his dismissal, turning away toward Omber's stall. "We Devans do not believe such nonsense," he said. "Go, priest, play with your poor excuse of a horse. Just stay far from me."

Nasr Yamut drew himself up to his full height and raised his arms. "I will curse you in the name of Suth!" he shouted, and Kyrem stopped where he was, glancing back in annoyance. Where he came from, priests did not fail to obey his command. But this one was beginning to glisten all over with a glow like small fire, and Kyrem saw that Nasr Yamut was quite serious and an antagonist to be reckoned with. There would be a combat of power, perhaps to the death.

Prowess of power. Kyrem had heard tales of such duels between sorcerers, tales mostly told to children by firelight. Devans did not believe in such things, or did not approve; not believing meant that as well. . . . But if he was to meet this priest on his own magical terms, Kyrem thought, he had better believe for the time. He would fight with his Devan magic, which had made the curses of the horse-birds but words to him, merest meaningless words; that was comforting—and it was comforting to know that Nasr Yamut feared him. Perhaps there was a sorcerer's power in him after all, somehow. There would have to be.

Kyrem turned back and strode up to the priest, facing him squarely, his scowl of vexation turning into a grin that hid his misgivings. "Go ahead and curse me, Vashtin priest," he said. "Just try it."

"Kyrem son of Kyrillos—" Nasr Yamut spat out the name.

Kyrem felt the words, actually felt them, as a faint physical shock, as he had never felt the words of the cursing horse-birds, and for a moment panic seized him. What good was his body magic to do him? He had hardly ever used it except to guide his horse. *Auron, help*, he thought hazily; then, *I am a Devan*, but being a Devan no longer seemed of such importance. *I am Kyrem*, he thought; *I am myself, I will live. I shall not be destroyed.* And on the instant a great surge of will flowed through him, turning him rock hard and as pure as gold in his defiance. Words washed against him to no avail.

"—may all your dreams elude you. May you be cursed with a thousand failures and see your friends and followers turn against you. May the curse of Suth send you into exile in a bleak and dangerous land. . . . ."

Nasr Yamut stopped with a choking sound as his own words came flying back at him, stabbing him like so many knives.

For Kyrem was all talisman; nothing could touch him, and all such darts of enmity were turned back against the sender. He stood with a faint sheen on him like the surge or pulse of heat, blood heat, and he seemed bigger than he had been before; those who watched thought of a mountain or a standing stone, a menhir. He had not even needed to close his eyes. They shone jewel hard, jewel bright and black as jet, and they faced Nasr Yamut fixedly. The priest bore that stare and that unmoving presence only a moment more, then turned and hurried, almost running, from the stable yard. No one followed him. The onlookers stood like wood, not knowing what to think.

After a moment Kyrem stirred and let go of the conflict with a sigh, seeming to settle back into self. "Avedon has been good to me," he muttered.

And instantly all backs were turned on him as priests and boys and novices busied themselves with their work, half afraid and whispering among themselves.

"Have you heard the news from the stable, Ky?" Seda asked him that evening, and he stared at her.

"If you mean my bout with Nasr Yamut—"

"Of course not, blockhead. You know all about that. I mean have you heard the news of Omber?"

He came half out of his chair. "If they have attempted to harm Omber—"

"If they had, do you think I would be standing here so sweetly? But they did put him in a smaller bay, it seems. One of the sort wherein they tie the head to the manger."

"They—the scum—have they tied him?" Kyrem came to his feet, his face dark with anger.

"From what I hear. Not without difficulties. The epopts attempted it first, by Nasr Yamut's order."

"And?" Kyrem sat down again to hear, looking grim.

"They discovered that even the untamed frolickings of a pampered Vashtin oracle-bred are as nothing compared to the teeth and hooves of a determined Devan stallion." For the moment Seda sounded very much like a Devan herself.

"Damn them, I hope they have not upset him."

"Far less than he upset them. A broken jaw, a broken wrist—"

"Serves them right," Kyrem muttered. "I told them never to touch him."

"Then Nasr Yamut approached."

"I hope Omber kicked him in the head."

"Alas, no. Omber obeyed him. Nasr Yamut led Omber to the smallest stall in the stable and tied him there."

Kyrem slumped back where he sat, for the first time comprehending the full measure of his shame and Nasr Yamut's cleverness. Rage flushed his face, rage as much at himself as at the priest.

"Seda," he said, "I am an utter fool."

"You gave him that power." She had guessed.

"Yes. I am glad it was you who told me, and no enemy." He stood up, suddenly icily calm. "I had better go check on Omber."

"Not now. It is after dark. And it will not hurt him to be tied, not really. Do not let them think that you care overmuch."

He nodded, after considering, for she had a sense of things Vashtin.

"The king wants to see you," she added. "A late supper."

"Oh." He softened somewhat, even the hard set of his shoulders eased, and Seda looked at him curiously.

"It seems you think better of King Auron these days," she said, and Kyrem grinned at her.

"So servants do not know everything!" he teased. "Great Suth, Seda." He strode out of the door and out of earshot.

In the days that followed he spent much of his time with Auron and learned much and wondered much. And he exercised Omber for hours daily. When he and Nasr Yamut met at the stable, they ignored each other, the priest warily, Kyrem with scarcely veiled anger and scorn. The attempt to humiliate him through his horse seemed to him contemptible.

The other priests avoided him when they could. They knew their master.

Because he had no one to talk with at the stable, Kyrem tried once again to persuade Seda to come with him. "You never see Omber any more," he argued.

She was greasing his latest pair of new boots at the time—Auron was forever giving him gifts of clothing and footgear, taking vicarious pleasure, perhaps, in Kyrem's tall and youthful form with its heels that met the ground. Seda cared for each gift assiduously.

"You work too hard," Kyrem added.

She kept her eyes on the boots. "I do what the other servants do," she said, and Kyrem scoffed.

"Servant, my foot. You order me around half the time. Humor me for once and come with me. Omber will bounce about with gladness to see you."

"I can't," she said.

"Why not?" He sat down on his swinging bed and stared at her. Such a stubborn lad she could be in her own silent way. She sat silent for a long time, not meeting the demand of his gaze.

"I am a shuntali," she said finally in a very small voice, so soft he could scarcely hear her, and he whacked his hand on the pillows in annoyance.

"So? What of it?"

"The stable is a sacred place. Even lords and wealthy merchants are not allowed to go there. If I did, the priests would tear me apart." That last, even softer, and Kyrem's mood swung from vexation to amusement. He laughed out loud.

"Just let them try!"

She looked straight at him, and the look on her face stopped his laughter. "You don't understand," she said.

He decided to reason with her. "Seda," he wheedled, "you know Auron says there is no such thing as shuntali."

"King Auron is kind. The priests scoff at his kindness and do as they wish."

"After the way I saw him cow Nasr Yamut," Kyrem protested, "you can say he does not rule the priests?"

"This is Vashti and the king stays in his palace." She met his stare. "Outside of it, things go on much as ever. And I am a shuntali everywhere but here."

"Nonsense. You are my friend, and I am the Devan guest."

"Have you ever faced a mob, Ky?" She held his gaze, letting pathos show in her eyes, using her own past misfortunes for leverage on him. He saw what she was doing, but it did not matter, for a chill, irrational comprehension had crept in with her words. To be small, and to face the flung shafts of nine spearmen. . . .

"They used to throw stones at me, back in the mountains," she added. "Those were humble folk. But the priests are mightier, and crueler."

"Do you never even go out on the streets then?" he asked, his voice almost as soft as hers.

She shook her head, took her pot of grease and went away.

So on that day Kyrem went to the stable alone. But the next day Auron surprised him by offering to go with him. Auron, the king, who was in his exalted way nearly as solitary and circumscribed as the shuntali.

"I have never seen that mighty stallion of yours," he explained, "of which I hear so much."

"What if something touches those sacred heels of yours?" Kyrem was smiling broadly with delight.

"I will just have to be careful, that is all. Even a king has a right to go out once in a while, to my way of thinking. So let us be off.''

People in the street scattered before them, nearly hugging the house walls in their anxiety not to profane the sacred presence with a touch. Auron paid no attention, walking even more slowly than usual in order to safely traverse the tiles and bricks and cobbles with his buskins. He chatted easily the while, as if he went for such a walk every day of his life, but from the whispered comments and exclamations around him, Kyrem confirmed what he already suspected, that such an event was quite unheard-of. Never since his coronation had Auron been seen out strolling the street.

When he and Kyrem reached the stable at last, the priests took one look and busied themselves at the farthest corners of the place. Nasr Yamut was nowhere to be seen.

''Ah, the beauty,'' Auron murmured.

Omber stood still and splendid under no restraint but the light pressure of Kyrem's hand. ''So they do not all jump about with such frenzy,'' Auron mused.

Kyrem shook his head.

''And the ears too,'' remarked Auron. ''I am not used to them unclipped, but they are attractive, pricked forward so prettily. And he has a kind eye. May I touch him?''

''If I will it.'' Kyrem gave the silent command, and Omber stood quietly as Auron ran a hand along his smooth blue-black neck and shoulder.

''There, there, such a beauty,'' Auron murmured. ''Walk him about a bit, Kyrem, or what you will, while I greet the others.''

He went to each of the enclosed horse-bays in turn, chirruping to bring the horses over to him and patting them on their cheeks, rubbing their foreheads and the itchy places above the eyes. Kyrem watched this ordinary scene with an odd feeling of discomfort, wondering what seemed wrong or out of place until, with a small shock, he remembered that he was in Vashti and these were sacred steeds.

"You are allowed to touch them then?" he asked Auron. "Because you are king?"

"Because they belong to me." He summoned the nearest cluster of whispering priests with a shout. "Bring some of the other ones out, you fellows," he told them.

"Oh." Kyrem wondered why he was surprised. "I had assumed that they belonged to the priests or to the temple."

"In a very real sense they belong to all Vashtins, or to no one." Auron stroked the curve of a glossy neck. "Horses are of all things in Vashti most precious, most sacred. So the priests take charge of them from birth, bring them to human mothers for suckling—"

"I was raised on mare's milk," Kyrem said with some amusement, "and you Vashtins raise horses on yours."

"Yes." Auron smiled at him, a warm, contented smile. "It is odd. Well, when they have been accustomed to halter somewhat, they are let to run with the deer and the wild goats on the slopes of Mount Kimiel until they are past being yearlings, when the pick of the stallions are brought here. The rest remain, except for the foaling mares."

He hobbled carefully the few feet to where the flamens held several cavorting horses, and he gentled each in turn with a caress and a murmur. Kyrem followed him.

"And they are all yours?"

"No, not really. These, the oracles, are given to me as king and as the priesthood finds me worthy. But in any ordinary way they cannot be owned or bought or sold; they can only be given as the highest form of gift."

Kyrem listened in floundering amazement. He had often

found it hard to fathom Vashtin ways, but never so much as now. He shook his head, thinking intently.

"So the giving of a horse to an individual is a mark of honor?" he said at last.

"Yes. I have given three in my lifetime. One to a servant of extraordinary integrity and loyalty, one to a long-time steward, and one to a woman whom I loved when I was younger and not so set in my ways. None," he added significantly, "to courtiers. The horse is a gift of the heart."

Kyrem could well believe it, for a gripping spasm had taken hold of his own heart, subject to a thought he could not avoid as his hand rested on Omber's silky neck. In a moment he had managed to calm the beating organ and go on.

"Such a gift must automatically raise the recipient to the highest station in life."

"The concept of station," Auron replied dryly, "is not a legal formulation within the code of Vashtin law under my rule."

"I know, I know. But in effect. . . ."

"Well, in effect, yes. Those whom I mentioned are now persons of power and rank within their clans and guilds because they have that same honor to bestow. That is all to the good—they are worthy people. And the keeping of the horses is no burden to them; the priests see to it." Auron turned to scan the array of stalls. "Those three on the end there, chestnut, gray and rose roan. Those I may not touch."

Kyrem said nothing. He was still feeling an odd pain in his heart, and he returned Omber to his bay in silence, walked with Auron back to the palace in uneasy silence, and when they arrived, he went off to his chamber to brood. Seda had been there again. Clean linen towels lay on the washstand, neatly folded, and clean clothing lay on the bed.

Kyrem shoved the articles to one side and sat down to

think. He thought, on and off, for several days. In the end, fight it though he might, his conclusion was inescapable. Seda was a Vashtin. He had to give Omber to Seda, under Vashtin terms. He owed the shuntali everything, his life thrice over. And the gift of the horse, the highest gift, was the only way he knew of lifting his beloved stableboy out of the shadow under which she had been born.

Chapter Twelve

"Kyrem son of Kyrillos, prince of Deva, with his servant Seda, humbly presents himself," the doorkeeper announced. "Auron ataron, fire-maker, son of Rabiron, king of Vashti and emperor of the Untrodden Lands, grants audience."

"So, Kyrem," said Auron kindly, "what is it?" He could not imagine why the prince should have petitioned him for a private audience, a most formal affair, complete with footbearers, when he knew he could speak to him at any time. And for the matter of that, Kyrem seemed to be having trouble in stating his reason.

"Sire," he said, then stopped and put his arm around his little manservant Seda, drawing her forward. Seda looked as bewildered as Auron.

"Sire," Kyrem began again, "I have told you what I owe to Seda, my friend and comrade. And you know I owe him yet more since I have come here, friendship and loyalty beyond all expectation. As a guest under the protection of this house, I wish to make him a solemn gift. I adopt the custom of this kingdom of Vashti in presenting to him my horse, Omber.''

Auron sat too astonished and touched to reply. The prince had spoken firmly, but his face held far from steady.

"Think carefully, Kyrem," Auron said at last. "There will be no replacing the steed." Then he winced, fearing that he might have offended the mettlesome youth. But Kyrem replied evenly.

"I know. I have thought. But it has to be done." Their eyes met. "The gift of the heart."

The gift, Auron sensed, was as much to him as to the little shuntali. The trust and, yes, the love in that glance. . . . It was moments before he withdrew his gaze and moved it to Seda. There the boy stood with that trapped-animal look of his—and he ought to be overwhelmed with joy! What was wrong with the youngster?

"Seda," said Auron in gentle exasperation, "what is the matter?"

She wet her lips, moved them stiffly. "I can't," she whispered.

"What?" Auron could not hear.

"I can't accept Omber."

Auron could not understand. To him the horse was the Vashtin ritual, the Gift, and very fittingly presented. But Kyrem, the Devan, thought of the horse as a comrade and fellow creature and imagined that Seda did the same, and he had a reply ready for her.

"Omber adores you," he told the boy. "He loves you, you know that. Take him with all blessing."

"I am not worthy," she said.

"Everyone is worthy and no one is ever worthy of the Gift of love," replied Auron.

"But I am a liar!" For the first time she willingly met

King Auron's eyes, facing him in plea for Kyrem's sake. "From the day we met, I have been a walking lie, a wretched, living deceit—"

Auron straightened on his throne in sudden, terrible suspicion. "What are you saying?" he thundered. "Are you in league with his hidden enemy?"

She shook her head, trembling violently. Kyrem supported her with his strong right arm. "Seda," he appealed, "whatever are you talking about?"

She spoke without looking at him, but still, by the movement of her head and the pitch of her voice, speaking to him alone. "I am a girl."

"What?" Auron demanded.

"My flux has come on me, and my poor breasts, bound up. . . ." Seda spoke tonelessly, lifting her skinny arms in a gesture of defeat or despair, a gesture that cried for pity. "I can no longer hide it."

"A girl." Kyrem repeated the words without comprehension, then shouted as they came to rest in his mind. "A girl!" He turned her bodily, peered at her. "Why, to be sure you are!" he cried, grinning broadly with the delight of discovery. "I am an idiot not to have seen it before. You make a lovely girl."

"By Suth, my powers must be sadly on the wane." Auron sat astonished anew. "I ought to have sensed it the first time he . . . she . . . came into my presence, yet I cannot feel it of her even now." He stared at her, puzzled and unconvinced. "Seda, are you sure?"

"My organs are."

Auron bestirred himself, drew his feet up and put the buskins on them. "You two," he told the auburn-and-alabaster footbearers, "take her or him into the next room and find out."

The girls rose gracefully, their filmy gowns floating about them, and glanced at each other in confusion.

"Do it," Auron told them in some small annoyance. "You've known organs enough of either sort, and don't try to tell me otherwise."

They left at once, taking Seda with them, she looking awkward and earthen next to their porcelain perfection. Auron sat staring at Kyrem. "So, Prince," he said slowly, "you have befriended two muddled untouchables."

Kyrem shrugged. "Both of you befriended me first. And we do not have untouchables in Deva. Here—they are returning."

The footbearers whispered their report to Auron, and he nodded and sent them out of the room. Seda came straight to Kyrem, looking pale. He did not notice it, for his eyes had fallen willy-nilly to the small puckers that her young breasts made in the fabric of her shirt.

"You need not have bound yourself up for those," he teased, smiling. "Why, they are scarcely larger than freckles."

She ignored that. "You can't give me Omber," she said.

"To be sure, I can and I will!" he stated, annoyed. "Talk sense, Seda! How did you come to be a boy?"

"I'm not certain. I was little, in rags, no one could tell—"

"Wait," said Auron. "He—she looks faint." He came down from his dais and, lifting her, seated her on it, found wine for her, taking it from a compartment right under the throne.

"And . . . and I had to be a boy unless I wanted to be a whore," Seda faltered.

"What?" Kyrem exclaimed.

"A female shuntali is customarily put to prostitution," Auron said in a low voice, and Kyrem turned on him with a savagery that surprised even himself.

"This is your vaunted Vashtin piety? Your people revile me because I ride a horse, a beast, and care for it with all love. Yet they think nothing of enslaving unfortunate women?"

"Kyrem!" Seda snapped, reviving.

"I have told you, the condition called shuntali has no legal status in my kingdom." Auron sounded very tired. "But custom dies hard. . . . I admire Seda more than ever for her ingenuity."

"It just happened," she said quietly. "And then . . . I couldn't have traveled with Kyrem had I been a girl. He is too honorable for that."

He stared at her, all his righteous wrath forgotten, sensing her meaning and realizing that things would never again be the same between them, that he had forced a drastic change. And slowly he too sat down on the steps of the dais.

"So, Prince Kyrem," Nasr Yamut taunted, "your cata-mite has turned out to be your concubine, ay?"

The two footbearers had spread word of their discovery quickly. The whole palace was full of the news that Seda the boy was now a girl, and even the stable, apparently, where Kyrem had come to find some peace in communion with Omber.

"Of course it is to be expected," Nasr Yamut went on. "You Devans are so fond of mounting, you hardly seem to know where to leave off."

The priest stood a bit too close for his own safety. Kyrem swung out with lion quickness and hit him hard in the mouth. Nasr Yamut fell sprawling, sullying his yellow robes with the dirt of the stable yard, and in the same instant Kyrem realized with sickening certainty that he had done exactly what Nasr Yamut wanted of him.

"Blasphemer!" the priest screamed as blood started from

his split lip. "Infidel! To attack the body of Suth's anointed fire-master!"

All the priests in the place ran to the defense of their stricken master, and for the first time in his life, Kyrem found himself facing a truly angry mob. Men were shouting, and some were brandishing broom handles and the like. Kyrem could perhaps have held them off with his personal magic, his presence, but perhaps not—he was tired, and it seemed to him that the day had held tumult enough. He chose the obvious way out. Omber stood close at hand. He vaulted onto the steed and galloped through their midst; they scattered before the horse's driving hooves, and in a few moments prince and mount were beyond the stable gates and the city gates and away.

The free wind of the open farmland was balm. Kyrem let Omber gallop until the horse slowed to a walk of his own accord. Then he drew him to a halt, laid his head against the black silky mane and sighed. He would have liked to have galloped all the way to Deva. But after an hour or so of roaming among the gentle hills that surrounded Avedon, he turned back and started home—Auron's city was home to him now, and Auron awaited him, and he did not know how he was going to manage the priests, and he did not greatly care.

He walked Omber quietly through the city, in no hurry. At the stable gates he found a troop of Auron's household retainers awaiting him, and raised his black brows at the captain in inquiry.

"We're here for your protection, young my lord Prince," the man explained, and Kyrem had to smile.

"What, does King Auron hear everything?"

"Sees everything, my lord." The men ranged themselves to either side of Kyrem as he dismounted. Priests watched from a sullen distance as he cared for Omber and put the steed in his stall. They would not attempt to harm the horse, Kyrem felt sure, or fairly sure, since the stallion was a sacred animal. Such must have been Auron's reasoning also, or he would have seen to that matter as well.

Auron was awaiting Kyrem for a late dinner.

"Where is Seda?" Kyrem asked him.

"In the women's quarter. They're fussing over her and trying to find her some clothing." Auron looked up with a tilted smile. "It is going to take some getting used to, that Seda is a girl."

Kyrem nodded in weary and wholehearted agreement and lapsed into his chair.

"What in the world did Nasr Yamut say to you?" Auron asked.

The prince shrugged. "Something about Seda and me. Ignorant insults."

"Why did you not just turn them back on him, as you did the last time?"

Kyrem laughed softly in a sort of despairing wonder; he had not told Auron about the last time. Then he sobered. "I don't know why not," he said. "I just felt . . . spent, and I reacted in anger. I am sorry I have caused trouble."

"Trouble would have come soon or late anyway," Auron said. "The priests think they run Vashti, and to a large extent they do. All the ceremonial nonsense that hems the king in, the proscriptions, the sacred silliness, is largely of their making. They want power; that is all they understand. Nasr Yamut has had an eye on you from the first day you arrived, sensing power in you, seeing you as a piece in some game of power. But he does not know what game."

"No more do I," said Kyrem. "Do you think Nasr Yamut

could be the one who set those horse-bird demons on me, and the archers?''

"What do you think?'' Auron turned the question back on him.

"I think he has not the means,'' said Kyrem. "Nor the imagination.''

"No more do I,'' said Auron.

Kyrem was weary in more than body and went early to his bed and took it ill, though he did not say so, that an unfamiliar servant waited on him. He did not know that Auron spent most of the night on the alert, watching with his mind's eye from afar the shadowed form of a splendid blue roan stallion within a stall in a hostile stable.

"I can't get used to it,'' Seda said. "This being a girl, I mean.''

She wore a long indigo skirt with a paisley overskirt and a fringed maroon sash, a white cotton embroidered blouse with a paisley shawl and a lapis brooch. Her scraggly hair had been rinsed with henna and trimmed into a semblance of style and symmetry, then practically hidden under a beaded headdress. Her thin face gazed out plaintively from amidst the finery.

"You are yet half a boy at heart,'' Auron told her. "No wonder you fooled me so. Your body is still thinking of riding through the mountains.''

"And I still want to give you Omber,'' Kyrem said.

They sat around the table in Auron's private chamber, holding impromptu council. The matter of Omber had to be settled, and the matter of the priests added urgency to that of Omber. Auron sat back in his chair and his eyes turned sleepy; for several moments he stared at nothing, and no one spoke or disturbed him until he blinked and came back to them.

"Omber is munching his morning grain," he told Kyrem.

"Good. Do you think they would treat him as well if they knew he is Seda's?"

"It is hard to tell what priests might do," said Auron. "They do not always react as other men."

"Keep your horse," said Seda. "I . . . I think I am going to have to go away."

"But why?" exclaimed Auron. Kyrem sat silent, his face taut.

"I . . . ache," she said softly. "I have felt it since I became woman—a sort of pang, an empty feeling, as though something is missing, some part of me."

"Your twin," said Kyrem through dry lips.

"Maybe. I don't know for sure. I have dreams sometimes, and I feel a sort of . . . of whereness, eastward, toward Deva. That alone would not have made me leave you, Ky. But everything seems different now that I have put on these skirts."

"Don't," he whispered.

"But I can't stay with you in this body. I don't have— strength. Someday I may be a woman, but I am nothing now. I must go."

"Stay," he begged. "You'll have Omber, you will be someone. Auron, tell her!"

"I'll still be a shuntali. You can't change me from one thing to another just by giving me a horse," said Seda rather sharply. "And I cannot shelter in your house forever, Liege."

"So you will go to find your twin," said Auron slowly.

"Maybe. And maybe my mother and father. Perhaps something has changed. Perhaps they will accept me now."

"You are very brave." He stared straight at her, but his eyes misted over with thought or more than thought, so that she sat still and scarcely dared to breathe, wondering what he was seeing in her.

He stirred at last and spoke. "I would be willing to protect you for as long as I live," he said. "But that may not be so long after all, and you need more than protection, you need . . . you need heart's ease, this quest of yours, call it what you will. And let me say a thing to you: Do not underestimate your own magic as you search. I have had a sure sense that you are, or you could be, more powerful than I, as powerful as Kyrem."

"I?" she murmured, looking at him in puzzled disbelief.

"Do you not think too highly of my power," Kyrem told her wryly.

"The powerless are often powerful." Auron looked serenely at air, straight between them. "But for the time, there is a problem. We know what is done to female shuntali here, and you can no longer be a boy, Seda; neither your body nor your heart will allow it." He turned to his hostage and guest with a gesture of decision. "Kyrem, give her the horse as a Devan," he said.

A storm of protest arose from both of them. "But I am not taking Omber!" Seda cried, and Kyrem hotly held to the Vashtin ritual of the Gift.

"As a Devan?" he shouted at last. "But why?"

"So that she may ride it," said Auron. "Have some sense, you two."

The words cut through the tangle of their emotions. They stared at each other, finding the beginning of agreement in that look.

"Very few Devan women ride," said Kyrem slowly. "Those who do are generally the daughters of warrior chieftains, nomads, who wish to show that their daughters as well as their sons are proud and valorous."

"Excellent," said Auron promptly. "Let her be such a Devan princess then. And so you are, Seda, from this moment, and if anyone says or acts otherwise, let me have the correcting of him." There was a glint in his gaze, diamond hard.

"There will be a royal escort," he added, "and gold, and whatever you need to get you safely out of Vashti, lass."

"Thank you," she whispered, looking dazed and somewhat discomfited.

"You deserve all the aid the world can give you," Auron told her. "Remember that."

"How are you going to find your family?" Kyrem asked her.

"I remember a few things. And I hope my dreams will aid me." She hopped awkwardly out of her chair and gave Kyrem a shy hug. "I will take Omber," she told him. "Thank you. And I hope I can—I mean, I want—I will try to bring him back to you someday."

Chapter Thirteen

The next few days were spent in preparation. Kyrem passed the time rather tensely, avoiding Seda. Knowing she was a girl had subtly altered his perception of her, and seeing her made him uncomfortable. For the first time he had noticed that her features were, indeed, attractive, her eyes dark and expressive, her hands slender. At the same time it guiltily disturbed him to remember how tireless, even tough, she had been during their journey and afterward, how he had depended on her as a comrade and an equal. She deserved all his love. Why, then, did he find himself acting condescending and slightly aloof?

"You look very nice," he said to her one day, meeting her in a passageway. Oh, the brotherly tone of that remark! He clenched his jaw in inward fury, but Seda did not see; she was looking down ruefully at her indigo skirt.

"How am I supposed to ride Omber in this?" she asked.

"Sideways. I have been working with him. He'll take you that way." What a treat that had been for the priests, to see the prince of Deva riding out woman-fashion. They had jeered heartily. But he had done it.

"I'll need some boots. These things are useless." Seda indicated her fringed and beaded sandals.

"I'll go see Auron about it." Kyrem took the excuse to turn around and start off, but Seda called after him.

"Ky—" It was an appeal.

"What?" He turned back to her, stiffening in apprehension.

"What the ruddy devil is there for me to do all day except clean my nails?" she asked with the sort of passionate intensity most people reserve for matters of romance or gold. Kyrem grinned with relief. She was no more ready for love than he was.

"Do you want to mend my shirts?" he teased.

"Son of Suth, no! Mend them yourself."

"Let us take a walk then. Have you never been down among the shops of the town? Come, I'll escort you."

The days went by far too quickly after that. Within the moment, so it seemed, it was time for her to leave.

On the morning of the appointed day—one auspicious to travelers, according to the stars—Kyrem was up before dawn, making his way down to the stable to ready Omber. There, under the sour surveillance of the priest on duty, he groomed the horse and set about braiding the black mane and tail. Seventeen braids for the mane, including one over each intelligent eye; he tied the ends with red wool as he went along. Seven braids for the tail, all along the top of the bone, and the rest of the hanging, spiral-twisted hair gathered into a single great knot. When he had finished, he fastened the red riding blanket onto the horse, checked the hard blue hooves and led, not rode, his stallion out of the stable and up the brick-paved street to the steps of Auron's palace, where he knew Seda would be waiting.

There she stood at Auron's side, almost hidden amid a crowd of servants and soldiers and the onagers they were to ride and pack donkeys with their silly little fringed headstalls. Her mouth came open as he walked up.

"Kyrem," she demanded, "whatever have you done to poor Omber?"

"You should talk," he replied, staring pointedly at her short, beaded braids. Then he relented and explained. "It is Devan custom. The braiding and knotting ensures that the luck of the beast will go with the new owner."

"I thought you Devans didn't believe in luck," she said.

"You're a Devan now," he told her. "Remember. And we are a bit more careful in regard to horses than we are with other things." He grinned sheepishly.

"Well." She swallowed. "He looks lovely. Will you help me up?"

He set her on Omber wordlessly. Auron reached up to hand her a cloth purse full of gold.

"You know your way?" he asked anxiously. It had been agreed she would take a northern route, indirect, to avoid the ill-fated Kimiel pass where Kyrem's retainers and Auron's patrol had come to woe.

"Well enough." She sounded almost brusque. It was an awkward moment, for no one knew what to do or say, not even Auron. She left finally with very little said. She thanked the king, thanked Kyrem obliquely— "It feels good to be back on Omber," she said. Then she rode away with Auron's gold beneath her shawl and her retinue around her.

Kyrem watched her progress down the street until she turned toward the city gates and disappeared behind shops and houses. Then he ran for the steep spiral stairway of the watchtower. Coming out at last into the cuplike enclosure under a brilliant turquoise sky—those bright skies of Vashti, every day the same—he saw her pass through the gate and traverse the terraced fields beyond—peasants hard at work pouring water on the crops stopped their labors to look at her—then he saw her ride beyond the terraces of red earth into the gently rumpled meadowlands. She would disappear behind a sparse hedgerow of stunted thorn and reappear in the pasture beyond, disappear again into the fold of a hill. He watched her grow smaller and smaller with distance. Finally, near midday, he lost sight of her for good in the heat haze of far away, and he could only assume that she still existed.

There was not much for him to do after Seda left. No horse for him to groom and caress and exercise, no lad for him to tease. He even missed his former colloquies with Nasr Yamut. Since he had no excuse to go near the stable, he never saw the priest at all, not even to exchange insults. His friends among the servantry were busy during the day. Perforce he spent much of his time with Auron, and perforce he learned much of Vashti's affairs and of Auron's ways of dealing with them. Auron's ways were often different from Devan ways. Kyrem watched and thought and sometimes made judgment.

"Might I interest you in learning the runes, lad?" Auron asked him.

Kyrem had been taught to scorn such skill as in the realm of scribes and clerics, underlings, but he needed ways of passing the time. He applied himself to the task, and within the week he was able to decipher at least parts of the documents Auron placed before him. They were mostly compilations of Vashtin law. He read them with interest until they raised questions they did not answer.

"Have you no works of philosophy," he asked Auron over dinner, "or lore—wisdom, if you will?"

"Such matters are in the province of the priests, and they

distrust writing, even in the mystic glyphs." Auron smiled enigmatically." They keep all lore very much to themselves. What is it that you wish to know, lad?"

"The power of the stone Suth and of the jewel between its eyes."

"All concerning that statue is shrouded. I can tell you only what is the popular knowledge, which may be either wisdom or folly."

Kyrem settled himself to hear, and Auron leaned far back, closing his eyes and trying to remember. "There is a sort of rhyme, or jingle . . .

> *"Blue is for love, red for desire.*
> *Beware, fool, of Suthstone's fire.*
> *Those who to that jewel aspire*
> *Learn the ways of wealth or death*
> *Or the name of true desire."*

"Anything else?" Kyrem asked after waiting a while.

"Not really."

Kyrem stirred restively where he sat. "But what is the name of true desire?"

"I have my own thought on true desire," said Auron, "but you may have another."

"Let me hear your thought."

"I think that the true desire of every soul is heart's ease, the peace within self."

Kyrem shook his head. "I know nothing of that desire," he said.

"From what I have heard, from what I have seen in vision, I think it is such heart's ease that comes on one in the Untrodden Lands. Where the powers be, where Suth feeds on melantha. Power with peace at the core."

Power for peace, power not for domination? "I know nothing of such power," said Kyrem.

"I think you know it better than you deem, lad."

From time to time—for want of anything better to do, he told himself—Kyrem would climb to the cup of the watchtower and stand there looking off in the direction Seda had gone. On the morning of the tenth day after she had left, he stood there for hours in a lethargic condition, so listless that he hardly stirred when Auron himself came up the steep steps, puffing slightly and having difficulty with his buskins and at last teetering silently beside him.

"What do you see of our lad, any more?" Kyrem asked him idly after some moments had passed. He knew that Auron spent an hour or two every afternoon in his trancelike, sleepy-eyed state.

"Our lad that turned out to be a lass?" Auron smiled; then the smile turned bleak and faded. "Nothing," he said. "I see nothing of her any more, for she has reached the mountains, and the sight of those regions is withheld from me, I cannot tell why—whether by the waning of my own powers or by the will of some strong one who contests me."

Kyrem's Devan skepticism would not let him believe in Auron's hidden enemy, but he was feeling too languid to argue with him about it. "Well," he said, "it is no more than the ordinary lot of men, not to be able to see afar."

"I saw her last three days ago," said Auron, "and she was well and content then."

"Good enough," said Kyrem.

They were silent for a while. "Won't you come down, lad, and eat?" Auron asked finally.

"Wait." All Kyrem's torpor left him in an instant; he straightened and stood taut and keen. A dark blot was growing in the azure blue of the sky. It swept toward them rapidly, ever larger, and Auron gasped.

"It is one of those—"

"Demon things," Kyrem finished for him.

Looking as large as the sky, it flew directly over them, circling the slender point of the tower roof, its great black wings nearly touching the tiles, its baleful, blank white eyes glaring, red-rimmed, out of its grotesque equine head. Black hooves hung heavily and clattered against each other. Flinching back in spite of himself, Kyrem drew his sword. But the weird horselike thing did not come close enough to let him use it. "Gone," it said, a wailing roar out of the black cavern of its mouth. "Gone—gone—gone—gone. . . ." It flew away, still chanting, the words dying on the distance like echoes.

"Great Suth," Auron murmured, shaken. "He has grown strong. He reaches to Avedon now!" But Kyrem did not hear. He stood like a lance, motionless, staring away toward the place where they had last seen Seda.

"I should go after her," he muttered distractedly. "But how? Onagers are not fast enough. Take one of the sacred steeds—"

Auron looked at him in an alarm that verged on panic. Kyrem did not notice.

"They are half wild, I know," he went on, nearly babbling. "But with my personal magic I think I could school one to obey me." He turned to leave, took one long stride toward the stairway. Auron caught at his sleeve.

"You'll have every priest in the kingdom shrieking for your head," he said. "Or mine."

Very true, Kyrem knew. Already there had been demands for a royal apology on account of his "attack" on Nasr Yamut and the resultant show of palace force. Auron had ignored the uproar. If Kyrem had been thinking, he would have noted how unlike Auron was this concern with the shrieking of priests; he would have looked at him and seen his fear, terror, the real fear, of the hidden enemy. But Kyrem did not know that fear, and he was thinking only of Seda.

"Is there no way I can thieve a horse?" he demanded, frustration heightening his tone. "From the mountainside, perhaps, without their knowing?"

"No!" Auron stepped forward with reckless haste when Kyrem mentioned that dreaded holy mountainside, nearly falling off his buskins. Kyrem's outflung arm caught him.

"Sorry," Kyrem murmured, startled by the violence of Auron's reaction.

"You are lending too much credence to the things," Auron said more quietly.

The prince stared at him, puzzled, sensing something amiss, but he had never met subterfuge in Auron, and he failed to recognize it now.

"I give no credence to omens," he said with proper Devan spirit, "and curses cannot hurt me. But that black thing was sent by someone. Some schemer—"

"Your enemy then. Not Seda's."

"I suppose so," Kyrem acceded. He conceived only of a political enemy. He refused to think of any other sort.

"Whoever it is, then, likely wants only to send you off on a wild chase."

Kyrem said nothing. He stood looking away to the north and east.

"Stay," Auron told him, "and wait and see what happens next. If you refuse to rise to his bait, he will be forced to expose himself."

Waiting. The one thing Auron would be best at, the one thing Kyrem liked the least. He did not speak the thought. He stood silent. Seda ought to be well out of his reach by now, reason told him. The chase would be not only wild, but futile.

"Kyrem?" Fear in Auron's voice. Kyrem was too Devan to know what fear it was: Auron's ingrained, almost inborn terror of venturing forth into the wilds, he who knew only buskins and palace walls. The prince of Deva saw in Auron the anxiety of one who faces hostile priests. He was loath to make trouble for him.

"I will stay," he said heavily. "For the time."

In no way could he know, in no way could Auron surely sense, how Seda had been coaxed away from her course by the force of a strong and mysterious will, drawn as a shadow is drawn after the sun, by a beckoning that seemed no more fearsome than the beckoning of a river curve toward what lies beyond. She sensed it only dimly herself. She did not know her own power; how was she to suspect that such a power would take pains to ensnare her? For in her own reckoning, she was a cipher, of no account to anyone except perhaps as a target for the random flinging of stones.

It was the faraway other who felt Seda's presence most surely those days. Waking or sleeping, tending to the quiet routine of her work or lying on her cot at night, she listened—a bright dreaming hummed in her always, beneath her conscious thinking, constant, like the tenor of a song. Something had changed; the body she dreamt of was no longer that of a boy, or not entirely. And it was washed, pampered even, and the clothes were new and pretty, the full blue skirt spread and floating over the great stallion. Riding, riding, always riding and dreams of riding, past the blue shelving rocks of the foothills, the goats that fed on the pink and powder-green lichens of them, uphill, strength and surge of the mighty mount and his fox-pricked ears before her face, tawny leap of chamois fleeing away before them, cool mountain breeze in late summer heat, crisp dusk and fresh dawn, vistas beyond belief and sunrise and the blue wilderness rose and the running of the yearling horses on the northern flanks of Kimiel. The other no longer fretted about the visions, their strangeness, their pertinacity, or even the eerie sense that they were growing ever nearer. She had become used to them, they amused her over the dull spinning of thread, and they were so beautiful now that she felt sure there could be no harm to them.

Until one day suddenly, in the midst of a skein, arrows flew, many arrows, and men screamed and blood ran; she went pale with the force and shock of it. And the great horse, hemmed in on a narrow mountain trail, could find no escape. Rough hands dragged her down from her sideways seat; she kicked and fought and in a moment the horse found an opening and leapt away without her. After that, all was nightmare.

For days and weeks thereafter she went about pale and silent and clenched in helpless nightmare. Her mother saw it and questioned her repeatedly, but she could not explain what had happened to her, was happening, and her mother did not know what to do for her.

Kyrem passed his time in Auron's dwelling much as ever, but the place felt different since the visit of the horse-bird, as if foreboding filled it, and the prince grew apprehensive, irritable. There was no news of Seda; he expected none. Waiting—for what? He observed that Auron was waiting also, busily, almost strenuously. The king spent many of his days in a taut sort of trance, and many of his nights, Kyrem found, in some sort of vigil, to no avail. Auron wore a strained and anxious air.

Nearly a month after Seda had left Avedon, the waiting ended. A messenger lad came running from the city gates to the palace, and at his urgent pleading the doorkeeper admitted him to the room where Kyrem sat with Auron.

"The horse, Sire! The horse, my lord Prince," the lad gasped, falling to his knees.

"What, now, what horse?" Auron asked soothingly. "Has one of Nasr Yamut's beauties taken colic?"

"No, my liege, the dark horse! The prince's, that was gone. It's outside the gates!"

Kyrem gave Auron one startled glance, then sprang up and ran. People in the streets parted before him. Panting, he reached the gates within moments, to find them closed. The gatekeeper awaited him.

"Go through the postern, good my lord Prince, and come around the outside. The horse is half mad, and we are frightened of it."

A long, wild neigh rang from the other side of the gates. Kyrem tingled at the anguished sound of it.

"Are you sure it is Omber?" he demanded.

"Go see." The gatekeeper pointed toward the steps that led upward to his guardroom.

It was Omber, gaunt and frantically pawing at the hard red ground, his tail loose and bedraggled but the braids still in his mane. He looked like a specter of Suth. Kyrem could see why folk were afraid of the stallion; the sight chilled even him. Then hot anger surged through him, anger that the horse had suffered, and pity and love for the animal that stood waiting. He took the steps three at a time, going down.

"Open that gate," he commanded where he had no right to command, and the man did it instantly. Kyrem had not time to move a step before the horse had met him, stood under the shelter of his hand, and Kyrem rubbed the whorl of the forehead in greeting, stroked the forelock, and Omber lowered his head, sighing, laying his muzzle against Kyrem's chest.

"Great Suth," Kyrem whispered, still caressing the horse. "Great Suth forgive us all, where is Seda?"

Chapter Fourteen

Auron joined him at the stable as soon as he could, hobbling in on his precarious buskins. "Has Nasr Yamut caused you any trouble?" he asked.

"I walked through him." Kyrem's lips were set in a thin white line, and white heat of anger flickered about him. Auron smiled at his own question; no one could have stood against Kyrem just then. Though in a moment he himself was going to have to try. . . . Nasr Yamut was nowhere to be seen.

Omber stood gulping a generous feed of oats.

"Do you think Seda sent him back to you?" Auron asked.

"Not like this. She wouldn't have done that. And he wouldn't have left her unless . . . unless something was very wrong." Kyrem set to work brushing the horse feverishly, undoing the braids in the mane. "Something has happened to her, as we were warned it would. I should have gone to her long since." He did not say that Auron had prevented his going when he should have gone. Courtesy and affection prevented his saying that, but they did not keep the angry thought from his mind. Auron sensed it as a harsh red flash, a hot, painful sensation, Kyrem's fury and despair.

"I will send a patrol out at once," he said, instantly aware of how feeble the words sounded. The last patrol had not yet returned. Kyrem set down the brush and faced him over the horse's rump.

"No," he said with a gentleness that belied his anger, "no more patrols. I am going to go after her myself. It can no longer be said that I lack a mount."

"You cannot go, Kyrem," Auron said, as he had hoped he would not have to say, as he had schemed not to say. He spoke just as gently as the prince, but Kyrem heard the settled certainty in those soft words. White flame of wrath threatened to warm his reply. He restrained it.

"Why?" he challenged as quietly as he was able. "Because I am your hostage?"

"Because you would be in grave danger. All events prove that. Kyrem, I would as soon go myself, leave Avedon for the first time in my reign and let my kingdom fend for itself, as allow you to venture forth."

The king in his buskins, teetering off to rescue Seda. . . . The image, ridiculous, flickered through Kyrem's mind before he realized with a dizzying shock that Auron spoke as of something utterly impossible.

"But I must go and—"

"You are to stay here. I took oath on that, you know, when your father entrusted you to my care."

"My father is probably the one who has set hirelings to kill me as an excuse for war." In his rage and dismay, Kyrem spoke what he had only felt before, dark feeling below the threshold of thought.

"You cannot really believe that!" Auron exclaimed.

"I—no." Still there was a niggling doubt, for Kyrem had

known very little of his father's heart. And shame. . . . "But who then?" he appealed, annoyed to find himself suddenly near boyish tears. "I know now it was not you," he faltered. "And nameless enemies are of no use."

Auron bit his lip, face to face with a wound he had failed to heal. "I will put a name to it for you," he promised. "By Suth and all his seven sons—" It was a solemn oath, but Kyrem turned away.

"You cannot, not here in Avedon. And I cannot wait. I must go find Seda at once. Omber is tough; he will take me to her, or at least to where he left her."

"Kyrem," Auron warned, "if I were to let you go off and you were lost, the consequence would indeed be war."

The prince did not think so highly of his father's love. He felt beyond much thinking of any kind.

"If Seda is lost, none of it matters," he muttered. "I should never have let her set off without me. I should have gone after her at once—should have told her—should have known. . . ." *That I love her!* Auron heard the thought as clearly as if it were his own, as clearly as if the words were spoken. They wrenched at his heart, but then he steeled himself. Kyrem was putting away the brush, gathering up gear. "I will need some provision," said the prince.

"You are not going," Auron told him in a different tone of voice, and Kyrem halted his preparations to look at him.

"Surely you will not forbid me."

"Already I have forbidden you. What must I do to make you see?"

But Kyrem saw clearly enough, as he had seen one day through the crack of a door. The monarch stood there, eyes alight with a cold stony glow, jewel light, no color and every color, Auron son of Rabiron, king of Vashti and emperor of the Untrodden Lands. His power of the throne and his heartache.

Rage rose up in Kyrem, a pyre, bonfire, conflagration of fury. Auron had deceived him. Invisible chains had been on him all along, Auron's shackles of power. Well, let Auron see his, Kyrem's, power. He had magic perhaps just as strong, innate magic. Wrath and stubborn will swelled and hardened him, making him—it was true, in a jewel flash of clarity he knew it was verily true—a fit opponent for the Vashtin monarch. Exultation filled him, crystal hard.

"I am a match for you, Auron," he averred, meeting the king's eyes with his own of blazing black.

"I have never doubted it."

"You cannot command me."

"Perhaps not," said Auron evenly. But his small, plump body did not yield its presence, nor did the focus of his eyes give way. All the force of his kingship was committed to the battle to keep Kyrem by him, a desperate battle, nothing held back. For a long moment they clashed in invisible combat, and in that moment Kyrem realized that their conflict would destroy one of them, snap one of them like a twig while the other remained; there could be no other outcome unless it destroyed them both. . . . And he loved Auron as himself; how could he risk harming him? In an instant all wrath and warrior will drained out of him, leaving him shaken and blinking.

Auron saw, heard it all, rage and struggle—and then the love in that yielding. Now he held Kyrem's gaze and could not speak.

"Surely I am not really your prisoner," said the prince bitterly, and Auron found his voice.

"I love you as a son, I who have none."

Kyrem looked away, had to look away, was allowed to look away.

"Set me free then," he whispered, "and I will come back to you."

To set one's children free. Such was the role of the parent, and Auron knew it well, he who had parented land and people for many years. Now Kyrem had adopted him with a few whispered words. That one plea served to sever him from kingship and bring tears to his androgyne eyes.

"Go with all blessing," he said softly, hearing his own words with faint surprise. Kyrem looked at him, then came around the horse to meet his arms. Unshakable bonding was in that embrace.

Several hours later Auron stood in his watchtower alone, looking out at the hills where Kyrem had gone at the gallop. Disappeared like Seda, gone, and when he reached the mountains, there would be no way of knowing, moment to moment, whether he still lived.

"Gone," Auron breathed.

Something dark appeared in the eastern sky, a flying thing, growing larger. Auron silently watched it sweep closer, not wanting to believe what he was seeing. The grotesque horse-headed thing, black wings that seemed to blot out all light, malevolent white rolling eyes, bared yellow teeth, mane all in a tangle like black cobweb, and those pitiful hanging hooves. . . . The demon flew so close that he could feel the waft of its great wings, and he stood still, fixing it with his glare.

"What agent sent you?" he demanded of it. "Who is your master?"

The demon did not reply. "Gone—gone—gone—" it started to chant.

"In the name of Suth, answer me, effigy!" Auron roared.

"Gone," it mocked, "all gone," and then it flew away.

*   *   *

Seda sat watching the old man from her place against the
damp wall of the cave. Old? He might not have been so very
old, but he was bent, glaring and grizzled, the color of mud
flecked with dirty snow; she had to think of him as old. She
was on Mount Kimiel, after all, the holy mountain, where no
one came except a few priests and the sacred horses. The old
man lived in the seer's cave. If he were Suth, then she did
not like Suth and might as well be in hell ice. He sat with a
young raven on his finger, whispering into the place he
judged to be its ear.

"Kyrem is dead," he whispered over and over again.
"Kyrem is dead." The word he used for dead was *nihil*,
unbeing. "Kyrem does not exist."

"Kyrem is dead," the young bird peeped mindlessly and
obediently. The old man stroked it and put it back into its
wicker cage to await the nighttime, when he would undertake
the magical ceremony that would transform it into a thing fit
to strike terror and consternation in those to whom it took its
message. He chose another raven to work with meanwhile.
There were dozens, perhaps as many as Auron's horses.
Their stench filled the place. The old man spent all his
daytime hours feeding them, training them and caring for
them tenderly—far more tenderly than he cared for his prisoner.
It was not by choice that Seda sat against the wall. A leg iron
secured her to the rock.

"Kyrem is dead," the old man instructed the next bird.

If he were Suth, then Suth was a liar. Kyrem had been
alive and well when she left him, Seda knew. So the old man
had to be a liar. How she hoped he was a liar. Why was he
keeping her, she wondered. All the others had been killed.
And he never looked at her except to curse her. He was
fluent in his cursing, far more so than his birds.

"The devil take you and leave his clawmark in you and bend all your bones," he would intone, handing her a meager daily ration of food. "My curse on your eyes, your legs, your sexual organs. May this food grow fangs inside you and do you no good. May your teeth rot until your breath smells like that of a carrion dog. May your fingers grow together and your ears fail you. Shuntali! Shuntali! Devan dog. You are dead. You do not exist."

She listened to him impassively, pulling her shuntali's toughness like an invisible cloak around her, letting the curses bounce off her like flung stones that did not break the skin. Bruises did not matter unless one noticed them, cried about them, and she had given up crying some years back. Besides, the old man lied. Why then should his curses be true?

"Liar," she said softly sometimes, and he would strike her, cuffing her on the head, and take away the food before she had touched it.

It did not matter. She sat with her back against the cold rock, expecting nothing, caring for nothing, wanting nothing. For until she let something matter to her, he could not hurt her overmuch.

The magical transformation of raven into demon took place within the dark penetralia of the cave, the darkest of darks, cave within a cave, where no one could see, neither the sorcerer nor his prisoner. It involved the invocation of the simurgh, primeval god-rival of Suth, and of Suth as well, the dark Suth to be joined with the dark spiritous bird, raven become more than raven, soon to be demon. Vibration of great wings filled the cave, and the bell-like ringing of hooves. The sour air grew tense with the conflict and uneasy mating of invisible presences. And with the dawn, a wicker cage stood empty and a black demon took wing. "Kyrem is dead," it shouted, then flew off toward the sunrise, toward Deva.

Within a few weeks an unaccustomed visitor thundered into Avedon. Townsfolk screamed and scattered before the hooves of his steed. Kyrillos the lion, king of Deva, was a big man, dark and heavy-bearded, and he sat a thick-necked charger. Although he came with only half a dozen retainers, his sudden armed and helmeted presence struck terror in Avedon. Alarm bells began to ring.

Even as the seven riders pulled up before Auron's stately dwelling, Auron himself came gravely out to meet them, weaponless as always, walking down the long ascent of shallow stone risers in his buskins and his gently flowing robes. Kyrillos dismounted to speak to him and had his men dismount also.

"My son," Kyrillos demanded, his tone urgent.

"He is not here."

"Where then? You swore to me—" The king of Deva checked himself with an effort, waiting for Auron to answer.

"He is off on a quest in the hills yonder." Auron looked back the way Kyrillos had come, and Kyrem's father shouted in reply.

"Off roaming? But of course he has his men with him?"

"No, my lord," said Auron steadily. "They were all slain on the way hither. And Vashtins do not ride horseback. He went alone."

Kyrillos snatched at his sword, and every man of his did the same. But the king of Deva froze with his hand on the hilt.

"Draw if you like," Auron told him. "My guards are

under orders not to defend me. We stand outside the household walls."

"I do not understand," said Kyrillos tightly. "Has it not been well between him and you?"

"It has been very good."

"I thought as much. And between us as well. I trusted you. Yet you have let him go off alone, into danger—"

"Your son is not a sheep, my lord, that can be tethered by the foreleg," said Auron rather sharply. "He has grown since last you saw him. I had to let him go or else put him in chains—and we both know that would not have served our purpose."

"Do not speak of that," Kyrillos muttered.

"I swore to you that I would cherish him as my own," Auron went on, "and I have done so, even to the point of letting him be a man. If you judge that I have broken faith with you, then my body is at your disposal. But I must warn you, Kyrem would not think kindly of you for slaying me." Auron spoke so evenly, he might have been discussing a matter of mere ritual.

Kyrillos glanced back at the mountains as if already searching for his son. "He might yet be alive," he said grudgingly.

"Indeed, I should fervently hope so! What has made you think otherwise?"

"Horse-headed birds." Kyrillos heavily took his hand away from his sword. "Black demons of ill omen, spreading rumor of his death around my kingdom. Have you seen or heard of any such creatures here?"

"Both heard and seen." Auron stood looking away toward distant Mount Kimiel with narrowed eyes. "I have spent men upon men seeking the enemy on that mountain," he declared, "and hour upon hour, day upon day, and to no avail. It is time and past time that I went to beard this mystery myself, in my own person. Take me your prisoner, king of Deva, so that I may ride with you.''

Kyrillos shook his shaggy head with a slow smile. Challenge was in that smile. ''I have no horse for you,'' he said. ''You must find your own.''

''Why, then, I will.'' Auron turned toward the sacred stable.

''And you will never be able to manage it in those things,'' Kyrillos added, staring meaningfully at Auron's buskins. ''Have you no boots, or sandals even?''

''I will find some.'' Auron kicked off the buskins, sending them flying up into the air, but he had to grasp at Kyrillos's outstretched hand to do it; his legs nearly collapsed under him, and he gasped with the pain, his calves fully extended for the first time in thirty-seven years. . . . His eyes closed and his head swam with the sickness of his agony. Then he brought the forces of his mind to bear on his body. Slowly he straightened, opened his eyes, stood with stockinged heels flat on the pavement. He let go of Kyrillos and faced the Devan king, standing quite erect.

''Come in,'' he snapped, ''take refreshment, make provision.'' Then he stalked up the many stairs and inside, giving orders as his servants gaped at him in greatest consternation.

Half an hour later, in breeches and Kyrem's spare boots, his smaller feet swaddled in wrappings to fit them, he walked to the stable and took Nasr Yamut's white-headed favorite from its regal bay, and no one halted or gainsaid him.

Chapter Fifteen

The brigands—criminals and mercenaries and outcasts of all sorts—who lived on Mount Kimiel understood vaguely that the power of the Old One made it a refuge for them. They served him. Their encampments formed defenses around his mountaintop cave, defenses nearly impossible to penetrate undetected. They brought him food and young ravens from the nest and oddments to feed the birds. These offerings might as well have been their sacrifices placed on an altar, the old man their god rather than their master, for they feared him and bowed to him as much in worship as in service. Nameless One, they called him. Odd that things most holy and things most despised were similarly shunned. Seda also was nameless in that place.

There were perhaps fifty of them, the brigands, enough to fill a sizable village, but few people knew of their existence. When they found it necessary to rob, they struck quickly and at scattered places, leaving alone most of the villages that stood nearer and the travelers who journeyed close at hand.

The few priests who wandered the mountain for the sake of the sacred horses knew of them, but they kept silence, for Nasr Yamut had commanded silence. Nasr Yamut sensed the power on the mountaintop, and he liked to study power; he watched, waiting for events that could be turned to his own advantage. Always he took care to withhold all thoughts of such possibilities from his mind when he was near Auron. The Vashtin king sensed only the presence of an enemy, not that of his minions, for his presence masked theirs.

One other person knew of the brigands: the prince on horseback who moved quietly between the black-trunked trees, searching and always searching for an opening. But he was only one, and no fool, and he could do no more than guess what awaited him.

Sometimes he could hear the talk of the guards, but it did not help him much. Their master kept them mostly in the dark.

"I wonder why the Nameless One would not let us attack the foreigners," a sentry asked his companion.

"He wanted them to get through to Avedon. He is hoping for trouble." The other laughed. "He likes trouble, that one."

"Then why will he not let us go looting if he likes war so much? And what is his game with that shuntali?" The sentry shook his head. "I don't understand him."

"We have only his word that she is a shuntali. I thought at first that she was a Devan. And she acted like one, she had that damned pride of theirs. For a while there he couldn't touch her."

"Well, he has touched her now." The man laughed nastily. "Oh, yes. He has touched her."

The old man had found a way through Seda's defenses to the needful center of her being.

There, at the core. By cleverness and a malicious persistence and the mad insight of sorcery he had found it, the tender place, the still-bleeding scar of the umbilical that had been torn away too soon. Seda could say and say to herself that it did not matter, but to her young, half-grown body it did matter, very much; one needs a mother at least until the bones are fully formed. Mother love. . . . The Nameless One could scarcely remember mother love, and to him it truly did not matter any more. Only for that reason had it taken him so long to understand. When at length he did discover, did comprehend, he smiled slowly, a cruel smile. And when he spoke to the girl thenceforth, he began in the name of that abandonment.

"Where is your mother?" he would chant, his words as offhand as villagers' flung stones. "Were you not born of woman, that you have no mother? She flung you away with her curse, like the offal you are. Where is your precious prince? Where is your lover? Bastard, you have none. Dung of Suth, all turn their backs on you. May your eyes cross. May your breasts droop and your bones bend. I curse you with the curse of your mother and your god. May you have a hump on your back and warts on your face. May you be as withered and sterile as Vashti, as harsh as Deva. The curse of all who worship the name of Suth be on you. Bastard, shuntali! You are dead. You do not exist."

His coldhearted intensity stunned and bewildered her. His words struck deep now, deeper than any stones of passion. Why would he not kill her more simply? What had made him hate her, Kyrem abandon her, her own mother hate her, everyone hate her? She was accursed. . . . But it was more than hatred in him, something even more chilling. Something made the lawless robbers heed him, listen to his ravings, do his will. There was a certainty in him that seemed almost supernatural, some secret knowledge. . . . Perhaps he was Suth. Had she not always borne the curse of her god? But why had he chosen to reveal himself to her now?

"Shuntali! Shuntali! Devan dog! You are dead. You do not exist."

"The dead do not wish for death," she whispered back at him once. The god lied. But he did not bother to strike her any more. He knew that his words now hurt her far more than blows.

At first Auron stayed on his horse only by reading its thoughts and anticipating its movements, then hanging on with hands and heels. That first day of riding was the most grueling physical trial he had ever endured. The sacred stallion was wild with freedom and ran like a crazy thing, with Kyrillos and his men urging their own steeds after. It made, as Kyrillos drolly said, a merry chase. Only a body softened by years of inaction kept the white-headed stallion from leaving them behind entirely in its mad career toward Mount Kimiel. It ran itself into a lather. By evening of the first day the company had covered nearly half the distance to the foothills, albeit erratically.

In days to follow, Auron learned to guide the horse by the movements of his body to some extent, and by a tug at the long lead rope still attached to its headstall. He never learned to control the animal very well. Most of the time it simply trailed after the other mounts. But it was all new to Auron and both exciting and unsettling to him, even this small experience of his own powers of the body, he the sacred king who had never had much parley with his body, his self. In the discovery of this new facility, he hardly noticed how his other powers were gently fading away from him, how he seldom slipped into a visionary trance any more, how he scarcely noticed Kyrillos's thoughts even when the Devan king stood at his shoulder. There was small occasion for the use of such powers those days, among those he trusted, and even in his court days he had always employed them with discretion.

They traversed the thorny foothills and gradually entered on the steeper land of the true mountains. It was autumn at this height, the blackthorn leaves rustling and turning the color of copper. Auron knew that Kyrem had come hither from Avedon, but farther he had not been able to follow him with his farseeing sense.

"Can you scent the spoor of the lad now that we are closer, friend Auron?" Kyrillos asked him.

Already Auron's face and clothing had taken on a weathered look, and he straightened on his mount and glanced around him with a new keenness. Then he closed his eyes, still seeking just as keenly. All the men waited expectantly, and even the horses stood quite still. But when Auron opened his eyes at last, he shook his head, and his face looked haggard.

"One presence on this mountain masks all others," he said, "and it is not Kyrem's. It is both powerful and malevolent."

"Could Kyrem yet be here then, even though you cannot find him?" asked Kyrillos.

"He could yet be here."

As long as there were villages or even scattered homesteads on the mountain slopes, it was not difficult to trace Kyrem's path. A horseman was no common sight in Vashti, and even weeks after his passing, folk still talked of him. He had gone straight up into the thickest of the black-trunked forest. There no one dwelt, or at least so it was thought. Though these folk lived peacefully enough, there was a certain cautious unease on their thoughts, and few men ventured to take the way that Kyrem had gone.

"Why not?" Kyrillos wondered aloud as they rode. He was a shrewd man, never one to hold back where something might be gained, if only knowledge. Nor would he shrink from challenge; his was a bold spirit. "Is this the Vashtin way, to sit tight always?"

"Perhaps." Auron gave him a tilted smile. "You have seen how long I sat tight. But it is more than that, I think. Those folk know surely enough what I have also sensed, though they will not say it."

"But what sort of sorcery is it that we will face here?"

"Hsst," Auron told him, softening his tone. "Enemies ahead."

Kyrillos gave his men the signals for caution and silence and the unsheathing of weapons. Quite softly they drifted forward, for the rustling leaves had not yet begun to fall, and the horses moved quietly on the thick bed of duff and dropped thorns beneath the trees.

Archers. They did not see them all at once. Bows and plentiful arrows at the ready, the brigands sat eating a midday meal from their satchels, each with his back against the black trunk of a tree. One outlaw they saw, and then two more, and then more again, a dozen or thereabouts, and there might have been more yet. Then one of them saw Kyrillos. He did not shout in alarm, but grinned and gave a sort of happy hunting call and fitted arrow to his bowstring. Kyrillos pulled his horse back sharply as the shaft thudded into the tree beside him.

"Retreat," he ordered.

They galloped off. Arrows flew after them from rearward, and they could see that even in the short time since they had been sighted, they had very nearly been taken on three sides. Auron looked frozen with fear.

"Stop," he said. "There are more ahead."

"Are you sure?" Kyrillos demanded, pulling his charger to a plunging halt.

"Reasonably sure," Auron said tersely. "I can sense them only at quite short range."

"Which way should we go then?"

Auron pointed downhill.

"Of course," said Kyrillos dourly. But he went, and the others followed.

They rode around the base of Mount Kimiel and tried it the next day from another approach. Kyrillos sent two scouts ahead this time.

"You cannot spare the men," Auron said, worried. "You are likely to lose them."

Kyrillos glanced back in some annoyance. "They are canny men. They will not be taken unaware."

"Yes, but how can they hide themselves? Perhaps on foot—"

"Horses roam these parts, you say?" Kyrillos interrupted, his tone one of utter serenity.

"Young horses, yes."

"Well, there. We are simply horses, nothing more, from a distance. We are not likely to be trailed, at least not if we leave few human traces. And our mounts given us the advantage of speed."

"Enemies," said Auron tensely, and in a moment the two scouts came hastening back to warn their master.

They had not been seen this time. Breathlessly they felt their way around the hidden presence of the foe. But as the terrain steepened, Kimiel put up natural ramparts to stop them, stony barriers the horses could not manage, certainly not with riders on their backs. Then a shout sounded from above.

"Retreat," said Kyrillos morosely as arrows rattled down through the blackthorn branches and clattered against the rocks.

They retreated. "Yon archers' shafts give them some small advantage as well," Auron said dryly.

Kyrillos did not answer. He looked furious.

"Try again," Auron sighed.

And again and again over the course of the next week and more they tried to make their way up Kimiel, to no avail. After ten days or so of edging up the baffling slopes, scouting every step of the way and sleeping by turns at night, everyone in the party was worn down with striving. The autumn weather had turned damp and chill, and the coppery leaves were coming down, thinning the cover, sending up a loud crackling noise at their every move, so that they felt sure their enemies would at any time be upon them. Time and time again they had sighted brigands and eluded them, until it seemed to them that the whole mountaintop must be swarming with hundreds of foes. But still they did not know the name of their true enemy. And they had not found a sign of either Seda or Kyrem, nor did Auron sense any presence of the missing ones. In fact, Auron was sensing less and less.

"I wish I had been not so proud and had brought a few more men," Kyrillos grumbled. "I wish I had brought a hundred. We would sweep right up this inhospitable hump and—"

He slid into curses. Kyrillos was feeling the effects of strain.

"This is holy land," said Auron reproachfully.

"So much the worse, then, that these ruffians are at large upon it. What makes them so bold, I wonder."

"I think the intelligence that governs them senses our presence and places them in our way. So there are not as many as there seem to be." Auron shook his head, his weariness manifest in the down-tugged lines of his face. "Do not count on me for much aid any longer, Kyrillos."

"What do you mean?" the Devan king demanded.

"Quiet," snapped Auron. "What's that sound?" He was the most nervous one of the group—the effect, Kyrillos conjectured, of soft flesh and the contemplative life.

"Only wind in the trees," Kyrillos said. But it was not wind, and after a while they traced it.

"By Suth," Kyrillos exclaimed, "it is a force."

The waterfall appeared over a high reach of rock and wavered down to the depths of a gorge two hundred feet below. At its lower extremity winked a pool like an emerald eye, frothy white at first but then quiet, shadowed, intensely green and deep. Almond shaped, it trickled away into stream. Towering ilex cast a chill purple shade, and laurel bushes crowded the edge of drop, pool and gorge, drinking in the spray.

"By Suth," Kyrillos added, "there's even a trail."

It zigzagged down over rock and earth, ferns and fallen logs, to the water. Deer could have made it, or the roaming horses. Auron looked at it dubiously, but the steeds snorted at the scent of water, the men fingered their nearly empty flasks.

"Dismount," Kyrillos ordered. He did so himself and started to lead his horse down the trail. The others followed, edging down the steep bank that soon rose far above their heads.

"No!" a voice shouted from somewhere on the opposite bank. "No, it's a trap! Go back!"

"Kyrem!" Auron exclaimed, straightening and looking eagerly toward the sound.

"Get behind your horses!" Kyrillos roared at the same moment, and he shoved Auron behind his white-headed steed. More shouts sounded along with his, and groups of armed men sprang up along the bottom of the gorge as though sown by dragons' teeth. They appeared from behind rocks and bushes and yellowish laurel clumps, from grottoes, even from behind the waterfall itself. A shower of arrows flew up.

"Get your head down, Auron, would you?" Kyrillos snapped peevishly. "Was that really Kyrem?" he added in a different tone.

"I think so. Who else would it be? Oh, no. . . ."

The arrows lost most of their force in their steep upward flight. Stalling in midair as they did, they could almost be swept aside with a sword or an outreaching arm. No one had yet suffered more than a minor wound, though the horses were whinnying wildly and only Devan magic kept them in place. But Auron did not possess such magic. A sharp-honed arrowhead grazed his horse's shoulder, and the sacred stallion plunged in panic, screamed and plummeted into the gorge. The fall broke its neck. Dying, it lay half in the water, staring horribly, and the brigands stood frozen, gaping at the white-headed, Suth-like thing as if it were an omen of illest portent. Kyrillos pulled Auron to his side, behind his own steed.

"Now that is enough of this," he declared, suddenly straightening. "One of us is worth three of them. Take them, men!"

All drew swords.

"Auron, stay here with the steeds," Kyrillos ordered.

"Do you want to shame me?" Auron flared in uncharacteristic anger.

"Of course not. But you have no talent for this sort of thing, and you know it. Stay."

"I can at least be another body in the line. And I have no reason to hold back. I am coming."

"He can take position by me," said a quiet voice, and Kyrem came over the top of the gorge and swung himself down to stand beside them.

Chapter Sixteen

"Kyrem. By the most holy one, lad, they told me you were dead," Kyrillos breathed, and tears started suddenly down his face. The prince stared openmouthed at his father. Tears trickling into the big man's beard. . . . Kyrillos reached over to touch his son, and Kyrem moved a hesitant hand in answer. But no sooner had hands met and gripped than a shout jerked them back to the pressing reality.

The brigands had closed ranks. They had mostly spent their arrows, but they still had cudgels, spears, long knives. No longer scattered at the bottom of the gorge, they advanced on the steep slope with weapons raised, ready for the charge.

"Get back," Kyrem said, tugging at Auron but speaking to his father. Kyrillos mounted his horse instead.

"The steed and I can hold them here a while," he said. "Auron, move the men back up to the top there."

"No room to turn the horses." Auron stepped forward to stand at Kyrillos's fore. He looked very pale, but determined.

"Confound it," Kyrillos roared, and then his attention was

172

taken up by attackers at his feet. He beheaded one with a swish of his curved blade and kicked another back down into the gorge. Auron lunged, a clumsy attack, but the slope gave him advantage over the man he faced and the fellow toppled backward. Kyrem struck down the sword of a second attacker before it could touch him.

"Will you both," the prince pleaded, "just get *back*?"

"What, and let you be killed after all? I've come too far for that, lad." Kyrillos swished off another head, almost absently. "Get back yourself."

"They're outflanking us," Auron said.

"Line of battle!" Kyrillos thundered, and his retainers fought their way forward and took their places to either side.

It truly is very difficult for horses to go backward up a steep slope. Hard beset, the Devans tried to make their steeds accomplish this feat several times during the next hour, but they found retreat impossible. Their whole focus after the first few moments was to keep the enemy to the fore. If once the swarming brigands managed to surround them, they would be finished. The riders on horseback took great advantage from their height and their uphill position, but the attackers on foot were numerous and fanatically persistent. They had to be killed. As often as they were knocked tumbling down the steep bank into the gorge they righted themselves and came up again with weapons raised.

Kyrem and Auron kept to the center of the line, the prince nearly frantic lest the gentle Vashtin king should be hurt. But Auron had captured a lance, hanging onto the shaft of it with grim tenacity while Kyrem killed the proper owner, and he quickly learned to use it to keep enemies at a distance. He would prod them back down the slope. Those few who came closer, Kyrem dispatched. Between the two of them, they managed almost better than the mounted men.

"It's a good thing we're fighting Vashtins," Kyrillos panted, for the outlaws were making no attempt to kill or injure the horses, only the riders. Auron glanced up dazedly from his bloody work and stared at the Devan king.

"By Suth, so we are!" he murmured, shaking his head as though to clear the haze of battle fever from it. "These scum are Vashtins, after all. King and people—"

Kyrem caught the drift of his mumblings. "Auron," he warned, but he had scarcely spoken when Auron moved.

The Vashtin king strode forward into the midst of the brigands. "Halt!" he cried in a ringing voice. "I, your king, command you to throw down your weapons!"

"Auron, you ass—" Kyrillos muttered frantically. Then he ceased his martial labors in amazement. The remaining enemies seemed caught in uncertainty, standing where they were and staring at the one who confronted them, their long knives wavering in the air. Kyrem also stood with sword at the ready but, his father saw, in some sort of expectation. Kyrem knew Auron's power, and he did not know how much the past few weeks had weakened it.

"Drop your weapons, I say!" Auron shouted sharply. "To whom do you owe more allegiance than to your king? Tell me the name of your leader!"

The brigands whispered anxiously to each other. One man laughed harshly. "He's not your king!" he barked out, scoffing at the others.

"He rode the white-headed horse," an outlaw tremulously replied.

"He's a blasphemer then, to ride a holy horse, and no king. Death to him! Death to the Devan dogs!"

"By the old man!" It was a Vashtin oath that Kyrem had adopted, and he strode forward suddenly to stand beside Auron. "By my beard, I know you! Weasel-face, from the

inn! Come meet me here if you are a man." He handed
Auron his sword and drew instead his long knife of single
edge. "The rest of you, do as your king commands."

They did not drop their weapons, but they shuffled back so
as to open a sort of arena, still whispering among themselves.
Kyrem's old enemy came forward, carrying his knife and
laughing wolfishly. "Where are the dozen who rode with you
over the Kansban, dog?" he taunted. "And where is your
precious shuntali?" Kyrem went white with fury, and as he
raised his knife and drew a panting breath, his foeman crouched
and attacked. The fight was on.

Upward stabs, aiming for the gut. . . . Knife fighting was
not a poised and princely sport, and weasel-face seemed to
be an experienced brawler. Kyrem essayed a thrust and the
man caught his wrist, nearly pulling him onto his own wickedly
waiting blade; Kyrem turned in time and the blow raked
across his ribs, leaving a long track of red. Only in desperation was the prince able to tear himself loose from the other's
grasp, and he lost his footing in the struggle, going down to
one knee on the steep slope, nearly rolling into the gorge or
the ranks of his enemies, and then the other was on him with
knife and fist and even teeth; he held off only the knife. Dust
flew up as the two scrambled and grappled on the treacherous
slope.

Kyrillos watched from his mount, sweating but silent. He
would not interfere with the contest, no matter how badly it
should go, for he knew that every man, every son, must
someday prove himself in fight, even fight to the death. He
had already lost two sons that way, over nothing more sub-
stantial than women. But this son, so long lost, so recently
found. . . . He bit his lip to keep from groaning as Kyrem
took a shrewd blow. Blood stained the prince's cloak at the
shoulder. Kyrem was all heart, the other all cleverness. Heart

had to win. . . . Kyrillos stole a look at Auron. The Vashtin stood as pale as the pale horse of moonlight.

Then a roar went up from the men at his side. Kyrem was on his feet at last, rising like flame, all blood and fury. His weasel-faced foe lunged and kicked, but the prince met his thrust with an arm like rock, his foot with a booted foot; the man howled, and for a moment his knife hand hung slack, and Kyrem grasped it, gripped. The man shrieked again, feeling small bones crack, and the knife fell flashing into the gorge. Kyrem forced the other down and held him pinned, blade at his throat. The roar fell off to a taut silence as men of both sides waited to see if Kyrem would deliver the deathblow. If he did, Kyrillos thought tensely, the brigands were likely to mob him before he could rise. Barely moving, he tightened the grip of his knees and his will on his horse. He would charge to save his son, even if it meant his own destruction in that chasm.

"Where is Seda?" Kyrem demanded of the man on the ground. He got no answer, and pressed the knife harder.

"Who, the shuntali?" The words came out in drawling derision from under that blade. "What makes you think we dirty our hands with such filth? We are not Devans."

"You slime, I saw her!" Rage possessed Kyrem; his knuckles went white, and a thin line of blood ran down from under the knife he held. "I saw her in your horror of a cave—but what have you done with her since? Where is she now?"

"Nowhere!" The man laughed, a defiant laugh that was ghastly to see, for it forced the knife even deeper, and yet he laughed insanely. "The Nameless One sent her off to wail in the wind weeks ago. Nowhere, I tell you! We dropped her bones off the farthest cliff we could find. *Nihil est*—she does not exist." He hooted with laughter.

Kyrem gave the stroke, lifted the body at arms' length above his head and hurled it down into the stream. It lay there with the others, sullying the water. Kyrem turned and faced the ring of many watchers, and they did not move. Only a shadow moved, sweeping along the deeps of the gorge, and the black, winged demon above it, whinnying.

"Filth!" it cried, making for the outlaw forces. "Bloody, craven filth!" The men scattered and ran, scrambling along the steep bank. The flying monster came speeding straight at Kyrem, who glanced at it and wearily raised his knife, standing as though all the heart had gone out of him—but Auron threw his lance, and to his surprise, it found its mark. The horse-headed thing fell fluttering and spiraling into the gorge, where it lay black in the water beside the white-headed sacred steed.

Kyrem lowered his weapon and came slowly back to stand beside his father.

"Lad, let me wrap those cuts for you," Kyrillos offered, but he shook his head.

"So she is dead," he said to Auron in a flat voice. "I thought as much when I stopped sensing her presence. I could not win through to her."

Neither of them knew what to say to comfort him.

"The enemy awaits us," he told them grimly. "The true enemy. Up on top. Up at the cave."

The old man moved unhurriedly from cage to cage, opening each one, shooing out the denizens. The birds flapped off with insulted squawks and occasional mimetic curses. "Go lay eggs," the old man told them indifferently. Presently, as if in afterthought, or as if she were an odd bird of a different sort, he turned to Seda. With palsied slowness he brought out a key and unlocked the shackle from her leg. Staring at him, she did not move.

"Your bastard prince is coming," he told her with only a hint of malice in his voice. "Killed my captain for your sake, he did. Filth." The word might have applied to the captain, or to Kyrem, or to her.

Kyrem. Kyrem was dead, *nihil est*. Kyrem did not exist. Her mind would not move properly, to tell her whether he had really died or the old man lied, but it did not matter. Either way, he had abandoned her, like her mother. Coming—he came far too late. Years before would have been too late.

"Go on," said her captor impassively. "Crawl off somewhere. Surely you don't want him to see you the way you are, dead thing." He turned back to puttering among his birds.

She opened her festering mouth as if to say "thank you," but did not; human speech was not in her any more, nor were human emotions. Even her gratitude was scarcely human, for she hated it, hated herself as she dragged her crippled body across the dung at his feet. She crawled out of the cave and off among the thorny brush. She could not walk, for the curses had taken their effect, and her bones were bent, warped and useless, her teeth rotting, her skin covered with sores, her eyes burning and half blind. Remnants of her maidenly finery hung about her in filthy rags. For once the god had spoken truth: Indeed she did not want Kyrem to see her. Nor did she very much want to see him. She was full of pain and bitterness and wanted only to hide.

Omber awaited atop the bank by the waterfall. Kyrem vaulted onto the horse, helped Auron up behind him and led off at once, the others trailing after. He took them splashing through a ford above the force—the way, Auron surmised, that Kyrem had come to them some few hours before, though Auron did not care to ask; the set of Kyrem's jaw and the stiff feel of his back did not invite conversation.

"You know the terrain, lad," Kyrillos remarked almost diffidently.

"I have been trying to get through their lines for weeks," said Kyrem harshly.

Silence, except for the hollow sound of hooves on reddish rock and the whine of wind through black trees.

"The power up there," Kyrem said at last, "whatever it is, seemed always to know where I was, directed those ruffians somehow to stop me. I can sense that enemy now, Auron, and the curse. You were right all along."

"Of course," said Kyrillos, his tones bland and innocent. The others ignored him.

"When you came, you two, it focused on you mostly. I hoped I could win through after all."

"You knew we were here and did not join us?" Auron was shocked. Kyrillos, though, had lived his life by the warrior code, and he admired the courage of his son.

"It was a forthcoming thing to do," he said to Auron.

"But we were worried," Auron told Kyrem reproachfully. "We came here to look for you."

"I thought you came to look for your enemy." Kyrem tried to turn on the horse to see Auron's face, but he could not without stopping the steed. "Could you not sense my well-being?" he asked over his shoulder.

Auron shook his head, silenced, and Kyrem could not see the bleakness of his face. For his own part, Kyrem looked as pale as the mist wraiths over the Ril Melantha.

"It was no use anyway," he mumbled. "She was already gone. I don't know what they did to her. She just . . . faded away."

Without preamble the trees to either side of them burst into flame with a roar like that of great wings.

The horses reared before their startled riders could control them. The men clung on by the manes, brought the steeds down, forced them forward once again as more blackthorn trees blazed up with fire that popped and sizzled through their crooked boughs, making a blinding trail of flame all the way up to the mountaintop. Kyrem sent Omber straight through it, sensing challenge and rising to it scornfully. But then, in the very midst of the fire, they came to a barrier they could not comprehend.

They could see nothing, but they all felt it and came to a halt. It might as well have been made of stone, whatever it was; it barred them. They ventured along the steep terrain to one side and then the other, the fire following them each time. The barrier stood there as well.

"A wall of will," said Kyrem. "Nothing more."

The horses were becoming frantic. When they could be driven forward by legs and heels, they were manageable, but standing still under scorching flames and burning, falling thorns, they could no longer be restrained; they reared and fought, and all the riders' energies were bent toward controlling them. Only Kyrem seemed to have any inner strength to spare, strength of grief and rage. He brought Omber around to face the invisible barrier, and then, with a wild shout and a body clenched hard as rock, he sent the stallion plunging through.

Auron went with him, willy-nilly, hanging to his waist. And Kyrillos leaped his thick-necked charger through on Omber's heels with a lion's roar of his own. The others could not manage it. They let their maddened horses turn and run away, down the mountain, out of the fire, and the fire no longer followed them.

"We are within the shadow of that enmity," Kyrem murmured to himself or Auron or his father.

A mighty presence sought to crush them with its weight, its curse, its hatred. Hot fires of hatred. Fire filled the mountaintop, and the curse bore down on them like molten lead. They sagged under the weight of its unseen presence, and the horses slowed to the slowest of walks, their heads hanging, in spite of all urgings. And even though fire seared all around them, the way seemed almost as dark as night.

"We have to get out of this," Kyrem said, perhaps to himself, a small note of panic in his voice.

"Let him wear himself out on us," Auron said in reply, speaking directly into the youth's ear, his voice labored but calm. "We can withstand his worst. That is all I am good for any more, lad—enduring."

They endured, and the horses took them at a snail's pace forward until they came out of the burning trees into a stony clearing on the mountaintop. Heat and the leaden weight of unseen hatred fell away from them and their heads came up as, with a scream, the demons attacked them.

More than a dozen demons. Their hard, heavy black hooves hung down on their yellow legs, swinging like maces as they swooped low, shrieking and going for the head. Kyrem, who had witnessed this mode of attack once before, crouched over Omber's neck, pulling Auron down behind him, and sent the stallion cantering forward. Kyrillos drew his curved slashing sword and joined battle with the horse-headed birds.

The old man awaited Kyrem at the gloomy entrance of the cave.

The prince brought Omber to a halt and stared at him, all other sensations lost in surprise. The frailty of this ancient, his limbs protruding thin and twiggy from under a patched and grimy robe, his back hunched, his head emaciated and the thin hair on it grizzled with age. He seemed one to pity and succor rather than one to fear. But his colorless eyes stared far too bright from out of a brown and expressionless face, and Kyrem remembered how he had at first scorned Auron.

Warily he slid down from Omber to face his adversary. Auron remained on the horse.

"Why have you killed Seda, old man?" Kyrem asked, his voice low, his eyes never leaving those of the one he faced. "And why do you curse us with your enmity?"

For answer the Nameless One only stretched his lips, baring his teeth in a mirthless rictus. He stirred, slightly lifting the arms that hung at his sides, and the sorrel rocks of the mountaintop began to move. Omber neighed in panic as his footing shifted under him, and Auron hastily grasped hold of his mane. From somewhere behind them Kyrillos gave an alarmed shout. Kyrem did not glance around to see how the others were faring; he did not dare to take his gaze from the sorcerer he faced.

"So you command the forces of earth," he said to him. "It seems that I must learn to do that as well. You have taught me much." Power of his youthful will swelled within him, and he also raised his arms, though only as high as his waist, his hands spread in a calming gesture, palms downward.

"Kimiel, be still," he murmured, eyes intent but open and focused. At the same time, his adversary twitched his arms a bit higher, and the uproar of the earth increased. Trees began to sway and rocks to crack and yawn. Thin lips pulled back in a wider grin.

"Anka, be still," said Kyrem sharply, and all fell to silence with a thud. For a moment a flicker of surprise showed in the bent old man's bright eyes.

"Press, Kyrem," Auron said crisply.

It was too late. Already the ancient had regained his mental footing, and his was the next move. Fire and earth he had attempted already. Next came air. He lifted his skeletal arms above his nearly fleshless head and fluttered them like wings. So frail were his bones that with the wide arms of his threadbare robe trailing about them, they looked nearly translucent, like cloud wisp in wind, almost like the wings of a bird—

With a demented wail, a wild wind arose, the most keening and desperate of winds, the hot, strength-sapping south wind, and on the wings of the wind came birds by the thousands, starlings mostly, their own wings helpless, outspread but twisted, feathers awry, broken. Their squawking assaulted the ears of those on the mountaintop and the scorched, fusty smell of them stung their nostrils and the yellow of their beaks came at their eyes and their sooty bodies pelted them like stones, filling the air, a feathery up-piling hot flood of birds, eerily horrible. Kyrem felt as though he were choking, boiling, drowning in them, and he realized all in a searing moment that he was exhausted. Weeks and wounds and sorrow had drained him; he stood no more than a weary youth, callow and shaking.

Auron sat safe on Omber's back. "Auron," the prince appealed, "help!"

"I'm sorry, lad." Auron's voice sounded thin in the shrieking mistral. "I am just a cipher these days. You are on your own."

With a shock Kyrem realized that he would not have come to this mountaintop so boldly if it were not for the comforting feel of Auron's presence behind him. "You might have told me sooner!" he cried.

"I tried. Hurry, lad, your father—"

Wind or demon had unhorsed Kyrillos.

Sudden strength of rage poured through Kyrem, wrath—whether more at Auron or the old man, he could not tell; it did not matter. He was rock hard and immense with strength, and power filled him with a fiery sheen. "By Suth," he shouted, "now you spirit of the simurgh, cease!" And in the instant he spoke, the wind dropped to a dead calm and the birds flew away, crying plaintively, except for those whose bodies littered the ground. And the old man fell down against the stone lip of his cave—the sudden cessation of the storm had unbalanced him. Kyrem strode over to him and stood straddle-legged, towering over his enemy.

"Old One," he said grimly, "think not of water now, for that is my element."

Kyrillos came up to stand by his son, for the black horse-headed birds had flown away with the others. And Auron slipped down from Omber's back. And crouching like a verminous, cornered animal, the old man did nothing but stare. His lips covered his yellow teeth now. For a long moment they all stared, until at last they realized what had happened.

"Kyrem," Auron whispered, "you have called him truly, and he obeys you."

Kyrem comprehended at the same moment, reached down swiftly and caught the sorcerer by the cloth of his robe, jerking him upright.

"Old One," he demanded, "why have you killed Seda? What is your grudge?"

The old man spoke in the dry, rasping voice of defiance. "Curse you, Devan dog. Curse you, people of Suth. Die—"

But Kyrem was still in plenitude of power, and the curses came back at the curser, choking him. He stopped, his eyes wide and glaring. Kyrem glared back for a moment, then tugged his prisoner inside the cave, the others following.

There they found filth, dung; and an empty shackle against a stony wall. The sight maddened Kyrem. He shoved the old man up against the hard red rock.

"Why?" he shouted. "Why have you killed her?"

At first the Old One seemed not to hear. Then he let out a wild cackle of laughter. "Die, Devan dog! Shun-shun-shuntali! Shun-shun-shuntali!" he chanted, for all the world like one of his cursing demons. "Shuntali! Shuntali! *Nihil est*—she is dead. She does not exist."

Before Auron could stop him, Kyrem had cuffed the grizzled head that lay against the dung-streaked wall. The old man grinned like a skull and spat out a dark vomit of blood. Essence of his life had been in his final efforts, and it was all spent. He laughed again and quietly, spitefully, died. Wordlessly they stood staring at the body, and when Kyrem let it go, it slid down the cave wall to lie in a bony jumble at his feet.

A large owl sat on a ledge near the roof of the cave, looking on. It had not left with the caged birds, for it was no prisoner. It simply lived there, a wild thing, depositing little pellets of mouse bone and fur among the other droppings on the floor.

From her refuge in the laurel not far away, she who had been named Seda looked on as well.

Kyrem gave in. Stricken by sorrow, wounded, spent by weeks of striving and a day full of combat, once more the hurt child for a while, he turned to his father, sobbed briefly and collapsed. Kyrillos caught him and carried him to the cleaner air outside, where he laid him down. The prince did not come to himself. He lay in stupor and fever, and his father and Auron tended him far into the night.

A few at a time the stragglers of Kyrillos's retinue found their liege. They cleared away the broken bodies of many starlings, and they brought food. Sentries were set; they stood guard all around, against what they could not say, for the enemy was vanquished, slain or put to rout, but still they stood guard. Against death? A small camp fire had been built, and by it Auron sat, his hands on Kyrem's burning head.

"Can you not heal him?" Kyrillos pleaded.

"Can you not see that I am trying to heal him?" Auron answered in a low voice. "But that power is gone from me, all my powers are gone utterly, I am but an empty husk, no king and not even man. It is as that renegade had said; I am a blasphemer."

"Because you rode a *horse*?" Kyrillos's voice rose impatiently. "What nonsense. Try harder."

"It is gone, I say." Auron withdrew his hands, turned away his face. When Kyrillos spoke again, his tone was gentler.

"Well, go to sleep then. It makes no sense that we should both be up all night. The lad is tough; he will mend. I will take a turn at guard." Kyrillos strode off into the surrounding blackthorn forest, and finally, for a little while, Auron slept.

The night is very dark a few hours before dawn, and this was a black and moonless night. The sentries gave no alarm when a nameless thing crept quietly out of the underbrush and stole food from the kings' camp. Auron awoke and saw it as the shadow of a bad dream. But it hitched away as he blinked, and it was not seen again.

Chapter Seventeen

Kyrem lay in a stupor of sickness for three days, but his fever gradually abated, and before long, Kyrillos and Auron knew he would be well. He took water and nourishment, and the third evening he eased from restless illness into a deeper and more natural slumber. He slept soundly through the night, then awoke groggily at dawn to stare at the two kings who sat companionably at the embers of the fire, watching the brightening sky.

"I thought you were supposed to be enemies," he mumbled.

"Auron is the best of enemies," Kyrillos said gruffly. He came over and touched his son's forehead. He knew well enough that the fever was down, but he needed an excuse for the caress. "Auron has been explaining some things to me," he added. "Lad, I am truly sorry about the girl."

"Seda. Yes. So am I." Kyrem closed his eyes tightly in pain, thinking of her. "We were far too late to help her. My shame . . ." He could scarcely speak. "I did not believe in such an enemy. Malice, no reason . . . I could not believe."

187

"And I believed and could not go forth against him." Auron came over and sat down on the rocky ground beside them, weary but oddly composed, accepting of all that had happened. "I might as well have been a stone statue in that palace, a fixture," he added. "Not until you king of Deva came to knock me loose. . . ."

Kyrem came out of pain for the time, opened his eyes and looked at his father.

"Did you really come searching for me?"

"Of course!" Kyrillos's voice shook, and to his chagrin, he found himself close to tears, making that affirmation. The sight of his son threatened to loose a flood of tears in him, for too many years had passed without any.

"Do you understand your father now, Kyrem?" Auron asked. "Sometimes it is necessary for a man to stand back for a while—"

"Speak for yourself," Kyrillos grumped. A hard edge helped to bring his voice under control. "The truth is, lad, I have been several kinds of an ass in my life, and all of them are starting to catch up to me. Do you remember Alim, your old nurse?"

"Of course. Is she still well?"

"She's fine. She used to coddle all you boys, or so I thought. Don't mother them so, I'd bark at her. I had never had a mother and it did me no harm. . . ."

"And she would tell you that you didn't know how much harm it had done you." Kyrem smiled at the memory.

"Yes. Well, she was quite right." Kyrillos took a deep breath, trying to retain his fragile serenity. "Fortunately, she paid no heed to me at all, and she mothered you all she liked. I was always brusque with you boys, afraid of the way I . . . the way I loved you."

"And Auron?" Kyrem asked quietly after a moment. "What has happened between you and him?"

"It took me years to look beyond the tip of my own pugnacious nose and see that Auron is—well, what you know him to be."

"Wise and true."

"That and much more."

"You could have told me," Kyrem complained.

"No, I could not. You had to come to terms with him yourself. But there were other things," Kyrillos added awkwardly, "that I could have told you."

"Everything except why he had chosen you out," Auron interceded. "You see, Kyrem, your father and I had agreed that his favorite son should be my heir, since I have none."

"Auron, hush," Kyrillos growled. "You've stunned the lad, and he weak and grieving still."

"It will do him good to know how highly we have both thought of him," Auron said.

Kyrem slowly sat up, grappling with one concept at a time. "Favorite?" he whispered.

"Yes, Ky," his father answered. "I cherish all my lads," he added judiciously, "but there is no denying that you have been special to me. Your mother—" The king stopped.

"Who was she?"

"Heart. All heart." Kyrillos looked away. "I miss her still."

He could not or would not tell her name. Auron interceded again.

"Vashti needs the vigor your youth and prowess can bring it. The people walk like donkeys in the paths of the priests— but you are not one long to abide Nasr Yamut and his ways. And you shall be the emblem and agent of fertility for a sterile land."

"Your heir?" Kyrem whispered, marveling, and Auron laid a kind hand on his knee.

"My heir and adopted son. No longer will there be war between Deva and Vashti."

Over the eastern steppes the sun came up.

They talked no more, the three of them, until they had eaten. Kyrem ate everything they gave him. Then he stood up shakily and went down to the stream and bathed. When he returned, they could see that he felt stronger.

"The bodies have been cleared away from below the force," he said.

"Yes. The men have been busy." Kyrillos stared, for he knew Kyrem had not been that far afoot. "How did you know, lad?"

"I—I can sense things these days, sometimes. You have left the Old One in his cave."

"True. We piled the loose rock over him, the stones he jarred free with his earthquake. It seemed fitting."

Kyrem shrugged. "And Seda's bones lie nowhere hereabouts," he murmured.

"No. We searched for some few miles, but—" Kyrillos stopped with his hand upraised in a sort of appeal. "She could be anywhere, lad."

"I know. I have searched all around with my mind for as far as it can reach, and I find nothing on this mountain except horses and creatures of the wild." Kyrem sat down by the fire with them. "I wanted only to mark her grave. . . ."

"Exactly what are your powers these days, lad?" Auron asked quietly.

"My powers?" Kyrem blinked. "Why, much the same as ever, I suppose, except that I had to learn to deal with yon old man."

"Ah, yes," remarked Kyrillos. "Except."

"The most formidable of old men," said Auron. "For a month and more you were able to withstand his malice and elude the focus of his mind, and you grew to sense his presence and whereabouts and the presence of Seda in his cave, and in the end you withstood his every weapon and vanquished him. And now you are a seer. Think of Avedon, Kyrem. What are the priests doing?"

Kyrem smiled in wonder and amusement. "I cannot see that far," he said.

"I'll wager you have not yet tried. Focus your mind on Avedon, and see."

Kyrem's gaze grew faraway and his smile faded. "Yes, I see," he murmured after a long moment. "But Nasr Yamut is sitting on your throne—how can that be?"

"Not *my* throne any longer. *Yours.* I have left it, and all my powers are gone." Auron stood up, and though he had said his powers had left him, he looked leaner and stronger and keener of eye than Kyrem had ever seen him. "King of Vashti, are you well enough to ride?"

For a moment the title took Kyrem's breath away. But then he remembered that titles were only words after all. He arose and went to Omber, silently offering the sharing of the steed to his mentor and adoptive father. Kyrillos and his retainers started gathering up food and gear.

"I will not be a king who sits in the palace and wears buskins," Kyrem said very gently to Auron.

"No, I should think not!" Auron laughed softly, seeming wry but not at all affronted. "I should think not. And I believe the people are ready for the change," he added. "They admire you and will accept you, but for the priests. And it is time and past time that we dealt with the priests."

All was ready. Kyrillos and his six men strode to their

horses. Kyrem managed to scramble onto Omber, then reached down to help Auron up behind him. Kyrillos seemed to be waiting for something—the king of Vashti was to ride in the fore. Swallowing once, then lifting his head, Kyrem led the company off toward Avedon.

But before they had left the clearing, a dark shadow fell over the group and a familiar black monster flew overhead, its feathers whistling, the sound of mockery. "Curse you! Curse you all!" it cried, then swirled away.

Kyrem followed it keenly with his gaze. "So," he murmured, "the curse is not yet off the land."

"No." Auron spoke from just behind his shoulder. "The agent of it has died, but his minions live on. And the curse itself has long since been pronounced with power."

The curse of war.

"Then how is it," Kyrem asked, "that you can say there will be no more fighting, Auron?"

"Why, we will have to negate it, lad."

They rode away toward Avedon, and from its perch in the cave, an owl watched them go, and from the shelter of an evergreen laurel, other eyes watched them also, feral eyes, until they had rounded the mountain peak and dipped out of sight westward.

After they were gone, a nameless creature of the wild lived on the mountaintop alone. Small, hunchbacked and twisted, it dragged itself about on all fours and scratched for worms and grubs to eat, or gulped the occasional toad or newt. Remnants of skirt trailed after it, looking like bedraggled blue quills. The creature drank at the stream and would not go into the cave; it slept on the open ground in the chill that increased nightly. Yellow autumn moon waxed from crescent to full and waned halfway to crescent again. The creature found little to eat but made no sound, except once when it crawled down to the stream for water and glanced up at a darkening sky and saw the yellow moon. "Araah!" it cried out into the night, an echoing, animal cry. "Araah!" at the heedless moon. But then it drank and slept and did not cry out again.

When the creature awoke in the dim dusk of that dawn, a dark circle had formed around it. Black-winged demons to the number of a dozen or more stood there, stolid on their ridiculous hooves, their equine heads turned toward her in curiosity. What did they want, she wondered. She was not their master, that she should speak to them. She lay motionless, watching them, until after sunrise, and they waited patiently for her. Finally she stirred and crawled toward the laurel thicket beyond them, intent on something to eat, and their ring parted before her, but then they crowded after her. All day they followed her about, hopping along on their black hooves and fluttering their wings to keep balance, occasionally banging their noses when the weight of their heads caused them difficulties. They did not curse or mock; they seemed almost diffident, like uneasy children.

Something odd stirred in the girl-creature as evening drew on, and she crawled up onto the hummock above the cave to watch the sun set over Vashti. The horse-birds could not manage the slope with their clumsy hooves and had to fly up in order to keep her company. They arranged themselves in ranks behind her and sat quietly.

The sunset was spectacular, magnificent over foothills crowned with copper leaf of thorn. Golden light—memory was more feeling than thought, feeling of the golden-domed dwelling in Avedon. . . . And great orange plumes of cloud floated across the western sky—lifted wings above a crimson heart, a wounded breast, of sun that shot out a single ray of brilliant yellow into the blue dome of sky. Cloud shifted, caught the yellow light . . . the watching creature blinked, dreaming for a moment that she had seen a blue and yellow eye and the down-curved beak of a great bird. She had. Snake of lightning shot across the western sky, and with thunder sound, the simurgh flew toward her. On wings of flame.

It did not grow larger, coming nearer, for it was already as big as the sky; it merely condensed, like mist of cloud becoming droplet clear, every feather jewel clear and translucent, shining. Breast of ruby red and crest of yellow and yellow beak and great orange flares of wings. No, it was not a jewel bird, the girl-creature sensed; it was a bird of fire, sunset fire, crystalline fire, and the incredible plumes streaming from crest and tail, and the sheen of red wattles, red fiery flesh of head and blue eye. . . . It carried in its beak a small chalk-white snake that wriggled fiercely. But as it reached the mountaintop, it smashed the head of the snake against red rock and popped the silenced reptile into the gaping mouth of the waiting creature as if she were no more than a nestling.

She gulped it down at once. Food was food. But she felt it burning its way down her gullet and into her belly, and the earth beneath her clawlike hands and crippled shins seemed to soften, flesh of the Mare Mother, her only mother, answering her touch with warm touch, embrace. And in the bare mountaintop blackthorn trees she heard birds, and she understood their chatter, heard them telling the names of the insects they had eaten that day and the business of their families.

The simurgh threw back its crested head and gave forth with a harsh, brazen cry. Dazzled, the girl-creature saw that the inside of its mouth was the same cerulean blue as its eye.

And she understood its cry. *Your father was the last of the Old Ones,* the simurgh had cried.

"*Is that why you fed me?*" the girl-creature asked softly. She spoke no language of men, not then. She spoke a wordless language, her query a soft whimper, and the simurgh understood, as she had understood its cry.

Perhaps. Your blood is impure, but it runs strong. The simurgh shifted and settled its feathers, sending up spear-heads of light so that folk in the lowlands thought there was a conflagration on the mountaintop, fire to rival the vanishing sunset. It threw back its huge head and cried again. *I fed the Old One sometimes. But he did not worship me aright. He was full of spleen.*

The girl-creature understood about her father in a creaturely sense, that he had been and was gone. She did not understand in any human sense, to ask, Who was he? She merely said, "*You have no one to worship you any longer then.*"

It is of no consequence. I was here before men, before Mare Mother. I was here, sky was here, and long after men and land are gone, I shall fly.

"*What is it that you want of me?*" the girl-creature asked.

Learn, grow, heal.

She grimaced, for she also was full of spleen, and she felt too hateful to even hear the name of healing. "*Is that all?*" she asked, a hard edge of irony in her wordless voice. "*Nothing more?*"

For now, nothing more.

Chapter Eighteen

In the arid heat of the lowland Vashtin autumn, Kyrem returned to Avedon. He held Omber to the slow, prancing, ceremonial trot as he traversed the streets. Auron had dismounted at the gate and walked beside him, serene in his commonplace state, a vessel of power no longer. Kyrillos and his retainers rode behind. All the people in the streets turned and watched intently, seeing Kyrem, seeing Auron, and a power stirred in the city, its own power, as the news ran.

At the palace gate the doorkeeper welcomed his former master and the prince with a smile. "I am supposed to ask you what is your business," he told them.

"Such impudence merits no answer," Kyrem snapped. "Auron is still master of this dwelling. Let us pass."

"No, in fact, I am not," said Auron to Kyrem. "You are, by my express will. So go in."

Kyrem strode past the doorkeeper, and the man stood aside, his smile broadening. Auron followed. Kyrillos and his retainers stayed outside the household walls, tending

Omber and waiting. Within, the servants watched as Kyrem and Auron walked straight to the dome room. There they found a phenomenon much of the sort they expected.

Nasr Yamut awaited them, sitting firm on the throne. He had put off his priestly robes and wore the multicolored robes and jewels of the Vashtin king. Footbearers attended him, and a pair of winged buskins perched on the ebony stand at his side. On his shaven head rested the crown.

"I will not make you kneel," Nasr Yamut said, "as you are both of rank, or former rank."

"Get off that throne." Kyrem strode forward, letting his anger lend him force, put power in his voice. But Nasr Yamut kept his place.

"Yonder king is a king no more," he said. "He has abdicated his position, thrown aside the bonds of his office, abandoned his responsibilities. He is a renegade and a blasphemer."

"That last is for Suth to decide, is it not?" Auron replied in the quiet voice of an ordinary man. "I have abdicated, it is true. And if you have examined my documents of state, you will have discovered that I appointed an heir, who stands here with us."

Servants were quietly gathering along the filigree walls of the room, listening.

"So, it is for your own sake that you want this throne." Nasr Yamut turned a glittering look on Kyrem, jewel-hard and glittering.

"I want to keep a vulture off it, nothing more," Kyrem said, his tone not loud but forceful. "Stand down before I remove you bodily."

"Carefully, Prince, carefully," said the former priest in a voice poison-smooth. "The throne itself lends me power, and I have some of my own, as you know. Back away, before you are destroyed."

"Not likely," Auron remarked. Something in that offhand statement gave Nasr Yamut pause, for Auron was not one to speak emptily. He stared, glancing from prince to former king, and his voice grew shrill.

"I have those who will fight for me!"

A small stir sounded as Kyrillos entered the dome room and came over to report to his son.

"Several hues of priest are lining up out there," he said in carefully level tones, "with clubs and pitchforks and the like. Some bear more war-worthy weapons."

"Well then," came a new voice, "we will have to fight also, for our proper master." It was the doorman. Other servants looked at him and nodded, and most of the men among them went out.

"Shall I order a charge?" Kyrillos asked. Kyrem shook his head.

"Go, watch and wait." And his father nodded and left.

"In no way can you succeed, Nasr Yamut," Kyrem said, turning to the priest on the throne. "Your followers may amass without, but I will prevail within." He mounted the steps to the dais, towering over the seated man, and power of his will and his wrath filled him, making him seem both luminous and enormous. The two footbearers looked up at him and hastily abandoned their post, hurrying away. Nasr Yamut's stockinged feet dropped with a small thud to the platform.

"Get up."

The priest rose, standing awkwardly in the confined space between prince and throne, but his eyes did not admit defeat. They stared up at Kyrem's, still venomous. "My men are under orders," he said, "to attack if you force me from this dwelling against my will. There will be a slaughter."

"Your men will take the worst of it," Kyrem said. "Men on foot are no match for Devan chargers."

But he knew at once that Nasr Yamut did not care about the well-being of his priests, did not care how many of them fell if their bloodshed brought him a martyr's sort of skewed vindication. The tiled streets of Avedon would run red with blood on the fire-master's account, and the white plaster of the houses be splattered with it. Kyrem thought of his father and his six retainers waiting there outside. They were warriors, they would fend for themselves, but what of the smiling doorman and the servants? He looked with his mind's eye. Kyrillos sat his steed with weapon drawn, every sense alert, the servants ranked by him. Worse and worse—scores of townspeople were lining up for battle as well, some siding with the priests but most opposing them. The brightly colored robes of the priests fluttered like pennons in a warm breeze, and the brightly colored clothing of the Vashtin townsfolk bedecked the crowded streets. It might have been a scene of festive gaiety had its purpose not been so grim.

Only lately Kyrem had first killed a man, and he had not enjoyed it. Bloodshed had been no more appropriate on the holy mountain than it would be in Avedon. . . . He brought his gaze back to the traitorous priest before him, knowing how he hated the man, how he would like to punish him. He thought of that, and then he sighed.

"What do you want?" he asked Nasr Yamut.

There are three types of magic, the simurgh was telling the girl-creature. *The Vashtin magic, which is pitiful, all fear, and the Devan magic of vitality and will, which is potent, a good magic. But the mightiest magic is the earth magic of the Old Ones.*

She scratched for grubs all the while, scarcely listening, and the horse-birds hopped around her, now and then giving forth with a curse.

You who are nameless, you own this magic, the simurgh said, and the creature of the wilds stopped her grubbing to stare up at the luminous firebird that had adopted her.

Have you not felt your own power, little one? the simurgh asked. *You who have nothing, all the numina are at one with you, or you with them. You are a feral being, at one with earth. You are earth, and the huge power of earth is in you. Listen.*

She listened. Black demons surrounded her, still looking to her as chicks looked to the hen. "Curse you," they chanted. "Curse Vashti, curse Deva. Dung of Suth." But the human words sounded like nothing more than the cawing of ravens to the creature of the wilds, and in that cawing and croaking she heard the wordless meaning.

Oh, my poor body! This horrible, heavy head. Am I never again to eat anything but vile grass?

What I would not give to be able to catch a fat, juicy insect. . . .

Or a baby rabbit! How long has it been since I tasted rabbit?

My poor legs. Useless for hunting or perching. That sorcerer, what has he done to us? Why has he done this to us?

He has warped us, twisted us all out of our proper shape.

An owl flew out of the cave, out at the wrong time of day for its hunting, and it hooted mournfully as it passed over her on soundless wings. *You can heal them,* that hoot said.

I? she thought.

Get of the Old One, you can heal them with a word, the simurgh told her.

She lay scrabbling, all twisted spine and heaving ribs. "With what word?" she asked, her voice no more than a whine.

With your express command.

The thorn forest stood in silence as the girl-creature stalked a toad. Hunger made her impatient, and she missed her prey.

"Araah," she cried.

Little one, speak, the simurgh admonished her, lifting its blazing plumes; downy sparks fell from them.

"Curse you," a black horse-headed bird shouted. *Tend us, Mother.*

"Araah," the girl-creature said again. "*Be yourselves.*" But they were only demons.

No, little one, the simurgh told her more gently, its brazen cry muted. *The power is in words. The words of men.*

Was she human, to speak such words? She had almost forgotten, it was far less painful to forget, and no such words had crossed her lips for a full changing of the moon and more. She moved her tongue rustily, wet her lips, opened her mouth to bare her rotting teeth, but no sound came.

Mother, a demon beseeched her.

She moved her mouth again. "Be ravens," she said huskily, her voice hardly more than a whisper.

And the change came on them so quickly that she was never to remember it as more than an eyeblink. Black horse-headed grotesques were no more, poor parodies of Suth. Instead, ravens flapped up, cawing raucously, thanking her and praising the powers that be and flying off rapidly, on the hunt for food. There was no cursing in them any longer.

Now, little one, said the simurgh in trumpet tones of victory, *heal yourself.*

It was a task beyond encompassing. The girl-creature stared up mutely at the splendid god-bird that stood towering over her.

All it will take is that you should call yourself by name.

But she had no name that a mother had ever given her, whether Vashtin, Devan, or— Someone had given her a name once, but it was false, he was false, false. She had no true name.

That shred of memory, more feeling than thought, that memory of a kind and golden place. . . . She moved twisted lips to whisper aloud again.

"I will go down. Down to the lowlands, the warm place, down to Avedon. To Auron. Perhaps he will be able to aid me."

It is a long way, and the journey needless.

"Even so, I will go."

But how?

"I will crawl."

As you will, little one. The tone was sorrowful and kind. *As you will.* And the simurgh faded into sky.

"Documents of state will avail you no whit," Nasr Yamut said. "This former, fallen king mentioned your name in them, it is true. But such items are easily . . . unfortunately misplaced."

"So?" Kyrem shifted his weight, seeming larger with every moment. "This is a matter between thee and me, Nasr Yamut, which of us is of more prowess, and that answer we both know already, I deem. But folk stand outside with weapons in hand. And there is no need for shedding of their blood over a matter that is between us two only. So I ask you again, what do you want?''

The priest slipped around Kyrem, descended the steps of the dais from the throne. Only then could he free his gaze and turn his glittering eyes on Auron.

''My white-headed horse,'' he said.

''It belonged to me,'' said Auron imperturbably. ''Insofar as such a steed can belong to anyone.''

''Where is it?''

''Dead on Kimiel.''

''You took it to its death then. *Rode* it—'' Hot storm of fury was rising in Nasr Yamut. Kyrem checked it with a word.

''Priest.''

Nasr Yamut's eyes turned at once, again held by his, although they burned with hatred.

''What are your conditions to walk out yonder door and tell your followers to disperse?''

''One you have named already,'' Nasr Yamut said, his voice a snake hiss of passion. ''I am a priest. I am a fire-master still. You shall not slay me or defrock me or demote me or attempt to do so.''

''Done,'' said Kyrem indifferently, sealing the bargain with his word.

''You shall abide by the Vashtin customs of coronation.''

''Which are?''

''The taking of a bride. The symbolic horse-mating, for fertility. The sacrificial fire to Suth, at the grove. The immolation of the sacrificial horse.''

Nothing had been said of buskins or the constraints of

custom, and Kyrem determined to oppose them at a later time. "Done," he said.

"And for the sacrificial horse, since my own kingmaker has been destroyed"—Nasr Yamut did not bother to dim the light of malice and triumph in his eyes—"I will have that roan of yours, that Omber, and none other."

Kyrem stood for a moment speechless with anger. "By your own standards he is unsuitable!" he shouted at last. "Not pied, splotched, ear-clipped, uncouth—"

"None other," said Nasr Yamut implacably.

"Great Suth," Kyrem breathed.

"I will have eyes of lapis made for his head," the priest added with ghoulish zest. "For when we hang it above the charts with the rest."

This man could be bested, Kyrem knew he could. He, prince of Deva, had the power to make the priest crawl, and of the forces ranged in the streets, his was far the greater. But the thought of such a conflict in sunlit Avedon sickened him. One horse's life, against those of many hapless men. . . .

"I gave Omber away to a friend once," he muttered wildly to himself. "What, am I to do as much for an enemy now?"

Nasr Yamut grinned, awaiting his answer. His malice would be satisfied whichever course Kyrem chose. Auron stood silently by, and Kyrem would not look at him. He had to make this pact entirely on his own.

"Done," he said tightly to the priest. "Now put off those robes and go." And Nasr Yamut departed, gloating.

A moment later Kyrem strode out on the portico, raised one clenched hand high in somber gesture of victory. The crowd below cheered, cheered again and broke up into families and groups of revelers. The priests headed back toward their stable in a knot of ceremonial colors, their master walking bright yellow among them. Auron came out quietly to stand at Kyrem's side, looking around at white towers and brilliant turquoise sky.

"A heavy price was paid, I know," he said. "But unless I am much mistaken, the curse of war is off the land."

Chapter Nineteen

Storm spun out of the stardark over the holy mountain. Winter thunder flings kingdoms asunder, so the adage ran. To the folk in the lowlands and on the mountain flanks it was a fearsome storm, white flare of lightning and the terrible rumble of thunder, hooves of the black horse of death, death itself galloping in the sky, though far away—thankfully, far away. They huddled in their huts just the same. But the girl-creature of the wilds, exposed and naked on a rocky mountainside, did not seek shelter. Storm meant nothing to her, though she glanced up once and saw the thunder-steed plainly enough, black equine presence in the clouds directly over her. Lightning only served to illuminate her way. She crawled on, continuing her slow journey.

The roar of thunder was not clamor of hooves only. It was voice, it had wordless meaning, like the chatter of birds, like the cry of the simurgh—

Shuntali! Shuntali! You are dead. You do not exist.

Meaningless. But the merest shred of memory stirred. She

hissed softly at it. Hissing, she stopped, sat back on her haunches and stared upward into the vortex of the storm.

There, at the core. It was not the thunder-steed only, but—huge, growing, the immense melantha-black equine head, gleam of rolling eyes, bared teeth, white flare of—wings, wings of white flame, and the glint of a jewel black as jet. And on the lifted forelegs, the claws, bone-white talons as of a huge bird. Closer, closer, as though they would pierce—

Devilish claws. It was the demon, the dark Suth himself.

The devil take you and leave his clawmark in you and bend all your bones.

That wordless voice. It was only a small part of the vastness of the black bird-stallion, thunder of those blazing wings, roar out of the black abyss of night. She was merely a single small creature on the vastness of the Mare Mother's sorrel side. But she felt its focus on her.

Shuntali! Shuntali! You are dead.

She hissed again, and the hiss was her reply. "Why, then you can no longer kill me. Go away."

My curse on you. I have made you.

"Your curses have done their worst."

I have made you, I say. I am powerful; I am with the numina now. I deserve your worship.

"Yaa." She spat. *"I also am powerful. I also am with the numina. I worship no one."*

It was immense, the black terror steed; it was as big as the stardark sky. Corpse-white deathflame wings thundered over her; bone-white claws drove at her. So close that she could see the sheen of black feathers, black scaly legs. Feathered black steed with the clawed black legs of a vulture. . . . One taloned foot would be sufficient to pick her up and pierce her to the core. She did not care. Nothing could be done to her that had not been done already, no pain inflicted that she did not already suffer. But she was annoyed. A claw the size of a Devan saber slashed past her hunched shoulder—

She opened her mouth and spoke aloud, human words. "Go away," she said peevishly.

And at once all fell to silence. She looked up; the storm was gone, the sky clear and liquid, the stars powdered across it like pollen of the melantha floating in the dark river of time.

She crawled off toward Avedon, and if she felt triumph, no one knew it.

"I don't know what to do," said the mother.

The Devan noblewoman listened patiently, hiding her annoyance, though she was anxious to be on her way to Avedon. This was her most valued seamstress and needle-woman, and as often happened, such a servant became nearly a friend. It would not do for her to be unhappy; the work would suffer.

"She moves through her tasks, but she scarcely speaks any more, ever, and she scarcely seems to know me. She tells me to go away. I have pleaded with her. . . ." The woman fell silent, trying to control sobs.

Trouble with her daughter. The lady knew how daughters could be troublesome. "Did something happen to change her?" the noblewoman asked.

"Nothing! At least nothing that I know of, and I know of almost everything that concerns her. . . . I cannot understand it. At first she seemed dreamy, as they often are at that age, and I thought little of it. Then it was as though she were caught in a nightmare, possessed by something, bewitched. She would scarcely move from her bed. I was so frightened, and I could not help her. Now she seems a little better in a way. She does her work, but she does not speak, and it has been so long. I am so worried about her. . . ." The mother sobbed again.

The Devan noblewoman had seen the girl and did not think her bewitched, and she was growing bored with her servant's sniveling. Happily she thought of a solution that suited her own devices.

"Bring the little wench along with us," she said, "when we go to the Choosing."

"The Choosing?" The mother raised wet eyes, blinked.

"Have you not heard what I was saying? All these new garments that have to be made, that is what they are for."

"I was not paying attention," the needlewoman said humbly. "I have been so troubled."

"Well, I want you to come with us, and bring your daughter too. That way we can have an earlier start and work while on the road. Kyrillos has made a son of his the king of Vashti, it seems, and the prince must choose a bride at the festival of the winter solstice. There is to be a great Choosing for him, at Avedon, with girls of Deva and Vashti alike—any maiden may present herself. Perhaps the change and the excitement of the journey will help your daughter. Let her walk before him herself! If by strangest chance he should choose her, at least she will be well taken care of."

Though actually, the lady was thinking, this prince was sure to choose one of her own daughters, Devan noble maidens whom he had known from his youth. She would adorn them gloriously to draw his eye to them, and she would make certain that the needlewoman had no time to so bedeck her own daughter. The wench was not unattractive. But then, there would be many pretty maids in attendance.

"So let us get to work on these clothes, shall we?" she said briskly.

The needlewoman was working her mouth in consternation.

"But my daughter is only fourteen years of age," she managed to say at last.

"As long as she is of childbearing years, the younger the better, say I."

"Well," the woman murmured, moving toward the worktable, "perhaps it will be an opportunity for her after all. We are so—" She stopped short of saying they were poor. "Or perhaps," she added, "she will be the better for the change."

"I am sure she will be," the lady said kindly. "Now, about these headpieces—"

"Thank you for thinking of us, my lady," said the needlewoman, because she knew such thanks were expected.

"You are quite welcome. The headpieces are to be all in satin stitch."

The Choosing took place at the river meadow between Avedon and the sacred grove. Devans came in throngs, their colorful tents festive under cloudless skies—even the winters were mild in the lowlands—and Kyrillos and all of Kyrem's brothers came, and in spite of everyone's fears, the gathering turned into a celebration. Factions vied to outdo one another only in hospitality. Vashtins, invited to the Devan encampment, feasted on whole spiced lamb roasted in pits and admired the mettlesome horses. Devans walked in delight amid the tiles and mosaics of Avedon. Young women of both kingdoms strolled about heavily veiled so as not to reveal themselves before the fateful day. And on that day, not the traditional day for nuptials, but still a day marked as auspicious by the sun and moon, planets and stars—on that day Kyrem put on a tall red cap and took his place on a gaily draped platform, settling himself to choose his bride.

"Let the procession begin," Nasr Yamut intoned. Although his malice had not abated, he had been keeping it to himself, biding his time. In the deep of night his moment would come.

Musicians struck up a stately melody on pipes, reeds and tambourines. Half dancing, splendidly arrayed, the girls promenaded before the prince. The occasion reminded Kyrem somewhat of the ceremonial procession of sacred steeds he had seen in Avedon, and the maidens' draperies, he thought, were no more functional than those of the horses. Heavily embroidered skirts, tight-fitting bodices studded with gems. Glittering corsets that bared gilded nipples. . . . Some of the damsels wore only filmy scarflike panels that drifted as airily as cloud wisp, revealing the white young bodies within. Some wore even less, nothing but beads and gold bracelets and gold fillets in the hair. Somewhat abashed, Kyrem made himself look at the faces. Lips reddened with carmine, eyes glinting moistly between lids blackened with kohl, sometimes studded with tiny beads. No better. All sheen and shimmer, surface. . . . Strands of fresh-water pearls hanging down from delicate ears pierced all around the rim. More pearls looped through braided hair, dark or russet. . . . With a small shock Kyrem recognized Auron's former footbearers and smiled grimly at a private jest; these girls were supposed to be virgins! He knew no more than that about any of them, for his would-be brides were not introduced by name or rank or provenance. Some few he recognized under towering headdresses; those were the daughters of Devan nobles. Marrying one of them might constitute a lesser risk than choosing a bride unknown to him, a pretty whore perhaps—though it would be the best of policy if he could settle on a Vashtin bride—

One of the maidens had lost the rhythm of the graceful processional, had stopped where she was to stand staring at him, dark eyes wide. And all thoughts of policy vanished from Kyrem's mind. He jumped up, heart pounding, vaulted off his platform and ran forward to touch her arm.

"Seda?" he blurted, tears threatening. But it was not Seda; he knew that already. This girl was taller than Seda, fresh-faced and beautiful in a simple dress of white, and her long, dusky hair rippled down over her shoulders unadorned. All the hope and trust of a well-beloved child were in her look. She could not have been more than fourteen years old.

"Seda's twin." Auron had come to stand by Kyrem's side. "It has to be. The faces are identical."

"What is your name?" Kyrem asked the girl, trying to gentle his voice, trying to calm himself. For just an instant he had believed Seda to be alive, and renewed grief was piercing his heart.

"Sula," she whispered. The name meant sunlight, sunshine. This maiden was a Devan then.

"And you had a twin who was cast away?"

"I—don't know of any!"

That soft voice. This had to be. "I will take you as my bride," Kyrem vowed.

Kyrillos had come up in time to hear that, to hear something of a twin, and comprehend. "My son, you will be seeing ghosts all your life!" he protested. "Let the dead rest. Find a better reason to take a bride. This lass is too young."

"I can have no better reason," Kyrem flared at his father. "Why should I wed a stranger? Sula, are you here of your own free will?"

"I—yes," she breathed, though in fact she had scarcely understood what was happening. But now he stood before her, the one whose face she had seen in her dreams. And he must have seen her before as well, it seemed, by the look in his eyes. She stood in a trance of holy awe. This thing had been settled in the stars; she was a handmaiden of Suth.

"We will be married this very day, you know, this very hour. Will you have me? Are you ready?"

"Yes."

He took her by the hand and led her to the feast.

They ate little. The time was taken up by ceremony, the wine-pouring and symbolic sheaf of barley. Nasr Yamut hovered near, leering. Kyrem would scarcely speak before him. But as soon as he could, he took his bride again by her soft hand and led her away to the bower built on Atar-Vesth. In silence they climbed the steep slope between the flamelike trees until they reached the flattened blue-stone apex, the altar itself. There stood their bower, a leafy latticework of liana interwoven with grapevine and late starflowers. Under its fragrant roof lay bedding worthy of a royal couple, down-filled cushions piled high, silken coverlets.

The two stood gazing wordlessly. Kyrem had never done this thing, for the doing of it would bind him for life with a mystic bond, such was his being and genius. He felt more than a little afraid. What would this deed spell for him, contentment or woe? But the doing itself, that was nothing. He had heard the talk of his brothers, had glimpsed a few indiscreet conjunctions between servants. And only lately Kyrillos had instructed him.

"Go gently, take your time," the Devan king had finished. "You will have all afternoon."

Kyrem turned a soft glance on his bride.

"Do not fear that we might be disturbed," he told her. "My father and my eleven brothers stand guard around the base of this promontory."

That moved her to a small smile. "You trust your brothers?" Sula inquired, and Kyrem laughed aloud with delight.

"I trust my father's command," he said.

His laughter thrilled her, awoke some echoing chord in her; she had heard such laughter once or more in a dream. Her dark eyes widened, and he saw it, sobered and drew her to him.

At some small distance, out of sight of the bower and out of earshot, a girl-creature of the wild was hiding in a knot of grapevine, plucking the purple fruit. The tart grapes did not satisfy her hunger, for she had traveled far and with difficulty, and all the while an aching emptiness had pulled at her, an emptiness not of the belly, though the pangs of her belly were persistent enough. It was the emptiness of one in need of healing, wholeness, the same emptiness that had once pulled a shuntali turned Devan princess away from Avedon and that now tugged her back. Odd, the call seemed so strong. But then there was belly hunger too, and the smells of a feast on the air, almost unbearable. The girl-creature fidgeted in controlled anguish. She did not dare show herself in daylight. Come nightfall she would venture forth to find food and perhaps win her way through to Auron—she had almost forgotten that name, could scarcely envision the kindly face. Was it he who called her? Or something else that she sensed close, so close. . . .

No more than half thinking, no more than half human, she lay down in the brown loam beneath grape leaves and dozed. Had she not been mostly asleep, she would have been terrified by the sensations that overcame her, but as it was, in her emptiness and exhaustion, she accepted them unquestioning. Tingling, tingling thrill, ecstasy and ache in one, lips moving, moist, lips, and then a soundless music rising to a great mountain peak of tension, hollow, and then—full, fulfillment, a supreme fullness and wholeness and oneness with—love, pure joy.

The girl-creature opened her eyes dazedly. Someone had whispered her name. Sula. Her name, whispered so softly— but how could that be? There was no one with her, and she was nameless.

She felt stronger, and irrationally happy. Standing, she found that she could stretch nearly erect, and in a surge of new energy, she scrambled up a tree to reach the high-climbing grapes. There she stayed for a while, and not far away a slumberer dreamed of her.

Dusk, at last. She dropped down from her perch and moved off cautiously on all fours, down the slope toward a place where she hazily remembered the presence of food— led as much by instinct as by memory, dim vision of a place once visited, long before. Singing arose in the distance. There was no guard, for everyone had joined the feast; the prince and his bride had come down from their bower.

Chapter Twenty

He had awakened her with a kiss from an hour's gentle slumber. Sula. Sleeping, she looked all childlike innocence, but Kyrem had reason to believe she was a woman, or very nearly so, and she was lovely, and love of her suffused him; he could scarcely believe his incredible luck, that he was to spend the rest of his life with her. They went down to their supper, the two of them, all smiles and soft glances and the touch of warm hands. Kyrem could not stop smiling. And the best of it was that no one dared to laugh at him, not even Nasr Yamut, for he, Kyrem, would be king.

The others had feasted all afternoon; therefore what the prince and his bride ate was not so much supper as the continuation of the ceremonial dinner in many courses. They ate heartily this time. And as they sat in their places of honor on the platform, Sula's mother was brought to join them. Kyrem had sent trusted servants to find her. The woman had been in hiding since the hour of the Choosing, fearing her mistress's jealous wrath.

She came before the royal couple with a sort of humble dignity, kissed her daughter and answered Sula's embrace with a few tears and a smile. She was dressed in plain, dark clothing and she walked with a limp, but it was evident that she had once been beautiful, though her raven hair was now touched with gray.

"You will be kind to my daughter, lord?" she asked, or rather declared. "She is very young—too young to wed, really, but I have no husband, we are poor, and I knew she would never have another such chance."

"I have loved her for these many months," Kyrem said, "in the form of her counterpart, whom you spurned."

The woman went pale, but her gaze did not waver. "Where is the other?" she asked.

"Wait," Sula exclaimed. "Then it is true, I have a sister, a twin? I thought I remembered, I dreamt—but you told me there had been a baby who was dead."

"I could not tell you the truth," the woman said to her. "Best beloved, please do not be angry with me."

"But, Mother—" Sula gave her a hurt glance and turned to Kyrem. "You have loved her? Where is she?"

"Dead, indeed," he told her gently, "or I would have been wed with no Choosing. I am sorry," he said to the mother.

She stood pale but firm. "You think me a monster, both of you," she said. "Another woman my age would understand how it was in those days, how a young wife did what she was told—but now that I am older, how I regret it."

Indeed Kyrem had thought her a monster, many times, before he met her. She, the mother who had forsaken Seda! But looking at her, and thinking of Sula, he knew he must somehow have been mistaken. The monster had been of his mind's making.

"I would like to hear your story," he said. "Sit down." He rose to make a place for her on the platform, on the cushioned couch next to her daughter, and after a glance at him, she took it. He leaned against the table to face her.

"Tell me," the woman requested, "what was she like, what was her life like, how did she fare, how did she . . . die?"

"First tell me how her life began."

They talked through sunset and dusk and into torchlit darkness. It took that long for the tale to fully unfold. Sula was of Devan blood, but she had lived half her life in Vashti. Her mother and father had fled there from Deva before she was born.

"It is hard to describe the man," her mother explained. "I should not have married him. Parents, aunts, uncles, they all warned me against him. But I loved him because he could charm the birds. He was of the old wild blood, not Devan, older than Devan, feared. He was never really accepted in Ra'am, not by my family, not by anyone. I loved him; he was handsome, he was intense, he needed me. No one else would pity him as I did. Then there was a poisoning of an important person and he was blamed. He was beaten and driven out of the city. That night I stole from my room, took food and followed him. I found him and nursed him and we were wed by the ceremony of his ancestors, in secrecy. Then we made our way by foot over the mountains into Vashti. My family was searching for me, but we eluded them."

The man was used to living by his wits. The pair wandered through Vashti earning their food any way they could, sometimes stealing it. Those were hard days, but good, the woman said. Finally an opportunity offered, a cottage was secured, a permanent dwelling place. The man was clever and could do whatever his lord required of him. The woman was a seamstress at her lady's command.

"It was terribly important to him that we should be accepted," she explained. "He tried in every way he knew to be settled, respectable. It was impossible of course. We were Devans, intruders, upstarts in the lord's affection; we were never much liked. But he thought that maybe in time, if we adopted the customs. . . ." Her voice trailed away, and she stared at an empty place, air, beside her daughter.

"So that is why we had to abandon the other babe," she said.

No one spoke, and after a while she went on, reluctantly, as though forced by something within herself to relive a time she had long tried to forget.

"When she was three, the very day after she had turned three, he took her away to the Kansban and left her somewhere with only her clothes for shelter. . . . I cried for weeks. I loved her, even though I had never been allowed to give her a name. And I grew to hate him."

"He had crippled you as an adultress?" Kyrem asked.

"Yes. On the day the babes were born. Of course he did not really believe that of me; how could he? But the custom had to be followed, even if it turned him against his loved ones, against nature. . . . He became a stranger to me. Yet I had to do as he said. I was only a wife; I could do nothing without him."

"Mother, is that true?" Sula exclaimed.

"No," Kyrem answered her.

"I thought it was true." The woman stretched her mouth into a bitter smile. "Later, when he left me, I found out how false I had been, to myself, to my poor baby, my child."

"That was when I was seven," Sula gravely informed Kyrem. Already she had lost much of her silence, her shyness.

"Why did he leave?"

"He had gone mad as a jay," Sula said.

"I had felt it coming for years," her mother affirmed. "Our house had filled up with hatred. I blamed him for all my pain, and he twisted the blame away and cast in on Vashti. He went through his days dealing pleasantly with the people he encountered, trying to be liked, trying to be no longer different, and all the while inside him I felt menace building, growing, and I could not help him, I could scarcely help myself. He moved farther and farther away from truth. He became a living, walking deceit, a poisonous man—"

"Had he actually done that poisoning in Deva?" Kyrem asked curiously.

"I do not think so. But because people thought he had—it took years for the change, but he became capable of such killing."

Living her days as though in a trance, watching as the bird watches from the cage, a dozen times she had thought the crisis must come, and a dozen times it had been pushed a little farther into the looming future. Finally one day the man erupted with an eagle's scream, or the scream of some raptor stranger than an eagle. . . . The woman caught hold of the girl and ran out of the cottage before he could reach them. He took his club, a vicious weapon with knife blades embedded in the tip, and he went through the village knocking down walls and pillars and everything that stood in his way, sending people fleeing before him, spitting and shrieking the whole while. Finally he stood in the empty village square, amid desolation, and pronounced his curse. Those few who hid nearby heard every blasphemous word. The woman heard some of it too, as she clutched a few salvaged belongings and fled with her daughter toward Deva. The man cursed Vashti and Deva, the two kingdoms of Suth, the places that had scorned him, and he cursed every soul in them. He cursed them with the most powerful of curses. He would set them like stallions at each other, wreaking war upon war until the streams ran red with blood, even streams where no streams had been before, until not a mother's son stood whole upon his legs and the winds were full of the wailing of inconsolable women. The wild things and the flying things would help him, he said. All free things hated Vashti and Deva. Vashti and Deva! They had taken from him his manhood and his child; he would be avenged!

"And then, so I later heard, he went up to the holy mountaintop," the woman concluded. "It was as well; he could do little harm there. I have heard no more of him, these seven years past, and I did not go back to my family for fear that he would find us. Sula and I supported ourselves by our sewing, made ourselves a humble home. We were poor, but we lived simply, we survived."

"He killed her," Kyrem whispered. His face was ashen.

"What, my lord?"

"He killed his own daughter, the source of all his sorrow—I mean, she for whom he mourned—twisted, twisted!" Kyrem hid his face momentarily in his hands. "He killed her and, in a way, himself," he said at last. "Though I struck the blow. . . . How horrible. Did he know? How could he have done it, knowing. . . ."

Sula stood and put her arms around him to comfort him, and the woman reached out to him as well, her face as hard and white as the walls of Avedon. "It is better," she said flatly, "that they are dead."

The evening was taking a darker turn. Weird, whistling music began, and Kyrem straightened himself, his face growing still and grim. "It is time for the horse ceremony," he told Sula.

The music came not from the instruments of the musicians, but from elsewhere—the priests. They came slowly advancing and playing on flexible pipes called snakes, each one fashioned from the windpipe of a sacrificed horse, the cartilege cut into a mouthlike vee at the end, a vibrating slit. The priests moved the pipes in sinuous, dancelike rhythms as they drew nearer, and the burbling, buzzing, whistling music undulated with the twistings and ripplings of the pipes.

Everyone listened, shivering. Sula listened breathless and wide-eyed, Kyrem with suppressed horror. The music quickened, but Nasr Yamut lowered his pipe and handed it to a novice to hold. From another novice he took a heap of bright garments embroidered in gold, and he brought them forward.

"Ceremonial robes," Kyrem explained, putting on his own, helping Sula on with hers. She had a headpiece to wear, her dark hair drawn back on either side to be fastened by its upraised wings of gold. Kyrem laid his red cap aside. His crown awaited him at the sacred grove, along with the royal buskins. He wondered how best to refuse the footgear. He thought of Nasr Yamut, of Omber and the death that awaited the sacrificial horse, and his heart grew sick, even though he had had weeks in which to harden himself.

"But you look like a queen now, child," Sula's mother murmured to her in wonder. "Such beautiful work—" She was examining the fabric of her daughter's robe.

"Mother," Kyrem said to her, "believe me, I know something of what you felt about the lost babe. I also have been forced to abandon one whom I love to a cruel and undeserved fate."

She stared at him, not understanding. He smiled at her and

shook his head. "Mother, when we go to the grove, stay close by my father and his men or by Auron, and I think your mistress will not dare attempt to harm you."

"I will not be able to go back to Deva with her," the woman said.

"Of course not. You are to stay in Avedon with us."

Then the warbling of the pipes sounded louder, and the priests ranked themselves in their order of colors, and Kyrem and Sula took their places just behind the leaders; Nasr Yamut, shining yellow in the torchlight, and his three epopts in green. The others fell in behind the novices and boys, all utterly silent; the pipes sounded shrill and clear in the chill midnight air.

Then, in solemn procession, in moonlight and torchlight, everyone walked to the sacred grove where few except priests had gone since Auron was made king.

Chapter Twenty-One

Omber was gloriously arrayed. He had been bathed in milk and his mane and tail combed with scented chrism before being braided with lapis beads and thread of gold; his very hooves were gilded. His headstall was of scarlet leather hung with scarlet tassels and glittering with gems; the largest one, a massive crystal jargoon, was centered on his forehead with the plaited forelock framing it. A great flowing torsade of finest gold chains adorned his neck and chest, and great flame-shaped wings of scarlet damasin rose from his shoulders. His body was draped with caparison of seven-colored baudequin over which lay a net of gold, and the whole of him was bestrewn with powder of real gold; even the fine hairs of his fetlocks had caught some of it, and he shone starrily in the night. People murmured in awe as they approached him.

Even with Nasr Yamut's aid—and many times Kyrem had bitterly regretted ever having allowed the fire-master to touch the horse—even with Nasr Yamut's assistance, the priests had been hard put to handle Omber, and that fact afforded the prince some dark satisfaction. "Years ago it would have been me going to the knife, lad," Auron told him, sensing his uncertain mood. "I feel, perhaps unreasonably, that I owe you a debt of gratitude."

"Quite unreasonably," Kyrem grumbled.

They stood in flickering torchlight. The moon had gone dark, and rumblings sounded in the sky. Omber was tethered at the base of the Atar-Vesth, the place of fire, and on his headstall the great crystal jargoon glimmered whitely as distant lightning flashed. Not far away, the white glimmer of the Suthstone answered the victim's borrowed gem. But that starlike glint continued after the lightning had dimmed; the effigy of Suth was awake and watching. Many eyes stared at it uneasily.

"There is a presence here," Kyrem muttered to Auron.

"What is it?"

"I don't know. Something quite wild. I felt it on Kimiel as well."

"A creature of the wild? Such are common in groves and unpeopled places."

"Yes—but this is no common creature. There is a power here." Kyrem stood with every sense strained, but learned no more; all was dark that night.

"Let the bride come forward to meet the scion of the god," Nasr Yamut intoned.

With only a single questioning glance at Kyrem, Sula went to Omber. She had learned from Auron what she had to do, and she had unlearned in Deva the Vashtin holy fear of horses; she had never ridden, but she knew how to greet a steed by rubbing its forehead. This steed wore a jewel on its forehead—Omber needed a special greeting. So she held her hands to his betasseled cheekbones, her face to his soft face.

Then, with the assistance of the epopts, she turned her back
to him and crouched for a moment between his forelegs.

The storm drew nearer, thunder sounded louder and lightning threatened, all was darkness and flickering shadows.
The Suthstone shone pulsating purple.

Crouching in the sheltering shadow beneath that great
stone Suth, the girl-creature gazed intently on the happenings.
She had eaten the bread and fruit from the niche in the
pedestal and, her belly at last full, had chosen this cavelike
nook to doze in. But now she was keenly alert. The presence
of a great golden knife on the pedestal troubled her. That,
and the crown and a pair of royal buskins—she faintly remembered having seen something like them before, and the memory stirred her to unease. But she did not recognize anyone in
the crowd before her, not in the dark and at the slight
distance; they were all featureless forms to her. Men, priests,
damsel, horse. She did not recognize even Omber in his
trappings, and she never considered that Auron might be
present, or Kyrem. What might be the weighty occasion of
state? And what was to be done to the hapless horse, the
stallion?

"Oh, glorious large-eyed horse of heaven. . . ." Nasr
Yamut began the sacrificial liturgy.

"Oh, glorious large-eyed horse of heaven," everyone
responded.

"Oh, glorious get of godmare and mistral,
Soon thou goest to join thy grandfather wind,
To speed along the easy, dustless ways of sky,
To canter on the yellow clouds of sunset
Where no hand of man may follow thee.
So let not the breath of mere life oppress thee,
Let not the knife of gold affright thee,

But, in the spirit world may there come wings upon thee,
Upon thy head, thy shoulders, thy fetlocks wings of gold,
Upon thy shoulders wings of fire and sunlight.
Let thee run the heavenly ways along with the seven wild sons of Suth,
And let Suth thy sire kiss thee with the greeting of horses,
Let thee know the blessing of Suth.
Go to thy doom in happiness, grandson of the mistral.''

From the summit of Atar-Vesth flames shot up. The bower had been set ablaze, and stacks of dried spiced applewood had been added to the pyre to make a fragrant conflagration suitable for the roasting of sacred horse flesh. But in the next moment a terrible crack of thunder sounded amid a blaze of lightning, and rain poured down, sheeting in a sudden wind. The trees tossed wildly, tossed and plunged like so many steeds, sending shadows flying everywhere. The Suthstone shone blue then yellow then green, blazing out like the lightning, then fading dim. The wind roared, and the fire hissed loudly in the rain. Folk huddled together in terror.

By the time he leads Omber three times around the fire, Kyrem thought eagerly, it will be drowned. The ceremony will be invalidated—

But Nasr Yamut was not so easily to be deprived of his victim. He moved at once into the liturgy for the immolation, leading Omber over to stand directly beside Suth's stone pedestal and taking up the great curved golden knife. He flourished it three times over his head and showed it to the onlookers.

"Knife of gold, knife of sunlight, with the stroke of this knife, the sacred king of Vashti takes possession of all that lies under the course of the sun, of east and west, of the four cardinal points, of all that lies under the running hooves of the horse of heaven, of Trodden Lands and Untrodden Lands; everything that lies under the sun, Suth gives into the possession of the sacred king of Vashti with the stroke of this knife. Such is the power of Suth.''

In the darkness and flickering fire-shadow and lightning and the greenish glitter of the Suthstone, it seemed for a moment as if the statue had moved. Everyone gasped and murmured. But Nasr Yamut, intent on his revenge, noticed nothing.

"Flamens, epopts, forward," he ordered. And the priests hurried to surround Omber. Sensing danger, the horse reared, struck out with forehooves—one priest fell. Omber attempted to bolt. But they caught hold of him by his trappings, dragging at him on all sides, struggling to immobilize him for the deathblow, not quite able to still him entirely. The whole group surged and flowed about the base of the statue. Nasr Yamut danced at the fore with ceremonial knife upraised, awaiting his opportunity. "Hold him *fast*, you fellows," he snapped, and with his free hand he caught hold of Omber's sensitive muzzle, sinking his fingers into the nostrils. Still Omber plunged. The golden knife wavered at his throat—

Kyrem had long since forgotten Sula, long since let go of her soft hand. He was shaking his head, glad of the darkness that hid tears, and he was whispering to himself. "No," he breathed, "no, it is all wrong, from beginning to end. No!" he shouted suddenly aloud. He leapt forward to seize the upraised knife and the hand that wielded it. Nasr Yamut twisted in his grasp, venomous. "Suth, stop him!" Kyrem cried to the night.

And all the priests fell back with a shout of fear as light blazed up, piercing light, for a great pattern had been broken.

The statue was moving. Flanges of red flame shot up from its shoulders, and the hard stone of its body had become supple flesh, and its forehead was shining, resplendent, and it was rearing where it stood, enormous. And from beneath its lifted forelegs another, smaller figure shot. Hunched, four-legged and lithe, it leapt to Omber's back, clinging like a shadow-tail between the damasin wings. "Demon!" someone screamed. On the instant it sent the horse forward with a leap into a headlong gallop, sweeping through the startled priests. The thing was a horror, every crooked bone of its body showing, but the thin, luminous face was unmistakable to Kyrem in that blazing jewel light. It was she, the only person in the world who could ride Omber save himself.

"Seda," Kyrem whispered, and he stood as though rooted, holding the golden knife and watching her ride, watching Omber run, watching the crowd scatter before them. Run far, Omber, run free—

"Great Suth be thanked," a voice said; it was Auron, come to stand beside him.

And in a roar like thunder, the mighty stone Suth left its pedestal—stone no longer but the most splendid of steeds; he leapt away and soared over the throng on wings of flame, screaming a stallion's scream, and all the people beneath him screamed, and many fell to earth in terror of the horse-god, but Suth wanted only to light the way for his earthly son. Wings ablaze, he swept over Omber, circling to match the speed of the slower mortal horse, the gem ruby-bright and flaring on his forehead. Then, with a swanlike dip of his head, he dropped to the ground to canter at Omber's side, and Omber galloped snorting.

Auron was jumping up and down by the empty pedestal. "Look at them go, both of them!" he shouted with unkingly abandon. "There will never by another night like this as long as Vashti endures."

Indeed it was awesome, the running of those steeds beneath a storm-lit sky, sheen of golden caparison and sheen of godly fire and that eerie apparition riding. . . . All stood watching soundlessly until Suthlight had faded into distance, until lightning and sacral fire had faded into darkness and only torchlight remained. Finally Kyrem stirred. He lifted his arm and flung away the golden knife he held, hurled away the blade of ceremonial sacrifice so that it disappeared into the hoofprint font of the Ril Acaltha. Then he turned to the empty pedestal, took the royal buskins and hurled them away in like wise; everyone heard the splash as they vanished into the dark water.

Nasr Yamut stood tamely watching him, pallid. Seeing his god come to life had shaken the priest badly; he had not expected such vitality from the stone thing he served.

Kyrem raised his hand in silent gesture of command, and the onlookers assembled near him, most of them as shaken as the fire-master. Sula stood with her mother, and Auron went and placed the shelter of his arms around both of them. Kyrem drew his long, curved sword halfway out of its sheath. "Is it peace?" he demanded of the priests.

"Ay," they muttered.

He sheathed his sword. "Am I your king?" he asked the people.

"Yes liege!" The response was quick and fervent. Another time he would have smiled, but his mind was taut with distress, and his lips tightened into a white line.

"Then I will take command," he said, "and honor whom I will honor, and appoint whom I will appoint. Nasr Yamut, come here before me. You priests, strike up that extraordinary music of yours once again."

They brought out their snakelike pipes at once and began to play. Nasr Yamut did as Kyrem had said, standing puzzled and wary. Kyrem had pledged never to demote him or defrock him, and though Nasr Yamut had no way of holding him to that pledge, he knew well enough that the prince, now king, would keep it. What, then, could Kyrem be plotting? The black Devan—

Kyrem began to speak in a carefully modulated, formal voice. "Nasr Yamut, fire-master, you have shown your power this night in such a display of mastery as we who have witnessed are never likely to see again in our lifetime. Storm arose at your command, and the spirits of the dark, and the very soul and genius and being of the stone effigy that we worship—"

"But it was our liege who called upon Suth!" someone in the crowd protested.

"Hush," Auron told the man. His eyes were sparkling with comprehension. Nasr Yamut's were wide open in uneasy surprise, but he was not one to turn aside praise, however unearned. He stood silent.

"—the very fleshly manifestation of Suth himself condescended to visit us tonight incarnate during this ceremony under your aegis." Kyrem wondered if he were making any sense. He was speaking the words just as they came to him. But the tone was right, and tone was all-important, irony veiled to all but the knowing few. . . . He straightened and held Nasr Yamut with his gaze.

"You have shown yourself in every way to be utterly beyond this mere mortal world," he said to the priest as the music burbled and shrilled all around them. "You are a man beyond the humble tasks of your calling, beyond human needfulness in any way, beyond the daily cycles of duty and care. Surely it is time and past time that you put on the white robe of the beyond. I hereby, with my express word, exalt you to the highest post of your priesthood. Be fire-master no longer, Nasr Yamut. I appoint you atarashet, he who goes beyond the fire.''

Too late Nasr Yamut saw the trap and opened his mouth to demur. ''I—my humble origins—surely—not deserving—''

''No one is ever fully deserving,'' Kyrem intoned. ''A new fire-master will of course be appointed from among the ranks of your associates.''

''I—my fellow priests, I do not deserve this honor—'' Nasr Yamut turned to his followers, flinging out his hands in desperation. ''Surely you do not want me to go from you!''

They continued playing their instruments, their faces expressionless except that all three epopts smiled. The whistling of the pipes sounded like mockery.

''Your humility becomes you, Nasr Yamut,'' Kyrem no longer attempted to veil the grim delight in his voice. ''But protest no more. Tomorrow, as the first official act of my reign, I will see you escorted to the bourne of the Untrodden Lands.''

Chapter Twenty-Two

The atarashet rode northward at dawn. Outside the city gates he awaited the dayspring, in vigil with all his priests, and at the first light they chanted the liturgy that would send him on his way. Then, white-robed, seated on a white onager, he left them. Kyrem watched him ride off in the pale light, an unimpressive figure amidst an escort of Devans on horseback. At the marches of the magical realm they would take his mount and leave him.

Kyrem rode forth at dawn also, eastward and at random, to seek Seda. His steed was a crop-eared stallion out of the sacred stables; he controlled it by sheer grim force of will and, to his disgust, by a strap around its nose. Behind him, sideways and still in her queenly robes, rode Sula.

It had been a short and sleepless and confusing night. First there had been the custody of Nasr Yamut to attend to, so that he would not attempt to elude the honor that awaited him. After that matter was taken care of, with the full cooperation of the epopts and flamens, there had been an

impromptu council. Sula and Auron and Kyrillos had seen
that Kyrem was more distraught than exultant, and the three
of them had questioned him until he had been forced to tell
them what ailed him. Or rather, Auron guessed, or came
close.

"That creature that rode Omber," he said.

"Seda," Kyrem replied.

"But—it looked more like a demon." Sula could not take
this in, and the others sat gasping.

"It was Seda. She is alive."

"Of course it was Seda," Auron murmured to the Devan
king. "Who else? Kyrem spoke of a power in the night. . . .
By the Mare Mother, Kyrillos, we are stupid."

"Speak for yourself," Kyrillos retorted.

Kyrem did not hear them, nor did Sula. King and bride,
chooser and chosen, they were gazing at each other, Kyrem
trying to think what this might mean to Sula, and she trying
to comprehend what it might mean to him and to them, the
union of the two of them, the bond, and he wondering the
same, and neither of them could speak for fear and pity.

"I don't know what he did to her," Kyrem said heavily at
last, "but from the looks of her, she might have been better
off dead in fact."

"Suspend that judgment a while," Auron suggested in his
quiet way. Hope hid in his eyes. Power in the night. . . .

"I must go after her at first light," Kyrem said.

"Do you not think she will come to us?" asked Auron.
"That she will want to bring Omber back to you?"

"I think, I thought, I sensed—that she wanted nothing to
do with us any more, that she wanted only to be left to
herself, like an animal that crawls off to lick its wounds.
Sula, do not tell your mother until we know more."

"My mother is sleeping," said Sula, "and I am going with you."

Half distracted, Kyrem scarcely looked at her, only shook his head. "Stay here, be safe, sheltered. I will bring her back to you and your mother."

"I am going!" Sula said more forcefully. "She is my sister; I will not be left behind."

Kyrem looked at her then, somewhat surprised by her tone. "Your sister she may be," he said sharply, "but she has meant little enough to you until now, whereas to me she has been a comrade and a friend. This matter is between her and me—"

"And me. I was there with you two, though I did not understand it at the time. I traveled with you through the mountains, rode before you when you were weak and sick, behind you when you were well, lay by your camp fire, roamed the night to steal food for you—"

"Sula," Kyrem whispered. All three men were staring at her, but she went on, undaunted.

"—saw you safely to Avedon, watched over you here in this palace as well, I recognize it. And when you gave her your horse as a gift of love, it was a gift to me as well. I felt her love of the horse and of you."

"So she loved me," Kyrem said tightly. "I thought as much. But the bond between thee and me is greater and lasts a lifetime, Sula, though I have known you only a day."

"I have known you longer, you and her. I felt her suffering when the Old One took her." Sula looked away then. "Terrible suffering. But she is not suffering now; I would know it if she were."

Kyrem came to her side, took her hand and looked at her.

"It is for our own sakes that we go to find her," Sula told him. "Not hers."

"I suppose that is true. But you can tell me where she is, what she is seeing, feeling—"

"If I went to sleep, perhaps I could." Sula settled herself deeper in her chair with a decided air. "But I will not go to sleep. You might forget to awaken me, and go off without me."

"No, you have to come along, I can see that now." He spoke softly, gazing off into the distance. "What can it mean?" he asked Auron at last.

"That Sula will make you a true queen," Auron replied.

"The lass is candid and courageous, for all that she seems half a child." Kyrillos bestirred himself and arose. "Well, lad, my felicitations. I know it will seem odd, but I have seen you are a man now. You will surmount this matter of Seda somehow, and I have a country to attend to. I had better be getting on my way." He embraced his son awkwardly and went out.

"On your own, Ky," Auron remarked, and Kyrem nearly smiled.

"And what of you?" he asked the quiet androgyne who had once been Vashtin king. "Auron, this dwelling has always been your home. I hope you know you are welcome to stay here as long as you live."

"Why, Ky, I have been here too long already!" Auron smiled and flexed his feet as if still luxuriating in freedom from buskins. "I am going to go a-roving and see this grand land of mine in fact, not only in dream. In the morning, betimes." He stood up, yawning, and also bid them good night.

"I cannot sleep," Kyrem told Sula. "You rest; I will not fail to awaken you. I gave you my word."

"But I will stay with you," she said, and they spent the

few hours until dawn sitting with hands entwined and heads together, very closely side by side.

"How will you find her?" Sula asked as they rode out in the dim morning. "Where can she possibly have gone?"

"Suth knows. Maybe back toward the mountains. I am searching. Can you sense anything, Sula?"

"Only that she lives."

Kyrem was a black river-falcon first, circling above Vashti, looking and looking with his eyes that could see a grasshopper at half a mile. The visionary process was not wholly controllable; sometimes he was the grasshopper instead and could see nothing but weed stems. But at long last, soaring, he caught sight of them far to the northward, glint of golden trappings and the blue-black horse with a dun-colored something clinging to its back. He turned his sluggish mount. Then he could sense the distant presence of Omber without seeing afar; he was an old saluki hound snuffling at a stale scent.

"I see them, I feel them," he said to Sula, and they were both content.

At nightfall, when the dusky melantha spread in the sky, they stopped in a secluded place between pasturelands and lay on the ground, and Kyrem made love to her again. And as they lay there, a warm rain fell down, moistening the dry red soil of Vashti. In the morning, dew lay heavy on the sere grasses. Kyrem stared at it, never having seen such a thing in Vashti before. Then he turned to his crop-eared steed without speaking.

It was the middle of the second day before he comprehended Seda's course, and his contentment left him all in a moment. He pulled the spotted horse to a halt.

"She is going to the lands beyond the bourne," he whispered. Sula stared at him in alarm, for his fair face had gone paler yet and she could feel his shoulders tighten beneath the cloth of his tunic.

"I do not understand," she told him.

"The Untrodden Lands, the place of the puissant dead! She is supposed to be dead—if she could neither go up as flame nor fly to the sun, perhaps that is why she has chosen this course." Kyrem suddenly lashed his holy horse across the shoulders with the end of its single rein, sending it leaping forward with a startled plunge. "Perhaps we can yet prevent her."

He rode the sacred stallion mercilessly hard for the next several hours. But as the day reddened, westward, he gave it up with a groan.

"They go far more swiftly than we. Omber is as hard as the blue stones, and this Vashtin steed no harder than a dish of curds."

Sula nodded. She had found a trance of her own, could feel the flying mane and strong shoulders of Seda's stallion even as she experienced the balky plodding of the other. She and Kyrem rode on, more slowly, after nightfall. But Seda seemed as restless as they, though she could not have known they were following. They did not gain on her.

She left them visible signs of her passing—baubles she had torn off the sacrificial steed and dropped like so much trash. Countryfolk would not touch the sacred trappings for fear of the wrath of Suth. They peered from their homes in dread and awe as the second steed went by on the bright trail—tassels, beads, a pair of flame-red brocaded wings, pieces of golden net, a glittering torsade. The gold Kyrem let lie, but once he stopped his horse and got down to pick up a jeweled headstall. And with an odd, aching look in his eyes, he touched the single great stone on the browband, the crystal jargoon that lay centered on the forehead.

Within a few days they passed out of settled lands, for no folk cared to live so near the magical realm. All was wild grassland, wind and sky. The chant of the atarashet began ominously to hum in Kyrem's mind, the liturgy the priests had intoned when they sent Nasr Yamut off to his doom.

> It's called the melantha, black lily of magic.
> It trails its pale leaves in the sundering water
> Of the river that flows at the end of the world
> Where there's no going over, beyond the white lily
> Of never returning, the lily of death.
> Men name it melantha, black flower of madness.
> It blooms on that far verge, and ever the seeker
> Stands pale on the near, yearning, calling, Melantha!
> Melantha! I see thee, black lily of magic.

He and Sula rode hard and silently, with strained faces and frightened eyes, until on the seventh day they came to the Ril Melantha.

"There it is," Kyrem said in a low voice, "and Seda is somewhere on the other side."

Sula nodded; she knew that.

The river ran deep and noiselessly, a great flow of smooth silver-gray, between banks on which the lilies clustered thickly—white lilies in the red soil of the Vashtin side, and black lilies, as black as black satin, in the strange black soil of the beyond. Kyrem stopped his horse short of the white lilies.

"Folk say that it is death to pass them," he muttered.

Sula made no reply but pressed the more closely against his back, shivering. A chill wind was drawing the warmth from her shoulders, and though the white lilies stirred and drooped in the wind, the haze of mist over the river hung as

still as a heavy tapestry. All beyond it seemed muted, yet
glowing like ancient gold.

After a moment Kyrem turned the horse to the left, the
west, and started riding slowly along the silent silver curves
of the river, all the while looking across it. Haze foiled his
sight. From what little he could glimpse, the Untrodden
Lands seemed to lie in soft folds that might hide anything,
some of them topped by trees taller than any in Vashti. Trees
stood also within the river curves.

And beyond one such clump of trees, on the far verge,
amid the black lilies, stood something white and very still. . . .

Nasr Yamut, white-robed. Standing in a mystic's trance,
he seemed not to see Kyrem.

"Balls of Suth!" Kyrem whispered, blasphemous in his
irritation. "Perhaps we can get by without speaking to him."

But as horse and riders drew abreast of Nasr Yamut, he
stiffened, stirred and came forward a step amid the melantha,
staring.

"My king!" he exclaimed.

Kyrem halted the horse and stared in his turn, for Nasr
Yamut had never before called him king.

"But what are you doing here, my liege lord? Vashti will
be bereft without you."

"I left a worthy steward," Kyrem replied. "He who used
to keep the door." He spoke slowly in his astonishment, for
there was a vast change in Nasr Yamut; his whole manner,
his voice, the very expression of his face, open, clear and
joyous. Unmistakably Nasr Yamut, yet somehow entirely
different. "What has happened to you?" Kyrem blurted.

"Happened?" Nasr Yamut stared, then drew back a step
from his own memories. "Yes, I see," he admitted. "I hated
you once. But now I am no longer afraid."

"You were afraid?" Kyrem was amazed, for of all seemings, the priest had least seemed afraid.

"Yes. Throughout my entire life, afraid of power. Others might wield power over me if I did not first wrest it away and myself hold sway. . . . But here everything is power, and where all are puissant, there is no domination. Danger, but no domination. When I came to his shore, a mighty king met me. Rabiron, the first Rabiron, welcomed me and took me to the palace of his ancestor Auberameron. Auron will be welcomed some day in like wise, and so will you."

Kyrem sighed and shook his head, no longer attempting to understand. Perhaps Nasr Yamut was mad. Black flower of madness, they called it, the melantha. "Seda is there, somewhere," he said. "She who is too young for yon far shore."

"She who used to be called shuntali? Yes. She is puissant, very puissant. Only one who is puissant may venture here without punishment."

"I must so venture, to bring her back." Kyrem swiveled on his steed's back to face his bride. "Sula, get down, take the food. Await me here."

"I will do nothing of the sort," she told him. "I am coming with you."

"You cannot! There may be that beyond the river which will destroy you."

"There may be that which will keep you from ever coming back to me. Then will I be the more slowly destroyed. How can you think I would leave your side?"

They sat glaring at each other at close quarters, there on the spotted horse's back, close enough to kiss.

"I will be the more likely to find strength to return," Kyrem said softly at last, "if I know you are awaiting me." But she answered him with a tilted, tender smile.

"It will not do, Ky. You cannot protect me. This peril is mine as well."

On the far side of the Ril Melantha, Nasr Yamut spoke as though once again in a trance, continuing his thought.

"She came across on that great blue roan of yours, came across clinging to the back of the swimming horse, and the stallion greeted me, and did not hold it against me that I had wished to slay him."

"I see," Kyrem muttered to Sula or the speaker. "Well— hold fast then." Leaning forward, drawn forward by the force of his will, he urged his crop-eared steed past the white lilies and into the water.

Ril Melantha was slow but deep, very deep. The horse's hooves churned in water, never touching bottom. The crossing seemed long, breathlessly long, though the river had not looked so wide. Turning once, Sula saw that Vashti seemed dim and distant through the mist. She shivered, pressed against the willful hardness of Kyrem's back, jewel hard, and did not look behind her again.

The sacred steed came out of the river with a plunge and a streaming of water, leaving deep hoofprints in the strange black soil of the bank, stopping amidst the strange lilies of black. Nasr Yamut came over and stood quietly by Kyrem's side, his hands tucked into the full white sleeves of his robe. Watching the play of mistlight, pale gold, on the former priest's still form, Kyrem knew suddenly, with certainty, that he could trust him. All things were different in this place of lambent haze.

"Where might I find Seda?" he asked him, and Nasr Yamut raised quiet eyes.

"You are right, my king, that she does not entirely belong here. She senses it herself—she will not enter the palace. She roams. But she is often to be seen in the meadow preferred by the horse. Will you allow me to lead you there?''

Kyrem nodded, and Nasr Yamut walked off northward, away from the river. After a moment's thought, Kyrem dismounted to walk beside him, leading the crop-eared horse with Sula yet on its back in her queenly robes. And so in silence they trod the Untrodden Lands. Kyrem looked down in muted surprise to find the earth so solid beneath his feet. All else seemed strange—the glowing golden haze, the water pure silver in the streams and ponds they passed, the trees so tall and all in crimson bud, the grass growing oddly pale out of the black soil, pale jade green and nearly as tall as the black lilies that swayed in no breeze but that of the horse's passing—

They sensed the presence of Seda before they saw her, Seda amidst the tall, soft-green grass and the black lilies. Nasr Yamut must have sensed it also, for he stopped as well as they.

"Let me go to her first," Kyrem murmured to Sula. "Please." And she nodded.

A horse was grazing in the meadow, a blue roan stallion— Omber. Omber as of old, freed of caparison, mane flowing silkily as he fed on the black lilies. Beyond him another creature also fed on the melantha, a creature hunched and creeping, stuffing the blossoms into a misshapen mouth with fingers crooked and greedy. She did not see Kyrem coming at first, the girl-creature did not. But Omber lifted his head and whinnied with gladness. Seda came up to look as would a shadow-tail, startled, then shoved herself away from Kyrem with animal speed and curled herself into a tight ball, head between her bony knees and hands, hiding against the earth. Only heaving ribs and a crippled spine faced him.

"Seda, please. . . ." he begged.

He tried to touch her, and she hitched away, still maintaining her hedgehog stance. "Go away," she said, her voice rusty from disuse and muffled against earth. "I am dead. I do not exist."

"Do not say that! You are one of the mighty ones; your saying it makes it so."

Omber had come up to Kyrem, rubbing a soft muzzle against his shoulder, and Kyrem stood still, accepting the comfort of the animal. He could have wept, cried out "Araah!" to the heedless trees—

"Take Omber and go," Seda muttered.

"No, indeed. He belongs to you."

"And you were going to let them kill him." She raised her head; anger gave her strength to do that, and she stared at him flatly. He wet his lips with his tongue, unable to answer. But then she sat up, all an awkward sprawl, looking beyond him, anger washed away by wonder. At a small distance, her face pale with horror and pity, Sula stood.

"Sister," Seda breathed.

Sula took a step toward her. Ten such steps would take her to her twin.

But before they could touch, before she could essay even the second step, there was a noise so intense, so sudden and overwhelming, that Kyrem clutched at Omber's mane to keep from falling, and only that grip of Kyrem's hand kept Omber from rearing up to flee. Lion's roar, thunderclap, rumble as of a thousand galloping steeds on the plains of Deva, but no, far greater and more vehement, a noise fit to stun reason, worse than earthquake roaring, a noise fit to sunder sky itself. And down came the terror steed, rending the luminous veil of haze and bringing with it, seemingly, the dark. And on clawed feet it landed directly between the shuntali and her twin.

Black, black, a thick-necked stallion with a feathery sheen on the head and shoulders and black plumes, black, sinuous plumes for mane and tail. Glint of white teeth and corpse-white flame of wings and those horrible bone-white bird-clawed feet. . . . And on the forehead, the jewel of glittering black. It was the demon, the dark Suth. Kyrem closed his eyes to the sight of it and hid his face against Omber's neck in all-embracing fear.

"Shuntali," said a dry, whispering voice, "Devan dog. You are dead; you do not exist."

Kyrem's eyes flew open and his head snapped erect. He knew that sere voice, bloodless and desiccated even when it had lived! Instantly his fear turned to consummate wrath, fury that suffused him, filling him with a glowing power so great that it shone redly in the mist far beyond the meadow. With a wordless noise very nearly like a lion's roar, he strode forward and faced the black bird-steed, near enough to touch.

"Old One," he commanded, "go away and trouble us no more. It is you who are dead."

Laughter, loud whinnying laughter, with the flash of chalk-white teeth. And behind all else the sound of an old man's wheezing mirth.

"I am the Old One," the demon said in that same snake-hissing voice. "But I am far more." And with those words the voice changed; instantly it was dark and immense, a voice fit to fill the world as thunder fills the sky. "You dare command me! It is you who must go away, small one, and quickly, before you are destroyed."

Though he kept hold of his power, fear crept back into Kyrem, and he glanced toward the one for whom he feared the most. Sula took a step forward, her second step, as if to come to him, or perhaps to go to her sister. But the black Suth reared up in threat, darting toward her its vicious foreclaws, and it gave out a roar that drove her back and sent her stumbling to her knees.

"Unclean, twin, unclean! Stay far, stay asunder! Step nearer and I strike, I the destroyer of the unclean! The Old Ones know the ways of twins—"

"Let her be!" Kyrem shouted, but knowing even before he spoke that all the power he could command would have no effect. This thing was far greater than he. If it should hurt Sula—but the demon turned back to him. And as it did so, Nasr Yamut stepped forward to stand by his side.

"My king," he said in a shaking voice, "we must hold firm."

Nasr Yamut looked as pale as the corpse-glow of the demon's wings. Growing desperation had made Kyrem mettlesome, and a last small shred of malice stirred in him. "I thought you were no longer afraid," he snapped.

"I have not been," Nasr Yamut said. "I have loved this place. But this black horse-creature moves counter to the order of it. Power turned toward domination—"

The terror steed came at them with beating wings and uplifted claws, sending them staggering several steps backward. Nasr Yamut caught hold of Kyrem's hand—not, Kyrem realized with a shock, to receive aid, but to give. Something touched his left hand as well—thin, twiggy fingers, Seda's twisted hand. With that touch he felt the pleroma of her pain, her despair, and of her love for him that underlay it. And he no longer cared if he were destroyed utterly, genius and spirit and soul.

"Now, by the numina," he shouted at the black Suth, "I am the emperor of the Untrodden Lands, and I bid you depart!"

Laughter. "Men lie. The holy place has no name and no emperor."

Hot breath, scorching hot as the mistral, struck Kyrem's face as the feathered horse of darkness drew nearer. He wet his dry lips.

"My friends lend me the power of their love," he said as firmly as he was able, "and with it I face you and command you to go."

"Only Suth commands the demon Suth." The terror steed no longer laughed. "Hence, petty king," it thundered, and with a single blow of one white-fire wing, it broke through the shield of Kyrem's will as if it were eggshell, seared him across the face with sickening pain and knocked him to the ground. Nasr Yamut lay unconscious, and Kyrem nearly so, but in his final defiance, so he thought, he forced his eyes to open, to focus. He stared up into the mouth of the terror steed, its great teeth bared as if to rend him—and by his shoulder knelt Seda, her thin arms over him, her verminous head near his own, staring up in like wise.

Her mouth stirred, that horrible wreckage of a mouth.

"Go away," she whispered.

"Ah, little one." It was the dry voice again, oddly tender. "Even you cannot command me hence. Not in this place."

"I bid Suth hither then," she said in a stronger voice, "Suth and the simurgh."

"You cannot—"

"I command the powers of the numina, and I bid them hither." Her words rang out in the lambent haze.

Stunned anew, Kyrem stared.

Far up in the mist a glow of brighter gold began, and spread, and bloomed, sunbursting, more swiftly than Kyrem could comprehend—and then there was Suth, Suth on wings of flame, so that Kyrem, who would not shut his eyes for all the terror of the demon steed now blinked for a moment in the pain of great beauty, for no horse of mortal kind could match Suth for beauty, the airy golden flowing of his mane and tail and the silver-gray sheen of his crest, his flanks, his fetlocks above hooves of aureate white. And the stone, the Suthstone glowing wine-red on his forehead beneath small and perfect ears. And his eyes, wise eyes. . . . He was all shine and glory, all goodness, and before Kyrem could more than think it, he came down, down out of the shimmering sky to the very place where the terror steed reared, and melted into the dark Suth, and stood on earth.

Utterly startled, Kyrem struggled to his feet, ignoring the pain of his blistering face.

There stood, not demon steed and the silver-gold Suth, but the single god on four glossy black hooves, his flanks black and white and tarpan-dun and gray as stone, all colors—it was Suth the spotted steed, for Suth and the dark Suth were one. And Kyrem met Suth's eyes, milky cloud-white eyes that seemed to look through him, that seemed to have known him forever and beyond forever. Only Suth could command the dark Suth. . . . The great god-stallion did not speak. But he arched his neck, laying his soft muzzle against his own chest, and courteously he backed a few paces, just far enough so that Kyrem could see Sula rising from the ground, standing pallid and swaying some several paces beyond him.

Gravely Suth inclined toward her his great head. With stumbling feet she ran to Seda and sank to her knees beside the crippled girl.

"Sister," she breathed, putting out her arms, and instantly Seda returned the embrace. And they clung together, foul and fair, health and unhealth, queen and pauper. And Kyrem looked at them, and swallowed, and looked beyond them toward Suth, the god-steed who was both light and shadow.

Then, floating down on fiery wings out of the resplendent mist—Kyrem felt his senses swirl as Suth raised his great head and whinnied in greeting. For the simurgh drifted down, the mighty bird of sky and sunset swept down and settled companionably on the back of the horse-god, shone yellow and red and golden on his shoulders, and two pairs of fiery wings blazed as one. The sky-blue eyes of the simurgh gazed past the cloud-white eyes of the steed.

"Seda," Kyrem whispered, and he walked shakily over to where the two young sisters still crouched, seeking heart's ease in each other's arms. They were weeping and talking both at once, their words a babble as of mountain water.

". . . empty place," Seda was saying.

". . . felt you," Sula went on. "Dreams, I did not understand at first . . ."

". . . where my name should be . . ."

". . . if only we had been born one, you need not have suffered so."

Diffidently Kyrem put his arms around Sula and the shuntali. "I love you both," he whispered.

Seda's anger was gone. "Ky—" She spoke only the single word, laid the scabby weariness of her head for but a moment against his shoulder, and understanding pierced him.

"Yes, I have failed you," he told her, the pain of saying it tightening his voice. "And I cannot help you now. But, Seda, there is power in you like the power of . . . of earth itself."

She raised her head and stared at him blindly; her eyes were as all-seeing as Suth's.

"Seda, hear me! You have the Vashtin magic as well. Your color is saffron, like your sister's, and your emblem is the sun, your element essence, your flower the acaltha, your jewel the yellow beryl, your luck bird"—he stopped, realizing that she already knew—"the simurgh," he muttered anyway.

Heal yourself, little one, the great bird told her, a cry as out of the bell of a trumpet.

But instead she laid down her head and sobbed, a dry, hurtful sound, that most human of sounds. A wounding human knowledge had come to her through Sula's touch. "My father did this to me," she cried out in her turn. "Our father did this to me." And then she hid her face in the rich fabric at Sula's shoulder and wept.

Kyrem could not bear it. He got up, seeking comfort, and found Omber and leaned against the horse, and Omber turned to nuzzle the young king's ear.

Nasr Yamut came to himself and rose to his feet, smoothing his white robe, staring at the two who huddled in the grass amidst the melantha. He stared longer at the great god-steed and god-bird just beyond them. How could they bear that fearsome nearness? But Seda and Sula seemed hardly aware of anything around them—

So it was that, when a soft equine muzzle came down to snuffle at their cheeks, both reached up at the same moment, unthinking, to rub the itchy spot at the center of Omber's forehead, where the hairs formed a whorl.

But it was not Omber. Kyrem stood stroking Omber and watching, scarcely daring to breathe, for it was Suth, the great Suth, snorting so softly and extending his arched and lovely neck so as to nuzzle the two faces that lay so close together—

And at once Sula's hand and Seda's hand touched the great stone that flashed green and red and golden between his wise eyes. And the stone blazed out like sunfire, blinding, so that their hands looked red and insubstantial on it, and the two girls sat stunned and terrified, unable to move.

"Say it, Seda!" Kyrem shouted crazily, irrationally; say

what? What was the name of the one true wish? Heart's ease, heart's desire?

Heal yourself, little one!

Tears on her face. . . . Her rotting, misshapen mouth moved. All that it would take was that she should call herself by name. Mighty eyes were on her, urging her, and she knew, she knew her own name, better than anyone believed. Struggle with sickly, crippled self lasted only a little while.

"Sula," she whispered.

At the word, Suth reared back with a great ringing neigh, a sound like bells of rejoicing and trumpet gladness, and the stone on his forehead shone pure white. And the simurgh sang out its own brazen note of gladness and blazed upward on wings of flame. And Suth also took to the sky with a snort of joy. Upward, soaring upward they both flew, spiraling about each other until they disappeared in golden mist. But no one watched them go.

For where two girls had sat amidst black lilies there was now but one, a young damsel in queenly robes, and she sprang up with a cry of surprise mixed with loss or gain, and Kyrem hurried to her, grasped her by the shoulders.

"Sula?" he whispered, looking into her wide, dark eyes. It was Sula's body, straight and shapely, for the god wore a comely body always, but—it was Seda somehow too, in a wry pauper's smile, in all-seeing eyes, in a lithe step toward him, the strength of thin fingers in his hand. She lifted those delicate fingers and wiped away the oozing burn on his face as if it had never been, leaving him comforted, comely and whole. Transcendence of suffering was in her, healing, and a sure knowledge of the ways of love. She and Kyrem embraced, but then they stood regarding each other as equals as well as lovers: She would make him a queen of unsurpassed wisdom and power.

"I am . . . grown," she said. "I am well."

"But—Seda?"

"She is well, well and happy, living, loving. Only the shuntali was ever dead."

"What am I to call you?" Kyrem murmured. "What is the word for light and shadow?"

"Call me Love." She took his hand.

Priestlike, ceremoniously, as though performing a marriage, Nasr Yamut came and stood before them and between them. In their clasped hands he placed a black lily. But the flower, when they took it, was white.

"Vashti has need of you," he told them. "Farewell."

Then they saw that white lilies bloomed all around them, and a deep and silent river ran; beyond it a white-robed figure saluted once and vanished in mist. Omber grazed nearby, among the white lilies, and also the crop-eared horse, the oracle.

Cantering back toward Avedon, she rode Omber, she the nameless queen. The king of Vashti rode the sacred steed.

THE CHART OF SEVEN

	HORSE	PLANET	SYMBOL	ELEMENT	JEWEL	FLOWER	ANIMAL
spring rains	white	Moon	☽	air	crystal	asphodel	unicorn
season of new leaves	yellow	Sun	✳	essence	yellow beryl	acaltha	simurgh
summer unto the solstice	red	Mars	✺	fire	sard	blood-of-Suth	lion
high summer	blue	Venus	⚶	water	lapis	blue rose	cloud leopard
season of turning leaves	brown	Jupiter	⊕	earth	jasper	duncap fungus	onager
autumn unto the solstice	gray	Mercury	♐	ether	chert	lady's hood	coney
winter	black	Saturn	☉	stardark	tourmaline	melantha	wild goat

ANDRÉ NORTON